Embers in the Outfield

STEFANIE CASTRO

Content Warning

If you would like to be prepared for any content warnings, please visit my website using the QR code below:

Spotify Playlist

If you'd like to follow my Spotify playlist for *Embers in the Outfield,* please scan the QR code below. Happy listening!

Dedicated to all those who run toward the fires of this world instead of away from it. You are the true heroes.

Prologue

KENNEDY

I LOOK OUT THE WINDOW, my little hand touching the glass, hoping to feel the last of the summer warmth. Even at such a young age, this clear September day is one filled with love in my heart.

My parents are sitting up front, singing a song from the radio that has them smiling at one another, you can feel the love in the car.

I got picked up early from school yesterday for a surprise. Mommy and Daddy took me to an appointment, and I was scared I was getting shots. I hate shots. But luckily it was a good surprise.

Turns out I'm going to be a big sister. The lady at the doctor's office put jelly on my mommy's belly that made mommy laugh, while Daddy let me sit on his lap. I saw my baby brother or sister on the TV screen. The baby kept hitting Mommy, but she said she couldn't feel anything. That made me giggle too.

We had a special dinner, and we got to pick out names for the baby. I got to tell the baby goodnight through Mommy's belly, and for some reason, my mommy started crying. I felt bad making Mommy sad, but Daddy said they were happy tears.

Maybe adults cry when they're happy. I cried last week because Jimmy kept pulling my hair in class. I stuck my tongue out at him, and Mrs. Jenerick said that was not nice. I told my parents not to name the baby Jimmy.

"So, Kenny, are you excited for the field trip tomorrow? I know the zoo is going to be a ton of fun, sweet girl." Daddy loves animals. He's a vetarimarian. At least, I think that's how you say it. My tongue gets jumbled when I say it out loud.

Before I have a chance to answer, I hear a horn approaching our car. Before I have a chance to turn my head toward the sound, there's a huge bang on the car, and everything goes black.

I don't know how long I sleep for, but when I wake up, I see Mommy and Daddy in the front of the car. I start screaming for them; smoke is filling the inside of the car, glass is all over the backseat, and my parents aren't moving.

Why aren't they hearing me? I try to yell louder, but still nothing. I look around me; I'm so scared, and my crying won't stop now.

I see people running toward the car, phones against their ears. I see some holding their hands over their mouths like I do when I'm watching something scary on TV. Why are they scared?

Soon, I hear the sirens. They're getting closer. I keep screaming for Mommy and Daddy to help me out of my seatbelt. I'm stuck in here, and I can't get myself out.

I see a man outside my window, which has a huge crack in it, trying to open my door, but the car won't open. The crack in the window changes his face, and something about the look on his face makes my heart beat faster. He looks frightened and that makes me scared too.

My screams continue as a large man moves the guy outside my window out of the way. The way the sun is shining into the car, I can't see his face. I look at his clothes, and he looks like the firemen in the movies I've seen.

My tears stop for an instant, looking over to Mommy and Daddy, telling them there is help here and that we will all be okay. They still don't move, but maybe they are being patient. I'm not good at being patient; Daddy says that when I am going to get ice cream.

He has a big metal thing that is making that awful noise again with the metal of the car, so I cover my ears, the sound making my heart beat faster.

He pries the car door open, and that's when he undoes the buckle for my seat belt and pulls me into his arms.

"I've got you," he whispers into my ear. I feel my fingers grab his uniform.

I miss what he says, so I look at him with a puzzled look. He repeats, "What's your name?" as he walks me away from the car. I try to look over his shoulder to see Mommy and Daddy, but I can't see them because the other firemen are blocking the view of the front of our car.

I turn my face to look at the fireman holding me. He gives me a small smile, and I notice how calming that is in the middle of all this chaos.

He's walking me to the ambulance. I see people waiting for me with stretchers. I take a breath and finally speak, hiccuping from all my crying.

"Ken… Kennedy," I say just above a whisper. I'm scared, and I want my mommy. Why isn't my mommy getting out of the car?

I point to the car, and then I remember. "Baby!"

That makes the fireman stop in his tracks. He turns around and yells, "Is there a baby in that car?" I can tell he's concerned now. I want to tell him there's a baby in my mommy's belly, but the words hurt to say. The crying has made my throat raw.

I see the fireman who's walking around the car shake his head at the man holding me.

"In her belly," I finally say, and I see the fireman bow his head, something sad moving across his face. Why does he look so sad? They just need to get Mommy out. She'll be okay, like me.

"Listen, I'm going to leave you with these paramedics. They will give you a blanket and check you for boo-boos. Okay?" Right when I realize he's going to put me down, I hold on a little tighter, much like a koala, which is what my daddy calls me when I hold on to him really tight.

"It's okay. Jackie is going to look you over, alright? I have to go help my friends."

I give a small nod, and he sets me down on a bed. The tears start to stream down my cheeks, and I'm worried that nothing will be the same ever again.

It feels like life is moving in slow motion around me. The people who saw the accident, plus others who are coming out of their houses, have horrified expressions on their faces.

I feel the cold of the stethoscope on my skin while a woman starts talking to me.

"Hi. I'm Jackie. Can you tell me if anything hurts?"

I'm sitting there for a few minutes, the tears still falling, as I see the firemen moving around me and trying to help not only my parents but the people in the truck that hit us.

One of the firemen comes up to Jackie and whispers, but his words carry, and I hear words that make no sense to me. "Her parents are DOA. Waiting on the coroner to arrive. The guy in the truck looks to have dislocated his shoulder from what I can tell. Trevor is with him now to look him over."

The lady, Jackie, nods, and I see sadness on her face. I should tell my mommy I don't want Jackie as a baby name either. I don't want any names that remind me of today.

"Alright, sweetie. Is there anywhere on your body that hurts?" I give a little nod, trying to keep from screaming because I just want my mommy. Jackie continues, "Can you point to where on your body you're in pain?"

I stare at the scene in front of me for a few extra seconds, hoping my mommy and daddy start to get up and out of the smashed car. I stare for so long, I think I'm trying to make my thoughts come to life.

I hear the paramedic's throat clear, and that snaps my attention back to her. I point over my chest, rubbing at that area. My heart hurts. That's the only thing that hurts right now.

My heart, which will never feel the same, is forever changed from one second in the wrong place. It's in that moment I realize that most of my heart died in that car today, along with my parents, on this warm Tuesday in September.

CHAPTER 1

River

13 YEARS LATER

"SO WHAT'S SO great about this girl?" I can't help but ask Ashton as we walk through his fraternity house.

The music is blaring, and it's hard for me to even hear my own thoughts. I promised Ash I would visit when I had a break, and this was the only time I could hang out with my best friend since we parted ways this past summer. It's now November, and a long weekend is upon us.

"Dude, she's the most beautiful girl I've ever seen. I don't know how to describe it. Like the world vanished when we locked eyes." I have to control the reflex of rolling my eyes as my closest friend gushes about this new girl he started dating.

"Okay, let me rephrase. What makes her different than all the other girls you've dated? I mean, Ash, my man, I know how big your heart is, but you have a tendency to look at every girl and see forever with her."

Ashton Caldon is a hopeless romantic. He's the golden retriever of our group, and it seems that title remains the same, even in college. My brother and I have teased him about it since we were in kindergarten.

"It's not like all the other times. You and Clay will meet her and see what I'm talking about." He's yelling over his shoulder as we make our way through the fraternity house he just got initiated into this semester.

Clay is my twin brother, who likes to hold it over my head that he's older by two minutes. Who knew one hundred and twenty seconds could hold so much power between siblings? We're what people refer to as mirror twins, where our features are identical but mirrored between one another.

Unfortunately, he won't be here to see our best friend, once again, throw all caution to the wind for this current love interest of his. Clay was supposed to drive up here with me, but he had a paper to finish before Thanksgiving break. He stayed behind in Boston, and I'll drive back home with Ash in the next few days for the holiday.

"It's like I have an ache in my chest when she's not around. I can't even find words to describe it." Does he have hearts in his eyes right now as he gazes off, thinking of this chick?

"You're fucked, man. I can't wait to tell Clay about this." I grab a bottle of beer and slap my friend on the shoulder. "Is she here yet? I need to see this girl who swept you off your feet." I want to add, '*Until the next one*', but hold it in.

"She texted me saying she's grabbing drinks. She's probably in the kitchen. I know she brought her roommate. You have to promise me to be on your best behavior." With that, Ash looks at me, his expression growing serious as he points his finger at me.

"I'm always on my best behavior." I smile, the dimples popping out to show I truly am loving and innocent—most of the time.

"Don't give me that, Riv. You and I both know you are what most would deem a man-whore. You fuck anything with two legs. At least that's how you were all summer. Has that changed?"

"Well, that hostility is uncalled for. Just because I have fun doesn't make it bad. Plus, after that shit Kailey pulled last year, I'm sort of within my right to have some fun. I mean, she fucked Benson at the party. And of all people, he was our fucking friend. And let's be fair—my brother is worse than me, and he's been that way far longer," I say somewhat defensively.

"What Kailey did was fucking shitty, I get that. But not everyone is Kailey," he adds, understanding in his eyes.

Kailey Davis was my high school girlfriend. While I was captain of the lacrosse team, she was the head cheerleader. Yes, while it's usually the football quarterback who ends up with the cheerleader, I was the one who did. And I felt lucky until I didn't.

She and I were the *it* couple. We had been together for two years by the time we started our senior year. We were planning to do the long-distance thing once we graduated—at least that was the plan—but she showed me real quick that wasn't going to work.

I swear, after Kailey showed her true colors, I could see the devil horns coming through. She was my everything until she wasn't, and it still hurts when I think about it. She went behind my back and not only fucked the football quarterback, Benson Briggs—yes, even his name sounds douchey—at a post-game party after one of my matches, but it turns out they were hooking up all fucking summer. I felt like the biggest fool; technically, I still do.

The fuckboy status started after that. I mended my heart by partying as hard as possible and finding a release wherever I could. And I honestly regret none of it. I am enjoying my life. My brother and I go to the same university in Boston, so we've been having a good time while we acclimate to this college lifestyle.

The moment I broke things off with Kailey, I started to open my eyes to the person she was. She was selfish, inconsiderate, and simply the devil incarnate. I can only chalk it up to the fact I ignored it because I thought I was in love. But in all honesty, she held my heart in her hands, and once I discovered her cheating ways, that shit stung. Am I coping? Yes. Am I doing it the healthiest way? Most likely not. But I'm eighteen, in college, and not really wanting a long-term relationship anytime soon—or ever, if I'm being completely transparent.

If my father's passing taught me anything, it's that life can change in an instant. I don't think I need to sit here and plan forever with someone when I'm enjoying what's right in front of me at this moment. I'm being careful, and I'm figuring my shit out.

One of Ash's fraternity brothers I met earlier, Jared, makes his way over, an energy drink in one hand and a joint in the other. Seems counterproductive.

"Guys, I think I just spotted my future wife." Did someone spike the Kool-Aid with something other than vodka because these guys are completely losing it. I came to the wrong party. I was under the impression this was a college campus, not the next season of *The Bachelor*.

Jared continues, "I swear, this chick is fucking hot. She's in the kitchen with Samara, grabbing a drink. Come to think of it, she's in my business class." He scratches his head, his eyes distant as he realizes where he knows this girl from. I've only known Jared for a few hours, and I can already tell going to class is an optional thing for him.

"There she is, man." Ash is tugging at my shirt while I'm swatting his hand away, in no way wanting to ruin this shirt. I just fucking bought it.

We make our way toward the kitchen, maneuvering through a large group of people surrounding what I imagine to be the jungle juice. Red solo cups litter the area. In the far corner of the living room is a table—a new round of beer pong about to start.

"Hey, baby. I missed you." Ashton wraps his arms around

a tiny brunette, his massive height having to bend down to nuzzle her neck.

A small smile spreads across my face. As much as I give my friend shit, seeing him happy is all I want for him, especially with the shitty parents life has dealt him.

Ashton comes from a loveless home. His parents were constantly fighting, causing Ash to hang out more at our house than his own. We welcomed him in, my mother feeling bad for all the pain Ash endured being in an emotionally abusive environment. The minute he turned eighteen, he came over to my mom's house and stayed until leaving for college. From what he's told me, his parents didn't even ask about his whereabouts, and he hasn't relinquished any information to them since leaving Boston for college.

A movement catches my eye, and soon enough, someone new is joining our group. I am immediately taken aback by her beauty. She's stunning: long legs, wavy blonde hair, bright blue eyes—she might be the most beautiful woman I've ever seen. My eyes can't help the involuntary movement along her body, taking in each perfect part of her.

She's taller than Ash's girlfriend by quite a bit. Now that her eyes have trained in on me, I can see she has gold flecks near the middle, and it's hard to look away. She's got a bit of makeup on, but I see a faint scar across her forehead that accentuates her beauty versus taking away from it.

I'm staring at this point, and I can't even feel embarrassed. This girl causes everything around me to go silent with just her beauty. Her bright blue-gold irises lock on me, and it feels like she can see into my soul with her gaze. I'm instantly breathless and forget simple words, like a fucking introduction.

You're freaking her out, Riv. Say something!

"River, I'd like you to meet Samara. Sam, this is River." I hear Ashton's voice, but it's hard to pull my eyes off the woman in front of me. I watch the blonde beauty look me over, at first seeming to take me in. Then her expression morphs into disgust as if I kicked her puppy or something. She's looking at me like she's trying to figure me out, and what I would have categorized as intrigue on my end turns to discomfort as her eyes narrow.

I'm pulled from this hypnotic state because my friend is snapping his fingers in front of my face. Finally, I greet the woman my friend can't stop talking about.

"It's nice to meet you. Ash is smitten." This pulls a huge smile from Ashton's girlfriend, and her grin widens. She's completely his type with a big smile, doe eyes, and that small-town girl vibe he's always attracted to. I see why he felt a connection to her.

I try to show Samara some attention, but I can't help but swing my gaze back to the woman next to her. I don't know what it is about her, but she's commanding my attention in a way I've never experienced. I keep stealing glances at her as I shake Samara's hand.

"Oh really? Is that so?" Ashton's girlfriend sips her drink from the straw and looks over at Ashton like she's undressing him with her eyes.

I swing my full attention to the beauty by Samara's side, the girl now looking utterly pissed. What did I miss?

"I know you," hot girl proclaims, her voice dripping with disgust.

Whoa. I know, with absolute certainty, I have not met this woman. I would know. I know I wouldn't have walked away from her, seeing as she might be the most captivating person I've ever seen in my life.

I can't help but pull my backward hat off my head and run my hand through my hair. It's something both my brother and I do when we are uncomfortable.

I let an easy smile cross my features, letting my dimples pop out for a little extra charm. I'm uncomfortable, however, wondering how we are connected when I don't even go to this school. I let silence be my answer because I have no idea who she is.

"Yeah, I do know you. You were at my senior prom. Did you go out with Shelby Peters?"

What the fuck? Of all the connections to have tonight, this girl knows a psycho. Wonderful.

"Um, 'go out' is not quite the terminology I'd use." I use air quotes to accentuate my words because Shelby is in no way someone I dated. I would never classify us as dating, nor did I want to go to prom with her. Fuck, of all the things to follow me, this had to be the thing. What fucking luck I have.

"What do you mean you didn't go out with her? She told everyone what you did to her." Now that causes the easy-going smile I was sporting to drop off my face.

I put my hands up as if I'm surrendering, not sure what she heard about me, but knowing the source, I can guarantee it's false.

"Listen, I know Shelby, but I haven't spoken to her since that night at prom, and I did nothing to her."

Even though I'm trying to diffuse the situation, my words seem to be making this chick angrier with each sentence.

"Right. I bet every guy that gets denied the back door says that."

What. The. Fuck?

Ashton nearly sprays me with his beer, and Samara's mouth hangs open in shock. Her eyes are volleying between her friend and me like she's engrossed in an episode of *Law & Order: SVU*. Great first impression award goes to none other than me.

"What the fuck are you talking about?" I literally have no idea what this chick is talking about.

I can't hide my irritation with my question, and I see my verbal pushback only makes this chick more annoyed.

From the corner of my eyes, I can see Ash bring his fingers to squeeze between his eyes, probably thinking I did something with Shelby at prom because I have been on a rampage since the Kailey debacle.

I went to prom with Shelby as a favor to my mother. Her best friend from high school, who happens to live in New York, has a daughter named Shelby. I'm not trying to be a dick, but Shelby has had a crush on me since we were twelve. Apparently, she couldn't find a date, so my mom begged me to take her to the prom.

Clay had a great time giving me grief as prom approached. Lucky bastard got out of helping Shelby because she apparently liked me more. We're fucking twins! How can she choose one over the other? I had no excuses as to why I couldn't take her due to the fact I had no girlfriend to shield me from this whole thing, so I went, and I vowed to never hang out with Shelby again if I could avoid it.

"Yeah. She said that she had to dump you because you said you'd only continue dating her if she let you, you know."

That last part she says under her breath, leaning closer to me, emphasizing with her eyebrows, yet keeping the actual words out of her mouth. I can see the discomfort etched in her features talking about this, but I decide I may as well have some fun if she's going to burn me at the stake. Of course I know what she's referring to, but now I'm annoyed and also intrigued that ass play is making this girl uncomfortable. However, calling me out on it seems to be completely fine by her.

"Sorry, I don't know. Please clarify." I stand up a little taller and cross my arms in front of me. If she's going to be pointing fingers at a complete stranger, I may as well have her admit it using all the words possible.

"You know what I mean. She said, and I quote, 'If I can't fuck your ass, I'm out.'" The karma gods must be throwing a bit of pity my way because right then, the music cuts out, and that last part is heard by everyone in our vicinity.

This girl's cheeks flame a deeper red, and I can't help but

laugh. It's a dick move, but at this rate, what do I have to lose? Apparently, I have the reputation of liking a little backdoor action or I'm not wasting my time, so I might as well just go along with it.

There are a few chuckles, and then the music starts up again. I can see the fumes nearly coming out of this girl's ears, and now I'm all in on making this encounter even more uncomfortable for her. I love how easily I've pissed her off, and we haven't even exchanged names yet.

"Yep, Skipper, you nailed it. That's how I roll." The nickname slips out, and I think it just made her angrier at me. This is really going great for me. First this girl steals my breath away, then she's breathing fire in my direction. I, on the other hand, am incredibly intrigued, attracted, and annoyed all rolled into one.

I'm definitely not the person she's accusing me of being though. Did I take Shelby to her prom? Yes. Did I want to? No. Was I dating her? Definitely the fuck not.

The ironic part is, Shelby was the one begging me to fuck her. She said she was still a virgin, and all she wanted was to go to college and not have to worry about it anymore. Come to find out, she didn't just tell people I wouldn't screw her, but that I wouldn't see her anymore because I only accepted her with anal involved.

Listen, I'm no saint, but I'm not a total dick. I didn't want to lead Shelby on, knowing feelings were involved on her side of things. Plus, I couldn't stand her, even on a good day. I'd have a stage-five clinger on my hands. That scene from *Wedding Crashers* where the actress says, "I'll find you," kept playing on repeat as she begged me to have sex with her that night. No fucking thanks.

Obviously, I had no idea she was going to return to school and tell a rumor to her entire class that I was a major asshole. I mean, I wasn't a dick about it. I let her down easy.

"Listen, I don't know what Shelby told you, but that's not

at all what happened. You want me to call Shelby right now and ask her? I can." I'm ready to move on from this conversation. What a turn the night has taken.

"Right. She's the liar, and you're the victim." Her eye roll nearly makes me see red. The nerve of this one. Fucking forget runway model; this one is off her rocker. Whatever attraction I had for her is out the door now. She might be pretty to look at, but man, does she make my blood boil. She's all fired up, and she doesn't even know me.

"I don't have to explain myself to you, sweetheart." I take a sip of my beer, completely over this conversation.

"Don't call me sweetheart," she snaps, the air around us crackling, and not in the hot way like I'd prefer.

"Okay, both of you, take a chill pill." That was Samara, while Ash rubs his hand down his face.

He's met Shelby before, and I know he finds this fictional story too far-fetched, even for her. Fucking Shelby and the damn stories she makes up. Maybe after I share this one with my mother, the PG version, of course, I'll get excused from having to see her anytime soon.

Samara tries to fix this dumpster fire of an introduction, which hasn't gone past accusations. She just went right in with the insults. I may have met Ashton's girlfriend, but I have yet to know who the firecracker is by Samara's side.

"River, I'm happy to finally meet one of Ashton's friends. Thanks for driving back with him for the holiday." Samara gives me a genuine smile. I can tell that she is the peacemaker of her group, especially with uptight Nancy over here. Too bad her friend can't take these pointers and use them to her advantage.

She gestures to the woman who's on the Shelby band-wagon. "This is my roomie, Kennedy. Kennedy, play nice." She glares at her friend, I think realizing that she needs things to go smoothly, seeing as she's dating my best friend.

I extend my hand, and Kennedy looks down at it, then

looks at her friend. They seem to be having an entire conversation with their eyes, and Kennedy finally relents, rolls her eyes, and puts her hand in mine.

"Nice to meet you, officially," I say in hopes we can have a truce.

She rolls her eyes again and huffs out, "Fucking dick," under her breath while attempting to pull her hand out of my grip.

I'm quicker and grip her hand a little tighter, pulling her closer to me.

I bring my lips to the shell of her ear and say, "Maybe you need a little ass play. But I think that stick might get in the way." I chuckle as I move away from her, trying to ignore how good she smells. Skipper huffs out a breath, and her mouth hangs open.

"Fuck you," she seethes through gritted teeth.

"Why don't you get on your knees and warm me up first," I throw back, and I know that now she might explode.

She storms off, and I can't help the laugh that escapes me.

Sam sighs and goes running to catch up with her uptight friend, while Ashton mouths, *Fuck you*, yet laughs because that shit was fucking funny.

No matter how gorgeous that chick is, her attitude is shit. Lucky for me, I won't have to see her anymore after today. Ashton will soon be onto the next girl he's envisioning forever with, and I can say goodbye to what I can guarantee is an uppity personality like Kennedy.

CHAPTER 2

Kennedy

PRESENT DAY

"YOU MAY NOW KISS YOUR BRIDE!"

Ashton brings his hands to cup Samara's cheeks and plants a small kiss on her lips. I see my friend melt into his touch, even after all these years together. She pulls him closer to deepen said kiss, and relish in the fact she's finally going to be his wife. After so much planning, I know how happy she's feeling right now.

The couple walks down the aisle, the ribbon bouquet Sam put together at her bridal shower clutched in one hand while the opposite arm intertwines with her fiancé.

"Now remember that the photographer and videographer will be capturing this incredible moment while you walk down, so make sure to keep smiling; make sure it's natural. You're going to walk all the way from the gazebo to the hallway where we started the procession. Got it?" Theresa, the wedding planner, beams like she's going to win an Olympic medal after this entire wedding is over tomorrow night. She moves her attention to us, still standing at the altar. "Now, the rest of you, keep your smiles plastered on. Do not give me any resting bitch face during the ceremony."

"That might be hard for Kennedy!" That comment comes from fucker, I mean, River.

I swing my gaze at him, narrowing my eyes in his direction while he looks mighty proud of his snide comment.

I still remember the moment we crossed paths ten years ago at that fraternity party. At first, my gaze locked on his because—now, this hurts greatly to admit—he was the hottest person I had ever laid eyes on. He had on a backward cap that night, which is my kryptonite. That might be why it took me a minute to figure out where I had seen him before. But the moment the lightbulb went off, he instantly soured my mood.

River Nichols has been a damn gnat, one I can't seem to swat away. And the asshole doesn't seem to get ugly. Actually, despite my attempts not to find him attractive, it's almost like he's even hotter today than that day a decade ago. Damn him!

I'm pulled out of my thoughts when Ashton speaks up. "I think we can manage that." He's down the aisle now, standing next to Sam. If he had it his way, they would have eloped and saved the hassle of doing a whole wedding. He isn't much for the glitz and glamour Sammie had always dreamed of for her wedding.

Add in that his soon-to-be bride has been a slight nightmare in the last few weeks, so I don't blame him. Sammie is usually sunshine and rainbows, always smiling and seeing the positive in everything. The only thing is, she's turned over a new leaf that I wish she had left unturned.

She has been snappy and exhausted, dark circles under her eyes, and has completely deviated from her normal bubbly self. Not sure what happened recently to cause this change, but I am now counting the hours until this wedding is over if it means my friend will come back to me.

Theresa calls out my name for me to begin my walk down

the aisle next, and I walk toward the one man I really hoped I would never have to interact with again.

As happy as I am for the bride and groom-to-be, the one downfall of this whole thing revolves around the fact that I'm stuck with River Dipstick Nichols as a partner throughout this whole wedding. Actually, he's been the downfall of this entire relationship between Ash and Sam. They got happily ever after, and I got a lifetime of staring at his smug face, along with mocking comments whenever he finds a reason. Honestly, the reason is usually my existence.

I make a show of rolling my eyes as I walk toward River, my annoyance fueling him to smile brighter, the dimples in his cheeks more prominent as I get closer to him.

"Why, exactly, can't I walk down the aisle with your brother?" I know how much it irks him when I choose Clay over him, yet I get a huge sense of satisfaction that takes over my body each time I bother him. I guess I'm as bad as him when it comes to irritating one another.

"Because we flipped a coin, and I lost," he says without missing a beat.

Clay and River are twins. Their dark brown hair, tan skin, and hazel eyes turn heads everywhere. The fact there are two of them is just a bonus for the female population. As the years have passed, I can tell some differences between them, but if you're not familiar with them, they could easily pass off as the same person, especially if River keeps his mouth shut. His smug remarks really set him apart from his brother. Actually, they're chiseled to perfection, but I'd never tell River that.

"Ha ha, very funny. I think in reality—" I'm interrupted by Theresa as we make our way down toward the area where Ashton and Samara just disappeared.

"Pay attention, you two. You're worse than my toddler," she huffs. I hold a laugh in because she's acting like we are taking off into space tomorrow instead of simply walking down the aisle.

"Yeah, Kennedy, shush." River agrees with Theresa, and I see hearts form in her eyes at him. What the fuck? Isn't she married?

"Figures you already have her wrapped around your finger. Dick." I roll my eyes again.

"You know, for the number of times you refer to me as a dick, I'm starting to think you're a little obsessed with him. You know, he's always down to play. All you have to do is ask." He waggles his eyebrows, and I use my elbow to shove him in the ribs. He huffs but lets out a laugh at the same time.

The moment we make it through the double doors and back into the hotel, we rip apart as if we're going to internally combust with the proximity.

"Kenny, I need you to talk some sense into my mother!" Sam is already red faced and irritated. "My Aunt Kay wants me to use a crocheted purse she made special for the money dance. I can't do it. Please help me out." She's got her hands in a prayer position, and I swear she's on the verge of getting on her knees to beg.

"What's so bad about the purse?" That's from River, and the moment he asks, I think I see regret mar his features.

"What's wrong with it, you ask?" Sam is now on the verge of exploding, and River takes a step back and puts his arms up in surrender.

I vaguely hear Ashton whisper, "Don't anger it."

"It's in the shape of a penis, River! A fucking penis. Who does that?" My friend is worked up, and now I am starting to fully comprehend why, and I might have to agree.

"Start from the beginning," I say, hoping to understand why her aunt would want to do such a thing for an event like this.

"So when I was little, I guess I told her I wanted her to crochet a purse for me. Do I remember this request? Of course not because I was FOUR! Four years old! This woman can't remember what day it is, but she remembers me telling her I wanted a crocheted purse. Cut to her finding a funny print on Etsy, which I assume someone would do for a bachelorette party or something, and she thought it would be funny... FOR THE WEDDING. A cock purse, Kenny. Imagine the photos." Sammie is ready to pull her hair out, and Ashton decides to come up behind her and rub her shoulders.

I try to rein in the laughter that's threatening to burst out of me as I absorb this information from my best friend. Too bad River can't seem to have the same maturity, and he busts up laughing.

"I'm definitely dancing with Aunt Kay tomorrow. She sounds like a riot." His laughter is now spearheading Ashton to laugh, and I have a feeling if they keep this up, Sam may not have a groom to marry tomorrow because he'll be deceased, and I'll have to help her get rid of the body.

"Sam, look at me." I get her attention back on me while the boys, because men they are not if they're this immature with a penis purse. "Show me who Aunt Kay is, and I'll go have a friendly chat with her."

I see Sammie's shoulders relax, and she starts to look out the window to find who in the crowd is the aunt.

The moment she spots her, she points her finger in the direction of her mother and a group of other women. "See that lady with the purple hat on? That's Aunt Kay. She'll likely have a crocheted purse on her right now. She has multiple in every color so that she can coordinate with her outfit." Sam rolls her eyes, irritation still radiating off her.

"Okay, I'll take care of it," I say and begin my walk back out toward the family that's sitting in the chairs outside. I've got my sights set on Aunt Kay and almost miss Dorothy, Samara's mother, standing right next to the penis purse producer.

Unlike Ashton's family, Samara's is full of love and laughter. They welcomed me with open arms when I lived with

Sam in college, and we've been tight ever since. Though I'm surprised I have never met Aunt Kay before.

"Oh, Kennedy, isn't all this just lovely? Sam did such an amazing job. Have you met my aunt?" Dorothy motions to the woman next to her.

"It's lovely to meet you both. Aunt Kay, is it?" I turn to the woman with purple from head to toe, and sure enough, she has a purple crocheted purse in the shape of what looks like an eggplant. I can't help but look down at it, and she catches me staring.

"Why make a purse in a simple shape when you can make it fun? Don't you agree?" I think my eyes double in size at the thought of the random items she has made into purses.

Clearing my throat and figuring out how I'm going to rectify this for the bride, I begin my story. "So I heard you made a purse for Samara for the big day," I say, and the aunt starts to bob her head in agreement, happiness evident in the way her smile takes over her face.

I hope the smile I'm sporting looks genuine. I'm slightly horrified by the eggplant I'm seeing in front of me and the fact that it's gigantic. I can't imagine the penis purse is any better, although probably hilarious as a gag gift.

"I'm so bummed out though. See, I had given something to Samara that was pretty special to me that we planned on doing for each other's weddings, and it was part of what she was using for the money dance. I feel awful because what an amazing gift you made her." I pull out my saddest face, hoping she feels sympathy.

I see her gaze swing from me to Dorothy, and sympathy etches her face. "Oh, you poor girl. I don't want to cause any problems between you and our beautiful Sammie. That's no problem. I don't mind if you give her your gift. It's just a shame. I spent so much time on the intricate details for her purse, and it will go to waste." She looks down, disappointment evident in her features.

I'm about to interject, to say maybe she can use it another time, when a voice speaks up behind me, "Oh, you know, Aunt Kay, I think what would really make this so much better is if you allow Kennedy to borrow this purse, that I know you must have put so much love into making, for her own wedding day."

I keep the smile plastered on my face as I look at Aunt Kay, but I'm fighting the urge to knee him behind me. Fucking River. He's such a jackass. Where did he even come from?

I turn around and face him, horror and irritation taking over my face. He sees it instantly, and I know he has no remorse over what he's saying.

"What a great idea, young man. That's lovely. I bet you would love it. Yes, let's do that. When are you two getting married?" Excuse me, what now?

It's both River and I swinging our gazes to the little old lady, horrified at the thought of spending forever with this chump by my side.

"Oh no, we are not dating!" I protest a little too loudly. River's gaze looks me over, assessing why I would jump to tell this woman we are not together.

"You see, Kennedy has had a crush on me for years, but I have had to let her down multiple times. It's such a shame to be obsessed with someone like me for so long, and I just keep saying no." He's got that smile again, dimples and all, for Aunt Kay.

River throws his arm over my shoulder without a care in the world. He continues, "I've offered her my brother," he points at his twin with is opposite arm, who's quite far away, "but she said it's either me or no one. You see, Kennedy can't really deal with all the attention I get from the ladies, and she's a bit jealous, which would never work. I can't just turn off my charm, right Aunt Kay?"

The giggle that escapes this woman is surprising. What

the fuck is happening? Is he winning over an eighty-year-old woman?

He pulls himself off of me and brings his arm out for her to interlock in his and begins walking off with her, laughter continuing as he speaks.

"I know you two don't get along, but I'm sorry to say, he is a handsome boy," Dorothy says as she watches them walk off. I'm still speechless, and Sam's mom is over here giving him compliments. Great, am I the only one who finds him unbearable?

"Yes, you are," Dorothy says, and that's when I realize I said that last part out loud. "It's okay; sometimes that's how the best love stories begin." My mouth agape, I swing my gaze toward her, and she gives me a sneaky smile and a wink.

She walks off, and I continue to stand there, now with my chin on the ground, in shock at what just happened. I'm here trying to help a friend out with a penis purse, and everyone is going gaga over this dickwad.

Typical River, winning everyone over while I'm left to seethe and apparently now a proud owner of a dick-shaped purse to go along with it.

CHAPTER 3

River

"WHAT THE FUCK is on your head, Skipper?"

Kennedy holds her hotel room door ajar for me to come in, but I can't stop staring at the contraption on her head. Seriously, what the fuck is that? She looks like George Washington right now.

She turns around, but not before I see her roll her eyes. It's Kennedy's favorite pastime when I'm around. I sort of live for those reactions from her.

"Why are you here, Riv?" Her tone is dripping with irritation, and it just fuels me forward.

"You've been summoned." I want to add, *'by the devil herself'* because lately, that sweet girl my best friend fell in love with is starting to grow horns on her head. Maybe she's spending too much time with Kennedy.

I walk through her room, taking in the tidiness of her clothes. Good thing she's not in my room because it's got things thrown about.

"Doesn't the dinner start at seven? It's six fifteen right now." She looks at her phone, her brows furrowing.

"Yeah, I don't ask the questions, especially with the possibility of getting my head bitten off. Do you know what's going on with Sam?"

"Honestly, I think she's just stressed. She was fine up to a few weeks ago, and now she's just always so upset." She grabs a bag and makes her way to the bathroom, and like a magnet, I follow her.

"Seriously, were you summoned to walk around my hotel room like a fucking puppy?" Her irritation is my content. I smile at her, and she huffs out her annoyance.

"Can we get back to your head? What is that thing?" I point at her head, and I can't even hide the confusion on my face. There's a weird rod that's got hair wrapped around it. I move along behind her to take in the entire thing with a little closer inspection.

"They're heatless curlers. I'm trying something new." She plops the bag on the counter and opens it up as makeup spills out.

"I've never heard of them," I say, still inspecting the device she's sporting.

"Wow. You're not in tune with all the new hair products available for long, flowing hair? That's surprising, Riv, with all the hookups you have." The sarcasm just rolls off her when it comes to her interactions with me.

"Do I sense jealousy, Skip?" I smile and wink. I get rewarded with yet another eye roll.

I watch her, fascinated by her beauty. Despite a decade since meeting her, she still carries the attention of everyone in a room. She turns heads whenever she moves through a space, her beauty overwhelming at times. I can't say my blood doesn't boil each time someone stares a little too long, but I push those feelings aside whenever I open my mouth. I don't know what life with Kennedy is like without making a comment that seems to get under her skin.

For the first few years, having this banter with Kennedy

rolled off the tongue. I was good at keeping myself irritated whenever she was around, but since Ashton and Sammie have been engaged and I have had to see her more often, I'm starting to crave these interactions. I have noticed I want to see her, and I want to get a rise out of her. She's strong, confident, and smart. She's the whole package, but it's too bad she hates my guts.

"Earth to River." She pulls me from my thoughts, and I think I was just caught staring at her.

"Take a photo. It will last longer," she scolds, then goes back to swiping the lipstick across her lips. Her soft, pillowy lips. Snap out of it, River!

Fuck, I think I'm digging myself a deeper hold here, whatever these feelings are that are creeping up with Kennedy. Unfortunately, I can't explore it because I can tell I'm alone in this emotional spiral that's taking place. I'm starting to feel a pull toward her, and she's still dowsing herself in River repellant.

"So how much longer? You know I'm scared of your best friend, and I'd like to live to see another day," I tell her, hoping I'm covering up my feelings well with my response. I can't come off as too nice, or she'll sniff this out of me and realize my feelings are shifting when it comes to her.

"I can be ready in a few minutes. Let me just pull the curler out." She begins pulling the hair ties out from the bottom of the weird hair contraption and unravels the hair. Soon enough, her long, blonde locks are on full display, and now my thoughts are deviating to imagining my hand grabbing said hair and holding it back as I fuck her mouth.

Damn it. I can feel myself stiffen behind my zipper. It's going to be a long night.

———

I'm seated across from Kennedy at the table, the dinner full of laughter and memories being thrown about our favorite times with the bride and groom.

I look over at Ashton, and he's looking my way, a pensive expression on his face. I lift my whiskey in salute, and he does the same, taking a sip and moving his gaze across the table. I wonder if he's noticing the way I can't keep my eyes off Kennedy for long throughout this dinner. I better figure out how to get this attraction under control.

Things were done in a different order than usual with Sam and Ash. The rehearsal dinner took place last night with everyone in the wedding and close family members that came out early to begin the festivities, but tonight is simply a celebration between the bride, groom, and wedding party. All of us have known each other for years, and it's been nice to catch up. I let my gaze wander across from me for the hundredth time tonight.

"Dude, you're being fucking obvious," my brother whispers next to me. I look at him and try to hide my annoyance.

It's hard to keep things from Clay. He noticed something was off with me when it came to Kennedy a few months back, and I confided in him, telling him how my feelings were shifting, yet I was alone in this turn of events.

Clay is usually the romantic between the two of us, but he's recently divorced, and this change in marital status has sort of hardened his heart. Abby, his ex, is the love of his life. I can't even say it in the past tense because she remains his heart and soul.

Their love was the strongest I'd seen until it wasn't. Seeing her leave and watching him crumble has been one of the hardest things I've faced since our father passed away. His pain is mine, and I hope he can start looking forward instead of hoping things will work themselves out with Abby. She's pulled away from all of us, not even attending the wedding. I understand she's in a lot of pain from all the heartache she has had to endure, but my brother lived through the same pain, and he's here.

"I'm trying, man. It's just not that easy when the feelings are getting stronger. I mean, look at her." I jut my chin in Kennedy's direction. She's consumed in a conversation with Jessa, her college friend. They're both laughing, and I can see the tears forming from whatever stroll through memory lane they're going through.

Soon, we hear the clinking of metal and glass, pulling our attention to the head of the table. Ashton and Samara stand up, their smiles genuine.

"We thought we'd take a moment to say thank you all for being here, not only tonight, not only for this amazing weekend we've been planning for months, but simply being the friends that walk through the fire with us. We are so incredibly grateful for the love and support through the years. Most of all," he looks over at his bride, "we're sitting here and realizing we couldn't have asked for better friends to call our family. As you know, I did not grow up with the best of people to call parents. When I met Sam, I didn't just gain a partner, but I gained a family in her parents. And we've gotten our found family in all of you. Thank you for putting your lives on hold to be here with us. We know things are busy for everyone, but having you here is really filling our cup. We love you all!"

I see tears coming down slowly from Sam's face, and they raise their glasses and cheers. We all hoop and holler, taking our drinks and clinking them with those around us. I'm next to the couple of the hour and clink my glass to Samara's. That's when I realize she's got water in her glass and not the trademark champagne everyone was given.

Kennedy's gaze has shifted, and by the look on her face across from me, she's connecting the same dots as me. We both look over at Samara and Ashton, who are smiling from ear to ear. When they take note of both of our faces, their smiles drop, and Sam looks like her eyes are going to pop out of her face.

"Sammie, I need to use the restroom. Please join me." Kennedy doesn't wait for an answer and throws her napkin down and pulls her best friend to follow her out to restroom.

Ashton takes the seat next to me and whispers, "Please don't tell anyone. We just found out. That's why Sam's been acting so agitated lately. I guess the hormones are not quite making her glow in the way people describe. She's sort of glowing like the devil holding his pitchfork in hell."

I snort at his comparison, and he shudders. "Seriously, dude, don't say a word," Ashton says right as my brother puts a twenty in my pocket.

"Fucker, how did you know?" That's coming from Clay, irritation marring his features.

"I don't know. I just threw it out there, mostly as a joke." I shrug. I honestly had no idea. I just made a joke last night when we were having drinks together.

"Shit, you knew?" Ashton says, his face paling. "Do you think other people know?" He's looking around the table, and everyone is already at least two drinks in, if not more.

"Naw, I don't think so. No one has said anything. I was just throwing theories out last night with Clay and guessed it as a possibility. He thought I was crazy to think it, so we made a friendly wager on it."

"So you guessed I was going to be a dad and thought instead of asking, you would make a buck off me instead?" As much as Ash wants to act pissed, it's not possible. You'd never guess this guy lived with insensitive parents the way his heart soars for others. I think he put a lot of effort into being his parents' exact opposite, but whatever the reason, he really is a good person through and through.

"Why not? I mean, times are tough. May as well make

some money when I can," I tease, taking another sip of my drink.

"Please don't tell a soul. No one knows. She's just a few weeks along, and I just don't want to get everyone's hopes up." His eyes drift to my brother, and Clay nods in acknowledgment.

Clay knows all too well how things can take a turn. We all absorb the past a bit in that instance, but I can't help but turn to my best friend and congratulate him. "Dude, I can't just sit here and not say something positive. I'm really excited for you. You're going to be an amazing father. The best father." And I mean every word of it.

Ash has always dreamed of getting married and having children. I remember him talking about it on the phone with me after he met Samara. He knew from their first date she was the one. Of course at the time, I thought he was full of shit, but now I see they complement each other well. I think he always wanted the opportunity to give a child the chance he didn't have with loving parents from the start.

"Yeah, man, congrats." My brother follows suit and smiles at Ashton. I know there's pain in his words, his thoughts most likely deviating to his own experiences with a life he thought was going to be filled with babies and memories to build, but he can't quite have the same optimism as Ashton right now. Luckily, he isn't holding onto it as he looks at Ashton with genuine happiness for him.

The ladies make it back to the table, their eyes puffy like they've been crying.

"You two okay?" Ashton asks as he pulls the chair out for his wife-to-be. The moment Samara is seated, Kennedy pulls Ashton in a hug. I can see her whispering something in his ear, and I see her embrace pull him tighter.

When they pull apart, I see fresh tears coming down her cheeks. The way I see her smile grow, genuine happiness radiating off her, the genuine love she has for them is palpable.

Soon I get an elbow to the rib, and I look over at my brother. "What the fuck, Clay?"

"Wipe right here." He points to the corner of his mouth. "You're drooling, dumbass."

Yeah, I'm royally fucked.

CHAPTER 4

Kennedy

"I AM HONORED TO INTRODUCE, for the first time, Mr. and Mrs. Caldon!" the chaplain announces to a room full of their loved ones. Cheers fill the room while Samara and Ashton officially share their first kiss as husband and wife.

I fight the tears that are threatening to spill down my cheeks as I watch my closest friend marry her person. The moment their kiss breaks apart, I see their happiness in the smiles they save for one another.

I hand Samara her bouquet as she makes her way down the aisle. Her smile beams as she walks away, and my heart melts for my best friend, knowing she has waited for this day for some time between her and Ashton.

It's my turn to walk down with my partner, and that's when my eyes lock on River's hazel irises.

He gives me his cocky smile, knowing it's killing me to have to be near him right now. He's been the bane of my existence since we crossed paths a years ago.

"Always a pleasure holding you close, Skipper," he mocks as my arm interlocks with his.

What have I done in this lifetime to deserve this shit on the regular?

All these years, we've been thrust together with events between our closest friends. Add in the wedding festivities for Sam and Ash, and we've been around each other all the time. He's found every single way to rub me wrong, yet it's become such a norm for me. I don't know what I'll do once we don't have all these wedding obligations to stick to.

Top that off with the fact that in all the time we've known one another, I feel like his looks have only improved. He's gotten bulkier the longer he's worked as a firefighter; his cut jawline leans more toward a GQ model than someone who is running into burning buildings. Much like tonight, with the tux he's sporting now, he's downright edible. Too bad the moment he opens his mouth, I'm reminded why I can't stand him.

"Wave at your exciting date," River says as his lips move closer into my personal space and whispers into my ear while we both smile as we walk along the aisle.

I will not dwell on the fact that feeling his lips this close to my skin is making me break out in goosebumps down my spine, and that feeling progresses down to my fucking core. Damn him and all he seems to be doing lately to my body. It's playing tricks on me.

I will not be sexually attracted to River. I repeat, I will not let my sex life intermingle with River. I should say lack thereof because I haven't had sex in way too long. That's probably all this is; my body is reacting to his proximity because I just need to get laid.

At River's little comment, I turn to the right to find Darius, the person who Samara's mother thought I would connect with. I think they met at one of the games at the stadium, and he has season tickets. That might be the most exciting thing about him. And I wouldn't call him my date. He's someone Dorothy thought I'd find similarities with, but I think my morning piece of toast has a bigger personality than him.

"Shut up. At least he has a brain," I jab, looking over to our left to find Karissa, River's overindulgent date, taking selfies by the flowers at the end of the aisle, trying to angle the camera to pick up some of the views if I were to guess.

"She's an influencer. She has to take photos for her job," he explains, although his tone lacks conviction.

"Yes, and she's dating you for your impeccable personality too," I say, as I know this girl is completely in it for the gram.

No offense to River, but the fact he's good-looking and a firefighter is a huge plus for women like Karissa. There's an opportunity to take photos with people in his firehouse, and I have a feeling she's all for the photo op and not the connection. I fight hard to keep from rolling my eyes, well aware photos and videos are being taken of us as we make our quick walk down the aisle.

Before we can walk through the double doors into the venue, we are stopped by a woman at the end of the aisle.

"Oh my gosh. You two are the most beautiful couple. Please tell me you're together." I assume from the silence she's met with, River is giving her the same disgusted look as I'm giving her.

I feel like any answer that isn't a positive one is going to burst this woman's bubble. I try to formulate a response that will soften the blow, but before I get a chance to kindly respond, I'm interrupted.

"That's so sweet of you. Too bad Kennedy doesn't agree. She dumped me after one date." He feigns sadness, looking at me like I tore his world up.

"The stalking charges you raked up afterward prove to trust my judgment," I respond, a smile plastered on my face, feeling proud of myself for the quick hit back.

An uncomfortable laugh escapes said guest, and we continue to walk out. The moment the double doors close, where we'd once separated contact immediately during the rehearsal, I feel River hold on an extra second longer. I can't help the confusion on my face. It isn't until he hears his brother's laugh behind us that he finally lets go of me, and I immediately mourn his warmth when we separate.

Clay is chuckling, and even with all their similarities, I do not see them as the same in many ways beyond their looks. Where River is the thorn in my side, Clay has a softer side to him.

As much as River is as irritating as a stone in my shoe, his brother is usually not too bad most of the time. He likes to have some fun, but for the most part, he is a little more mature than his twin.

Clay got married at a young age, and when he and Abby were together, I'd say he was all about the happily ever afters. That romantic side of his flourished with her. I hung out with her as she befriended Samara, and I tagged along when they had girl nights.

Unfortunately, about a year ago, they went their separate ways, and I've only recently seen pieces of the old Clay making their way back to the surface. To say his divorce devastated him is an understatement.

"You have something to say, Clay?" I move my hands to my hips, annoyance lacing my tone.

"What? What would I have to say?" I give him a bored expression, knowing something is coming.

"Oh, you mean the fact that you and my brother make a beautiful couple? I agree, despite the fact you probably sit at home with a voodoo doll poking his eyes out."

"Come to think of it, my left eye has been twitching lately." River ambles up to his brother, covering his eye in mock discomfort.

I roll my eyes and decide I shouldn't waste my breath. The night is young.

"Awww, you think I'd waste my time making a voodoo doll of you, Riv. Fat chance. Also, between the two of you,

you already know Clay is the worthy one." I pat Clay's cheek and wink, pulling a scowl out of River as I walk away, chuckling like a Disney villain.

It's all fun and games between Clay and me. We love to ruffle River's feathers, and I know it's a point of contention when I favor Clay over him as the better brother. I love to play off that when and where I can.

I hear Clay's laugh from behind me, followed by an "Oof, what the hell, River!" I smile, satisfied my job here is done as I approach the bride and groom.

"Congratulations, you two. I'm so happy for you both." I embrace each of them.

Last night, when I pulled Sam into the restroom to confirm the reasoning behind drinking water, she told me all about the pregnancy test. She kept apologizing because she didn't tell me sooner, but I think we all learned a lot with things that happened between Clay and Abby, Samara wanted to play it safe when it came to announcing her pregnancy with all of us.

Apparently, in all the wedding prep, she skipped a few birth control pills. She thought doubling up on them would do the trick, but not so much. She said Ashton is ecstatic, even though she was scared when she found out. The idea of jumping into parenthood is alarming yet exciting, all mixed together. With the chaos of the festivities, she's still having to remind herself that she's carrying a baby in there.

The moment she told me, my heart soared for her and Ashton. I cannot believe my best friend is going to be a mother. She's already glowing, despite the fumes that seem to constantly come out of her ears when she's pissed. Maybe the baby is taking all her calm. I guess time will tell.

I feel the tears well up as I pull away from Samara, my happiness overflowing as I take in my bestie and her husband.

"I can't believe we're married!" she squeals, grabbing onto Ashton's arm and jumping up and down.

The moment Ashton proposed, she's been knee-deep in wedding planning. She's been meticulous about each wedding detail, even before that gorgeous ring was placed on her finger. I think her future was laid out with this man the moment he took her out on their first date years ago.

"This has been a dream of a wedding, Sammie." I give her another hug, and soon, we're rocking each other back and forth, laughing as the tears stream down our cheeks.

Our moment is interrupted when the photographer grabs the attention of everyone in the wedding party, telling us to follow her outside to take photos.

My feet are killing me as I'm dancing the night away, and the wedding has been an absolute blast. From the moment the reception started, it's been one thing after another: toasting the bride and groom, cutting the cake, dinner, and now dancing. The night has been beautifully put together. Sammie's attention to detail has shown in the way everything has come together flawlessly from the ceremony down to the reception.

This DJ has been choosing song after song that keeps me from sitting down, and I know this was exactly what the bride and groom wanted. They had attended a wedding shortly after graduating college where the guests couldn't get their dinner until they answered questions correctly about the bride and groom. She said the hunger on top of the irritation was growing with each failed answer for their table. She gave up on answering after the DJ asked them what the bride's first word was. She said the night dragged on from there, with the DJ making up all sorts of games throughout the evening. She vowed her wedding would be nothing like that. She wanted it to be a night to be remember, but in the best way possible. I think Sammie got that wish in the best way.

There's not one wedding that's complete without the

classic song "YMCA" blasting from the speakers. I'm swinging my arms in the air, moving them to mimic the letters to the title of the song as I sing along. I look around me and see everyone laughing and taking in the fun surrounding them. It's then I realize many of the wedding party are no longer close to me.

The moment the song ends, "Freak-A-Leek" comes on, and I immediately spot Clay's eyes on me. The moment our eyes connect, he's pointing at me, moving those hips of his. If the Nichols men can do one thing, it's dance. Clay gets close to me and moves his hand around my waist. I move with him, my back against his chest, and once again get lost in the movements. I've always felt completely at ease around Clay, and we've danced together before. It's always been entirely platonic.

I hear a chuckle from him and look back to see what's got him laughing. I look in the direction of his gaze and realize he's chuckling at his brother, who's eyeing us as he dances with one of Sam's cousins, Taylor. Before I know what's happening, I see River say something to Taylor, gesturing toward Clay and me. Once River makes his way over, I feel like the temperature of the ballroom has increased tenfold. I'm not sure why, but the anticipation of River and I dancing causes my heart rate to spike.

Without asking, River juts his chin, and it seems to be all Clay needs to walk away from me. Clay quickly kisses my cheek and says, "Try not to bite his head off," before he saunters off to find his next dance partner.

As River gets closer to me, his strong hands take hold of my hips and move me closer to him. Unlike my movements with Clay, with River it feels electric. We haven't danced together in years, usually avoiding sharing the same air when possible. But tonight, something has switched, and each time his eyes have found mine, he makes me feel like my skin is on fire.

River points a smile my way, his eyes shining, and I see the sweat lining his forehead. He's been dancing as much as I have. I saw him moving his body with every woman on the dance floor, although now that I think about it, he hasn't danced with his date most of the night.

He's charmed everyone he's shared space with tonight. Each one is captivated by his beauty and his moves. I don't blame them. He knows what he's doing, and I can't help the way my mind deviates to how those hips would hit all the right spots in bed.

Where the fuck did that come from?

"I like you like this," River whispers in my ear, his lips grazing my skin, and I swear I feel my pussy aching in need.

I'm speechless for a second, trying to allow my brain to catch up with my body. Finally, words process and spill out. "Like what?"

"Quiet. Not inventing ways you could cut me up and feed me to the wolves." He laughs, his movements light, and I can't help but laugh with him.

"Yeah, well, you're making me feel good right now, so I have no complaints," I say and then wish I could immediately take it back.

He pulls his face away from me, probably in shock, then gives me that panty-melting smile where his dimples make my ovaries want to explode. I've apparently lost my mind.

He brings his lips near my shoulder, moving up my neck to the lobe of my ear. I am immediately turned on, and I feel the goosebumps lining my flesh.

"Oh, Skipper. You have no idea how good I could make you feel." His words surprise me, and I lean into his heat.

We continue grinding our bodies together, and the longer we're in this close proximity, the more turned on I'm becoming. The way our bodies sway in unison makes me feel like we're made for one another. And the more River moves his body against me, the more I feel my mind drifting to what else his body could do if we were alone.

The song ends, and River's face comes close to mine, and I'm paralyzed in place. Is he going to kiss me?

At the last second, he moves his face to my ear and says, "I think I need to grab some water."

And just like that, it feels like a bucket of cold water was dumped on me. Good thing because I swear I was in a trance.

I simply nod, and he pulls away from me and walks toward the tables. I'm instantly longing for his touch when he steps away. Following him would be a bad idea, so I continue to dance, but something about it feels muted compared to how I was feeling prior to River's movements.

I look around, hoping to find Mr. Exciting, a.k.a. Darius, but he's nowhere to be seen right now. Tonight I found out Darius works in finance, which isn't surprising with his colorful personality. He's nice enough, but I think my personality would squash him, poor guy.

My eyes connect across the dance floor with River, who is surprisingly not dancing with anyone. I stand there, my gaze locked on his, and his eyebrows rise. Before I can react, he's walking my way.

I decide I may as well grab some water myself. I start to walk off the dance floor, my gaze swinging around the ballroom, trying to find the bride and groom. They left the dance floor during that last song, where I was lost in a trance with River pressed up against me.

"Looking for someone, Skip?" River's voice pulls me out of my pursuit.

"Yeah. I don't see the newlyweds." I turn my head in search of our friends who were just dancing near us.

"They're headed out the door as we speak," River says as he points his chin toward the door to the left.

Right then, I see both of them bolting out the double doors and laughing. Sneaky little shits.

"Where's Karissa?" I ask next. "I haven't seen you dancing together much tonight."

"Oh, you didn't see?" I give him a questioning look, and he continues, "She found something interesting in your friend Darius, and they took off together about twenty minutes ago."

I gape at him, astonished we both got ditched. "You're serious?"

He chuckles, no anger behind his expression. "Like a heart attack. I saw them walking off. Let's just say he wasn't giving her information on spreadsheets." He waggles his eyebrows, and I'm surprised he's not more bothered by this turn of events.

I make my way over to the table River has sat at, the water pitcher in his hands. I pull a chair out and sit next to him. The moment my ass hits the chair, it's automatic that I feel the pain in my feet from standing all day.

"I'm sorry your date ditched you. I wasn't really giving Darius any attention during the entire wedding. I thought he was going to put me to sleep when he started talking about the latest Excel update. I mean, who cares about that kind of stuff?" I huff. I nearly plopped my face on my dinner plate as Darius droned on about his work and his excitement to see the latest installment on Excel.

I looked over at Sam during the meal, and she kept suppressing a laugh, covering her mouth with her cloth napkin. I kept squinting at her, completely aware she knew his personality was probably as bland as the professor in *Ferris Bueller's Day Off*.

"Don't apologize to me. I'll be just fine," he says. "I won't be crying over that not working out. I promise. I just brought a date because I thought it was best."

I've seen River date quite a few women throughout the years, but they never last longer than a few weeks. As much as Clay was starting his life as a husband early on compared to the rest of us, River was adamant about keeping his options open. I overheard him say he enjoyed his single life far too much and would let his brother take on the responsible sibling role.

"You haven't lost your moves, Riv." I wink at him and reach over to grab my glass of water. River must know what I am trying to get, and he moves at the exact same time. It causes his face to rest right at the crook of my neck, and I can't help my body's excitement at his proximity.

I take a breath and finally reach the glass. It takes everything in me not to turn my head and pull his lips to mine. He's so close, and I'm apparently really needing a release.

Fuck, it's been too long.

I sit back in my seat and take a big swig of water, closing my eyes and trying to calm down whatever my body is doing in response to River tonight. I'm the president of a fucking baseball team, and this right here—this attraction with a man I've detested for so long—is nearly causing me to lose my cool and mount him right here in the ballroom in front of everyone. I need to find some release when I get back to my room. I'm wound way too tight.

My job doesn't give me much time to focus on me right now. Looking at my life at the moment, baseball would have been the last career path I would have envisioned for myself when I was a little girl. I was all about princesses and glitter and finding Prince Charming.

Too bad life has a way of slapping some things out of our grasp. The moment I lost my parents, that part of my life also dimmed. I said goodbye to the moments when I saw life as a fairy tale and had to find a new normal to adapt to. Luckily, I had it better than those who may not have people who love them to take them in.

I was sent to live with my grandparents, who also lived in New York City at the time. I was there with them until I graduated high school. However, in the summers, my dad's brother, my uncle Thomas, along with his wife Gennie, took me in. They never could have children, and they spoiled me with each visit.

My uncle is the owner of the Boston Gaels, and the older I got, the more my visits became about business and how I could one day take over the company. My uncle still owns the team, but he recently appointed me as the new president.

I am the first female to take on such a position of power in the league, and that comes with more lows than highs at the moment. The media has not been kind with having a female in this position, so I'm going to do everything I can to prove that I am more than capable. It's a bigger hill to climb than a man would have, the double standard not lost upon me in my newfound role. But I know what a huge responsibility this is for me, and I do not take it for granted.

I stand up, grab my purse and shoes under the table, and put the glass down after finishing off the rest of it. Now that I've taken a few moments to rest, I realize I need to get to bed. My body is wiped now that I've given it a chance to relax after today's festivities.

"I appreciate the dance, Riv. I think I'm going to head to bed. It's been a long day," I say, turning around and making my way to the exit. I can feel him following behind me, so I turn my head to give him a confused look.

"I thought I'd walk you up," River says as he reaches for the items in my hands and pulls them into his grasp. What is going on right now? This isn't our usual interaction. Chivalry is dead when it comes to River and his actions toward me.

Of all our friends, I haven't put much thought into us getting along. However, my mind has wandered to the fact that if there were one person who could handle my strong personality, it would be him.

It's not something I've spent too much time thinking about because each interaction with us is always teetering the line of a nuclear bomb going off. But a part of my brain has always acknowledged that River would probably be the most compatible person for someone as uptight as me, even with our rocky introduction.

I stare as he moves ahead of me, my eyes on his back as I follow him toward the exit of the ballroom. My mind doesn't know what to think right now. From the way we moved on that dance floor to the way he's showing me this kind side of him, I'm unsure how to navigate anything past hate for one another. This is unknown territory for me and my brain when it comes to River Nichols.

As each year has passed since my parents died, I've allowed a thick wall to build around my heart. At first, it was a coping mechanism. But the older I get and watch my friends marry off and live lives with love and companionship, I see that I've really grown accustomed to an independent life.

It may have started as a way to keep me from breaking down when I was a child, but now it's all I know. I don't let people in. Much like River, I date, but I pretty much start everything knowing there's an end date attached to it. Plus, I barely have time to wash my hair, let alone commit to another person and give them my time.

Losing my parents and a sibling I never got to meet taught me how to maneuver through life with a huge berth around me. That space has given me the room I've needed to feel the control I've always longed for since that horrible day when I was young. I've felt like if I hold on to people around me with a weaker grip, maybe life wouldn't find a way to break my heart. So I keep people at a distance, and so far, it's served me well.

We're about to go through the double doors when someone is calling River's attention. She catches up, her smile nearly splitting her face it's so big. I recognize her as one of the many women he danced with tonight.

"Hey, River, hold up." The girl is out of breath once she reaches us. She's holding something out. I don't see what it is until I peer over and position my nosy self a little closer and realize it's her room key. I feel my eyes bulge, partly in awe this girl has balls and the other at the audacity. What if River and I were leaving together?

I have to internally roll my eyes at myself because what the hell is going on with this train of thought creeping in? I never think anything of River and his extracurriculars, and tonight, I have thought about how he could relieve the ache between my legs.

River's discomfort is evident on his face as he looks at the white and blue key card she shoved in his hand. If I didn't know him so well, I would miss it, but I can see he's embarrassed he has me as an audience right now.

He masks it well when he pockets the card and winks at the girl. I doubt it's the first time this has happened to him, but I still can't help the dumbfounded look that must be showing on my face.

He gives a slight cough and says to the woman, "Thanks, Cheryl. It was great meeting you." Her cheeks pink, and now I feel like I'm interrupting a moment here.

She smiles wider at him and then registers I'm still standing there. She gives a little wave and then runs off, her friends waiting at the table, clapping at her bold move.

My eyebrows arch when I look over at River, and he shrugs as if this is a normal interaction for him. I bet he's had many key cards thrust into his hands throughout the years, but for some reason, tonight, this feels weird between us.

We quietly make our way to the elevator, the awkwardness of that encounter latching onto me like water in the rain. I don't know why it bothers me that that woman thought it was completely fine to approach him while he was walking out with me. And I can't understand why I care either. The emotions of this wedding must be catching up to me. That's the only explanation.

My mind is tired, and the irritation is festering. The

moment we get into the elevator, I blurt, "So, you going to drop me off and go to her room?" The second the words are out of my mouth, I regret them.

I can see the shock turn to amusement in his gaze. I can tell he's ready to pounce at a chance to rile me up.

"Why? You jealous, Skipper?" I hate that he uses that nickname with me like I'm some ditz he can forget about at the drop of a hat. My irritation is bubbling at this point, and I have no right to feel this way.

"No. Just wondering if that's how easy it is to get you into bed." What is wrong with me? Am I giving this guy ammunition to fuck around with me?

"Awww, you taking notes?" Now the River I'm used to is back. Prick.

"You wish. Like most men, I doubt you can find her G-spot, so I think the only one who should take notes here is you."

He looks at me, and I think he's speechless for the first time since I met him. Finally, I got him good enough that he can't think of a comeback.

"Are you saying no man has made you come before?" I can't quite tell if he's about to make some asshole remark or if he's genuinely curious. I decide answering him is pointless and a waste of my breath.

I yank the items he was carrying for me out of his hands. When the doors open onto my floor, I rush toward my room, moving slower than I'd care to. The blisters the silver shoes left on my feet are aching as I walk down the hallway. River is trailing me because I can hear his footsteps behind me. Luckily, he's keeping his distance, and it's probably best. I've lost control of this interaction with him, and I just need to be left alone.

"Kennedy, wait," he pleads, but I keep walking, hoping the more distance I put between us, the more this feeling that's been creeping up all night will dissipate.

The moment I get to my door, I don't see River standing by my side, waiting for me to go inside. I see him pulling his own key card out and swiping it at the door to my left.

"Are you serious? You share a wall with me?" He's like a leach. I can't shake this guy.

"Looks like I do, Skipper." He follows that with a wink. Right then, I know he's back to the River I usually want to avoid.

"Don't worry, I won't be too loud." He gives me that panty-melting smile and strolls into his room, laughter continuing to fall out of his mouth while I grunt, exasperated by the way my night has ended.

I open my door and let it close behind me, frustration lacing each step further inside. I roll my eyes and look to my left. Knowing River is next door is making my blood boil. At least I have a few hours before I have to see him again at breakfast with Sam and Ash.

CHAPTER 5
River

I **TAKE** my time moving around my room. Everyone says grooms get the luxury of relaxing all day before they get married, but Ashton didn't get the memo. He was a bundle of nerves all day as if Samara wouldn't show up at the ceremony.

I can hear movement next door as Kennedy readies herself for bed. I can't help the jolt my dick gives at that thought. Why does that excite me?

I never told Kennedy I was next door to her. I let a smile creep up at the thought of her irritation when she realized my proximity. Then my mind goes to the fact that I think I spotted a little jealousy hit her this evening when I got that key card. I have no intention of hooking up with Cheryl even though she gave me the key to her room, but we had a good time dancing together.

Picking up my clothes piece by piece, I'm reminded of the aftermath of the chaos that ensued when I was last in here. Luckily, Clay decided to get his own room, giving me the freedom of a quiet night's sleep. My brother sleeps like the dead and snores as if he's in competition with a train.

I had to share a room with my twin my entire life growing

up. As expensive as living in Boston can be, I jumped at the chance to find a place all to myself. Clay didn't mind because shortly after getting our jobs at the station, he decided to fully commit to Abby and get married.

He's now in a one-bedroom in the same building as me, with Abby moving back in with her parents in California for the time being. The entire thing has been a messy divorce. I think the ugliness lies in the emotion still left on the table and not the material split of assets. There's still a lot of love between them, but I think the pain of their past is masking the love from being seen clearly.

Once I get my space cleared up, I start to undress, ready to take a quick shower and get to bed. Pulling my shirt off, I run my hands through my hair, and I can't ignore the one face that keeps entering my thoughts.

Kennedy and I have never seen eye to eye. Despite years of us intermingling, we've simply rubbed each other wrong. Somewhere along the way, though, my thoughts have veered, and now I can't shake this feeling that I want more with her. Being close to her tonight only intensified those emotions, and I can't shake it.

Now that I'm older and creeping closer to the age my father was when he passed, thoughts are clouding my mind about how alone I really am in my day-to-day.

I pull myself out of my thoughts once I've stripped down to my boxers. Grabbing the toiletries bag I packed, I open the shower to turn on the water, and that's when I hear it. A loud thud on the other side of the wall sounds. The rescuer in me kicks in, and I throw my bag onto the bathroom counter and run toward the adjoining doors that connect our rooms.

I put my ear to the wall in hopes it's thin enough that I would hear if she's calling out for help. I don't hear anything, but decide to open my adjoining door to attempt to hear a little clearer.

The moment I swing my door open, I realize her door is

slightly ajar on her side. I move slowly, fearing I'll scare her if she's directly on the other side.

I quickly call out, "Kennedy, you okay?"

I hear the water running but not much else. Shit. Maybe she slipped and hit her head. I take a step into the room and see she had started to unpack but must have given up and gone straight for a shower.

The moment I step in a little further and make my way over to her bathroom to see if she's injured, I hear the worst singing voice to ever touch my ears. The lyrics to "I Will Survive" are being belted at the highest volume imaginable and my ears may never recover. Thank goodness Kennedy's dream wasn't to be on stage because she fucking sucks.

I try to control my laugh and cover my mouth to ensure I can retreat into my room unnoticed. I'm almost back to our adjoining doors when something on her bed catches my eye. Holy shit. She brought a little friend with her.

I walk toward her mattress, the water still running in the bathroom, along with the shit vocals now filling the entire hotel room. I stare at the purple silicone dildo and am frozen in place. It's gigantic, and now I'm starting to wonder if that comment in the elevator was more a window into the fact that no man has found her G-spot.

It's got girth, along with some ribbing for her pleasure, and this rabbit-looking portion that I assume exists to rub her clit. A sneaky smile takes over my face. Here I was, trying to figure out how I'd have a little fun this weekend, and this just fell in my lap.

Of course, staring at it isn't enough, so like the fucking moron I can be, I pick it up and click it on. Soon enough, the entire thing is gyrating in my hands, and I'm trying to swallow a laugh at how comical this is. Oh, the fucking fun I could have with this, as I know Kennedy will be desperately looking for it later and come up empty.

I must be too focused on the contraption in my hand because I don't even hear the water turn off, nor do I notice the horrible singing has ended. Once I figure out something is different in my surroundings, I turn around to find a soaking wet Kennedy with a small towel wrapped around her body and what I can only describe as pure hatred etched across her face.

"What the fuck, River? You breaking and entering now, you perve?" She moves forward, ready to take me down, when I throw my hand forward, waving the vibrator that I now turned off, in her face.

"Ah, ah, ah, Skipper. I was just knocking to see if you were okay," I tilt my chin toward the adjoining door, "after hearing a thump in your room. I walked in and saw this fun little contraption all alone on the bed. I just had to check it out and see what keeps you company." I see her eyes volleying between my face and the dildo. I can't help the fun this is causing me, as she seems like she's about to blow. I think her eyes are turning bluer. If they were green, they would look like the Hulk.

"Get. The Fuck. OUT." Her volume escalates, and she stomps her foot. Actually stomps it like a toddler not getting her way. It's cute if it weren't from a woman who's barely covered with that hotel towel. I lick my bottom lip as my gaze sweeps her body, taking in the sight of her.

I push on, moving toward her, causing her to move backward until her back is up against the wall. May as well take our banter to another level, hopefully erasing this damn line we drew years ago. Also, I'm curious how far she'll let me go with my little plan.

I bring my lips near her ear, looking down to where she's holding her towel, her knuckles white while keeping herself covered up. The moment I begin to move my lips to speak, I can see her take a quick breath in.

"You know, Kennedy, it's too bad we aren't on better

terms. I wouldn't mind showing you that your silicone pal isn't the best at his job."

Then I switch the device on, the vibration the only sound between us, aside from our heavy breathing. I see the goosebumps pop along her skin, and that just spurs me on. I move the dildo up her arm and along her collarbone, down her chest, circling each nipple, hoping that beneath that towel, they're pebbling into hard points. I keep the device moving down until it's right above the juncture of her legs.

"I mean, can this tell you how wet you are for it? Can it tell you how good you taste?" I see her react to my words with the rise and fall of her chest, noticing the quick pulse through the skin along her neck.

I move the silicone mold closer to her body, and I see the slight movement of her legs parting, hoping to feel the friction of the dildo to relieve some tension. She fucking likes this.

I move my lips to the point of grazing her ear, the contact only pushing me further into this little game.

"Looks like you need a little release, Skipper. Is that right?" I move my gaze so that we are looking right at one another. I can see the speckles of gold splashed throughout her blue eyes.

I can see her having her own mental battle. She looks pissed that she's liking this as much as I am, and I bet that is infuriating her even more.

"That vibrator has been more successful in making me come than any real dick." She might be in shock that we're in this compromised position, but her voice is steady as she speaks to me.

She continues, "You wouldn't dare prove me right by making me come with my vibrator instead of your cock." The way she says cock is making my dick strain against the fabric of my boxers. I have never felt this kind of pull toward

Kennedy before. Of all the years we've played this little game of hatred, we have never crossed this line.

"Oh, to see you fuck this dick only to make you wish it were me? Yes, I would do that. Because I know all you'll think about is wanting me more than this moving inside you."

I smile, but before I can process what's happening, Kennedy drops the towel, and it's like the whole thing happens in slow motion. Kennedy Sparen is fucking naked in front of me, and I think I'm short-circuiting. She's perfect. That milky skin and those perfect breasts, her nipples peaked, my gaze trailing down her skin that looks like porcelain. The moment my eyes move back up to reach her face, I feel like I might pass out.

My mouth goes dry, and I can see she's surprised by her own action with the towel, but as if a switch has gone off, she brings her chin up and has that confidence I've learned to expect in Kennedy.

"What are you, River? All talk?"

I give her a cocky smile, rest my forearm on the wall, bringing my face mere inches away from her, and finally find my voice. "You're going to let me touch you with your trusted vibrator?"

She nods slightly and grabs her bottom lip with her teeth. The moment we cross this line, there's no going back. Who am I kidding? We've already crossed a line, and nothing will ever be the same.

I hold her stare for an extra beat, then move the silicone dick toward the apex of her thighs. She spreads her legs a little wider, and I keep my eyes on hers. It's like we are connected with this invisible tether, and we can't snap out of it.

The moment the vibrator touches her, she lets out a soft moan, her eyes closing at the relief she seems to have at the contact. I veer my eyes downward to watch everything unfold in front of me.

"Fuck, that's hot." I can't help the words that fall out of my mouth. I don't know if it's just been a while for me or if it's the fact I'm doing this to Kennedy after years of squaring off with her. No matter what the reason, this is becoming my favorite side of her, and now I want to push a little further.

I move the vibrator through her folds, seeing the silicone glisten with her desire as I move it back out. Soon I'm slowly pushing it in and out, her eyes slits, desire swimming in her gaze.

I get into a rhythm, and she grabs my shoulders, closes her eyes again, and tips her head back, pushing her chest forward. It's taking everything in me to keep from sucking one of her nipples into my mouth.

She's so fucking wet, it's nearly taking me over the edge watching her unravel like this. My dick is rock hard now, and I wish I could pull him out and give him a few strokes. But this is about Kennedy and seeing her come undone in a way I never imagined I would.

This might be the most beautiful thing I've witnessed, and I begin whispering into her ear.

"You like the way that feels?" She can't form words and simply mumbles a "Mmmhmm" while I continue to move in and out of her with the vibrator.

"Now imagine me moving in and out of you. Imagine me hitting that spot no other man has hit inside you. Fucking hell, I'd make you scream my name and ride me until you came so hard, you'd forget your own fucking name."

She moans and says, "Fuck you for making me wet with that thought, River." There's a side of her that's pissed she's liking this connection we're sharing.

I keep going, my pace getting faster. She's moaning louder with each stroke, and I feel like I'm getting high off her sounds.

Soon I can see her thighs shaking, and she lets go of one shoulder and grabs onto one of her breasts, pinching her nipple as she screams she's coming. I've never been jealous of a hand, but I'm envious of hers right now, touching her body in ways I want to touch her. After this little interaction, I already know I will be addicted to seeing her come in whatever way I can get it.

The moment she jumps off that cliff with my name falling off her lips, I start slowing my pace, and a soft smile spreads across her face. She brings both her hands through her hair, the wet strands sticking to her forehead. She grabs the bottom of her lip with her teeth and gives a little chuckle, her eyes still closed.

I pull the silicone cock out and see her glistening sex all over it. When I bring my gaze back up to meet her, it's as if reality has hit, and she's looking at me panicked.

I'm about to say something, hoping to diffuse the situation, when she speaks. "Well, looks like dildo: one; River: zero." A cocky smile now spreads across her face.

Game on, sweetheart. Game on.

CHAPTER 6

Kennedy

WHAT THE HELL JUST HAPPENED? I watch as River gives me that cocky smile, saying a quick, "Finders keepers," and walks off toward our adjoining doors. The muscles of his back move with his stride, a result of years as a firefighter, carrying loads of equipment up and down flights of stairs. I can't help but fight the drool that threatens to escape my mouth.

Throughout that entire interaction, he did not touch me once with any part of his body. His only touch was through my vibrator, and yet I still feel a void when he walks away from me. My body yearns for him to come back and touch me in ways that will leave marks on me physically and emotionally.

Despite keeping his hands to himself, I know he was turned on because I saw the massive tent in his boxers while I watched as he rhythmically moved my vibrator in and out of me. The word massive doesn't even suffice, if I'm being honest. I don't know how he walks with that beast between his legs.

I have never had a man do that to me, and I never thought it could be that hot. Even though he didn't actually touch me with his own hands, it felt more intimate than an entire night with a man in bed.

I'm still coming off my high, feeling as if I need another shower to cool off, when I register River's words. He took something with him on his way out. Taking in my room with a clearer mind, it dawns on me that he walked out of here with my fucking vibrator.

I also realize that I'm not upset about it. Instead of anger that he stole something that's mine, it makes me wonder what kind of game we can play for me to get it back.

A smile spreads across my face, and I try to concoct a plan on how my vibrator can be mine again. It doesn't take long for me to figure out how I'll gain control back in this fucked up dynamic we are building.

The exhaustion of the day is catching up to me, and my eyes feel heavy, sleep and my bed calling out to me.

Once I'm fully ready for bed and under the covers, it takes some time to get my mind to quiet down. I think about the River of today versus the River of ten years ago. I think about how attractive he remains, even more so as the years have passed, and how I keep finding ways to avoid the obvious.

Who said I can't have a little fun with a good-looking guy? I never said I needed to find forever with him. I just need to let off some tension here and there. What's the harm in that?

* * *

The next morning, I arise with the sound of a cart outside. It isn't until I pick up my phone that I realize I slept in. I was too distracted last night to remember to set an alarm. I shoot up in bed and begin getting myself ready to meet with the newlyweds downstairs for Sunday morning brunch.

Ash and Sam don't leave for their honeymoon until tomorrow. They wanted an extra day to recover from the wedding, along with getting some time in with me and others from the wedding party.

I get myself ready in record time and finally grab my

phone and text Sam that I'm headed down shortly. She replies with a winky face emoji, and I laugh. My best friend is consistent, that's for sure.

Since we lived with one another in college, she has been the queen of emojis. I think if a language could be invented where emojis were the only things used instead of words, she would champion that new communication method.

I open my door, slowly at first, to assess the hallway. The cart I heard earlier is now stationed next door at River's room. That means he's no longer in his room and likely downstairs.

I'm about to make my way to the elevator when an idea strikes me. Instead of going with my original plan to win back my vibrator, I decide to deviate. I was going to wait to pay him back for his little stunt last night, but now I've got something new in mind.

I peek my head into River's room, the housekeeper tending to the bed.

"Um, excuse me." The woman startles for a second before realizing I'm in the room. "I'm sorry to do this, but I left something here last night. Do you mind if I grab it?"

I prepare myself for more resistance from this woman, but she nods and goes back to making the bed. This is too easy.

I quickly find what I'm looking for and rush back to my room. Part one of my plan is underway.

About ten minutes later, I walk into the restaurant at the hotel and find my friends sitting in the back. It seems most of the wedding party has left, probably up early to enjoy breakfast together, while I'm over here strolling in nearly forty-five minutes late.

I cringe at the sight of the table with uneaten croissants and half-drank coffees strewn about the tables.

"I'm so sorry. I crashed last night."

Sam looks up from her phone, a genuine smile marking her features.

"Don't worry about it. Ash and I were a little late too." She waggles her eyebrows at that last part, and I make a motion to gag.

Samara laughs and goes back to looking at her phone.

"Sorry for the distraction. I'm just checking into our flight for tomorrow."

"You know you could have saved yourself the trouble if you had just accepted the offer that my uncle would have let you use his jet," I say as I put my purse down at an unoccupied area of the table.

Yes, I sound like a pretentious diva, but why not use the things we have at our disposal? Unlike my uncle, I am not as flashy as he chooses to live his life. I offered for Sam and Ash to use it as a wedding gift from me and my family, but she wouldn't hear of it.

They're headed to Hawaii for their honeymoon, something they've both dreamed of doing since they met. It's a long flight from this side of the States, so it makes sense to make the trip for a special occasion like their wedding.

"Stop it, Kennedy. We are already staying at your uncle's place while in Maui. We don't need to overstep."

I roll my eyes; this argument is becoming a bit of a repetitive game we are playing at this point.

I look around and survey the restaurant, then bring my focus back to my best friend. "Where's Ashton?"

Sam looks up but is interrupted by a voice I had prepared to hear, yet it still catches me off guard.

"He was making sure I was fed before he left me behind to care for his wife." River's voice, usually grating my nerves, is now something that causes that uptick in my heart rate. I'm surprised by the turn of events, but I try to tame my reaction.

Ashton chuckles as he settles next to Sam and kisses her cheek. She closes her eyes, almost like she's savoring every second they touch one another.

I swing my gaze over to River, his eyes looking me over,

most likely checking to see if what happened last night is having a negative effect on me. I try to give him a calm look back, then opt for a smile, and that seems to appease him. Whatever nerves he had, fearing something would change with us, dissipates quickly off his shoulders.

"Good morning, River," I say, trying to sound indifferent.

"Wow, not a 'fuck you' or 'drop dead' at this early hour? That's new." That's from Ash, and I look at him, panic taking over my features that he can see right through me. Am I giving off *River made me climax with my dildo* vibes?

"It's almost like she's let off some steam and has no energy to throw daggers in my direction," River answers, and I give him a glare in return.

I roll my eyes and don't even waste my breath with a comeback. Maybe there's more truth to what he's saying than I'd care to admit. I excuse myself to grab a plate and serve myself some breakfast at the buffet.

When I return, Ashton is talking about the new software he's helping build at the company he is working at.

"Yeah, the metrics are a little different, but overall, this framework is similar to platforms I've worked on in the past. Thank goodness because learning something new with the wedding going on at the same time, I think it would have been a nightmare."

Ashton looks over to his new wife and kisses her nose. The love these two have for one another feels like nothing I've seen before. Actually, scratch that, I have seen it—in my parents long ago.

I snap myself out of my thoughts when the waiter comes by asking if I want coffee. I don't have it in me to use words and simply nod, thanking him with a whisper. The memory of my parents is taking over my heart and leaving me uneasy as my friends tell us all about their plans for their honeymoon.

Grief is difficult like that. I'm constantly thrown into moments where my mind veers back in time to moments where I felt whole. Now, I just have little glimpses into the life I lost with them.

Ash and Sam begin to veer off into a conversation together while I'm eating some fruit quietly. I feel River's gaze on me more than I see it. When I look to my right, sure enough, his eyes are trained on me.

"You're awfully quiet," he says, his brows furrowed in concentration.

"How did you sleep, River? Any tent issues that kept you up last night?" I chuckle, and an amused expression takes over his face.

He moves closer to me, his voice just above a whisper. "As a matter of fact, I handled my tent issue a few times. It seems once wasn't enough. How about you? Were all your needs met?"

I instantly feel my panties dampen with the image of River stroking himself, but I keep my gaze on the plate in front of me.

"Oh, with my handy little stallion, my needs are always met." I wink, hoping to show how unaffected I am by his words.

Luckily, he can't read minds because he'd soon find out that all I want is a repeat, maybe without the silicone dildo and with the real thing instead.

An easy smile spreads across his face, his attention going back to something Ashton just asked him. My head is in the clouds, my heart racing, thinking about what I am going to do next.

River is lost in a conversation with his best friend, and Sam ran to the restroom, so I pull out my phone and decide to execute the next part of my plan.

I quickly hear the swoosh of the text being sent, and River

pulls his phone out, putting his finger up for Ash to hold his thought.

He's mid-sip of coffee as he unlocks his phone. Then he realizes his mistake because the moment the photo pops up for River to acknowledge, the coffee goes down the wrong pipe, and he's coughing incessantly. I pat his back while Ashton worries his friend is choking.

River is waving his hands up, hoping to convey the message he's okay, and I can't help slapping his back but smiling at him, knowing my photo worked him up.

He finally catches his breath, and he reassures Ash he's okay. Sam returns to the table, holding out her phone to show something to her new husband. They get lost in a conversation that seems to be an unspoken language between the two of them, and that leaves me to look over at River.

"You play dirty, Skipper." His choked words don't match the wicked gleam in his eyes.

"Oh, I assure you I'm squeaky clean in that photo. The only dirty thing present are my thoughts." I excuse myself, hugging my friends goodbye and wishing them a good honeymoon. I give a little wave to River, who is simply sitting there, speechless, gawking at me.

I know he was worried I was going to freak, but little does he know I don't back down from a fight, and I most definitely don't back down from something that might end in orgasms.

I walk to the elevator, feeling a little lighter after my little stunt. I used the opportunity earlier with housekeeping in his room to take the dildo back. But that's not all I did.

I had gone back to my room, stripped off my clothes except my lace panties, and grabbed my boobs with one hand, ensuring a nipple was being pinched with my thumb and index finger of that hand while the dildo sat right below my navel.

I captioned the photo with, "Looks like my vibrator continues to be the lucky one."

A laugh slips out as I make my way into the elevator, satisfied I was able to plant a tiny seed and maybe see where this little cat-and-mouse game will lead us next.

CHAPTER 7
River

I'M SITTING at the table with the new husband and wife, stunned by the photo Kennedy sent me. I'm trying to veer my thoughts somewhere to help the situation growing in my pants, but I cannot stop visualizing that fucking photo.

My best friend and his bride are looking at one another, talking about their upcoming trip and some things they need to grab before heading to the airport early tomorrow morning. To say I'm just a body sitting across from them is an understatement.

After years of banter between Kennedy and me, it should come as no shock she would send me a taunting photo like that. But something about the gesture still caught me off guard.

I tossed and turned last night—first, for the fact that we crossed a line, and I wasn't sure if Kennedy would chop my dick off for it or applaud it. Second, because I wasn't sure where this would lead us. I'm used to many different reactions from Kennedy, but this playful side is one I wasn't quite prepared for.

A smile spreads across my face, and it catches Sammie's attention. "What's that smile for?"

Something is unsettling about the way she's looking at me. I try to temper whatever is going through my mind to keep this little game I'm playing with Kennedy from being discovered.

I know Sammie, and she can sniff anything out of us. Shit, the moment I knew Ashton was going to propose, I didn't answer her call for a week. Turns out that was enough to set off the alarm bells for her, and she knew something was up.

"Just someone I hooked up with wants to hang out later." There, she won't ask too many questions.

"Oh really? Do tell." She gives me a Cheshire cat smile and looks over to her husband.

Well, shit. Now I need to make something up and hopefully stop this from going further.

"Um, not much to tell. It really was just a hookup. Nothing special. We fucked around last night, and I barely slept." The horrified look on Samara's face, along with Ashton looking pleased I got some, spurs me on to keep rambling. "I better get more coffee and go pack my stuff. Clothes were thrown across the room, and we—"

"Please stop!" Samara pleads as she puts her hands up, and Ash laughs. "Dude, we get it." Okay, so maybe I was a bit too descriptive. But it seems my plan worked, and I got them off the scent that something happened between Kennedy and me. I have no clue why I panic thinking she would assume the woman in question would be Kennedy but I'm a panicked state so my mind is in a state right now.

I look at Sam, and she has a pinched look on her face.

"Listen, I think my work here is done." I move toward my friends, giving them hugs and wishing them well on their trip.

"Oh, and don't do anything I wouldn't do."

I wink over my shoulder, chuckling as I hear my best friend yell, "The list is endless then!" At that, I hear a smack across what I assume is his shoulder courtesy of his new bride.

The moment I get to my floor, I take my steps a little faster than I would normally, hoping to catch Kennedy before she checks out of her room. I was going to follow her right as she left the table earlier, but I didn't want to come off as too eager. I look down at my watch to see she left nearly forty-five minutes ago. Shit, time flew.

But when I turn the corner, I'm greeted by housekeeping, Kennedy's hotel room ajar, and the employee vacuuming the room.

I can't hide my disappointment as I scan my room key and walk myself into my room. I don't know what I was expecting between Kennedy and me, but a part of me feels an emptiness that I was never expecting.

Whatever happened in the last twelve hours between us has left a lot of unknowns circling around my head, and the unease that settles in me at the thought that I won't get to explore this further with her is pushing the disappointment deeper.

I had called for them to fix something in my room while I was downstairs getting breakfast and housekeeping must have fixed up my bed unexpectedly. I move along my hotel room, gathering my toiletries and a few scattered items I need to throw in my duffle bag, when I hear a knock on my door.

For a second, I hope it's Kennedy waiting for me on the other side, but then my brother's booming voice carries over, and I quickly realize whatever line I crossed with Kennedy last night was much like a footprint in the sand. With this new day, a fresh layer of sand has been smoothed out, and I have to let the possibility go that the two of us could be more than enemies.

I open the door, and my brother's gaze is full of mischief.

"You lucky dog. Who was she? Where did you find her? The hotel bar?" Fuck, news travels fast. Damn Ash and his big mouth. He must have texted my brother right when I left the table.

My brother uses that twin instinct and eyes me a moment longer. "Unless you left out the detail that you were with a leggy blonde who seems to push all your buttons. Is that it, brother? Did said blonde push all the right buttons last night?"

I try to slam the door in his face and walk away, but the fucker kicks his foot out to stop it from closing. I can't lie and say my brother's attitude is truly upsetting me. Since Abby left last year, he has been a shell of himself. But in the last few weeks, I've seen him come alive again, and I feel like I'm getting my brother back.

"You better be careful not to hurt yourself. Chief Daniels will be pissed if you're out due to a foot injury."

"Oh, please. Chief and I go way back. He loves me. He said I'm his favorite," my brother says as he walks into my room.

"We've known him the same amount of time. He was Dad's best friend, and I think he is still pissed at you for making a pass at his daughter sophomore year," I retort, rolling my eyes.

I grab my duffle and swing it over my shoulder, hoping the hookup he was inquiring about has passed.

"That's been long forgotten. He loves me now." My brother puffs out his chest like he's the biggest and best between us.

"Keep telling yourself that." I roll my eyes and walk out the hotel room door, my brother trailing me.

"Don't think I'm going to forget that look regarding this 'mystery woman' you hooked up with." He winks. "I don't forget things that easily." He taps his index finger to his temple, as if I need reminding. My brother and I have that twin thing where we can nearly read each other's minds, and he will not let this go.

I grab my bags, swinging my gaze around the room to make sure I didn't forget anything. When I turn back to look at Clay, he's got a pensive expression lining his features.

"Hey, you okay?" Concern laces my tone.

"Me? Of course." He grabs one of my bags and strolls out. I know there's something up, but I don't want to push him. I doubt being at a wedding after longing for that life he had once built with his ex-wife is an easy transition.

Luckily, he seems to take the hint from my expression that now isn't the time, and we head to the valet to retrieve the car. The ride home is quick, and I can't wait to get back and rest off this headache that is in no way an alcohol hangover.

I think this headache stems from the realization that what started as Kennedy being a thorn in my side is now this unknown I'd like to explore. But she headed out before I could talk to her, and now I feel like the opportunity has passed.

* * *

"So, what made you want to be a veterinarian?" It feels like I'm pulling teeth on this date. To top it off, I'm going to have to find a new vet after this disaster.

"I love animals." Seriously? That's her answer? I work diligently not to roll my eyes, but I'm cringing internally at how awful this is going.

It's two weeks since the wedding, a timeframe I have felt each day that passed slowly. I assumed, even with Kennedy's quick departure from the hotel, I'd hear from her, but the silence was deafening. I have opened my phone, ready to text, at least a dozen times, but each time I'd write something out, it sounded lame, and I held back. As each day went by, it felt more awkward to reach out, and now, it feels like the opportunity is gone now.

I know Kennedy keeps herself at a distance from pretty

much everyone, but I honestly thought we would explore this new side we found between each other. In all honesty, I had been growing tired of this turmoil we always conjured up when we were around each other. So when things turned more playful and sexual, I was ready for it. But just as much as I haven't texted, neither has she. It's probably best we don't complicate things more. In all honesty, I'm finding more excuses the more I ponder the reasons why I've let the time lapse and I'm now sitting across this disaster of a date.

The woman across from me, my dog's veterinarian, is quietly back to sipping her tea. The boredom is palpable between the two of us.

This woman has been giving me the vibe she's interested in me since I started taking Lola, my three-year-old golden retriever, to her a year ago. She would treat my dog, but she's been giving me flirtatious glances for months now. When I came in to pick up Lola's flea medication, she ran after me, asking me out for a coffee.

As much as my gut told me not to accept the offer, I decided it might be better to throw myself back out there. This plan backfired quite quickly, I now realize.

I look down at my watch, maybe for the hundredth time, and see I'm inching closer to my departure time. Maybe if I walk slowly to Ashton's place, it would make sense to leave now.

"Listen, Tabitha, I just realized the time. I should get going." I thumb my finger toward the door to the small coffee joint we decided to meet at. "Do you want me to walk you back to the office?"

Did I mention I made sure there was an out-clause in this whole date situation? Maybe, subconsciously, I knew this was going to be craptastic, so I called Ashton yesterday to see if I could come by this afternoon. I haven't seen him since the morning after his wedding.

"Actually, I'm going to stick around. You can head out."

The eagerness is hard to ignore, and it's the most enthusiastic she's sounded since we both sat down here forty minutes ago.

Before I can say anything else, someone clears their throat behind me. I look over to see a man around my age, looking at Tabitha like she hung the moon.

I can't help but ask, "May I help you?"

The man ignores me and goes straight to addressing the vet seated across from me. "Hey, Tab. It's good to see you."

I see the flush of her cheeks and her smile grow wide. What is happening? "Do you two know each other?" Seems like a pointless question, but I honestly don't know what's going on here. I'm having a hard time connecting the dots.

"Hey, Danny. It's good to see you too." She takes a shy sip of her tea, batting her eyes at him and doing all the things I would have expected her to do while on a date with me, not this guy. Again, what the fuck is happening right now?

I keep looking between the two of them, waiting for someone to clue me in. "Oh, um, Danny, this is one of my client's owners, River. River, this is my ex, Daniel." The pieces are starting to fall into place.

I stand up, grab the remainder of my coffee, looking at Tabitha. "Thanks for joining me for coffee. I hope you have a good rest of the afternoon." She nods an acknowledgment of my words but keeps her eyes on her ex.

The moment I move toward the door to leave the shop, I see Danny taking the seat I just vacated. Either this was purely a coincidence, or this woman used me to make this man jealous. I could bet my left nut I was set up as a pawn in her little scheme to make him jealous.

"I nearly peed my pants." Sammie is retelling a story of Ashton when he went down the zip line in Hawaii. She's laughing so hard, there are legit tears streaming down her face.

"I wasn't that embarrassing." Ashton moans next to her, running his hand down his face.

"You're right. It wasn't the volume of the scream you let out; it was the pitch I'm talking about, sweetie." She pats his cheek mockingly.

I grab the beer sitting in front of me and take a swig. I have an easy smile painted across my face, enjoying this relaxed feeling I get when I'm around the two of them. For just a second, a pang hits my chest, wishing I had this type of relationship with someone.

My shifts at the firehouse have been nonstop lately, but the moment I walk through my front door, the loneliness becomes more evident.

Right around the time of the wedding, some of the guys at the station came down with the stomach flu. Clay and I have been covering some extra shifts, so I haven't had a chance to see my best friend and his wife since they returned from Hawaii two weeks ago.

As my mind has been consumed with thoughts of Kennedy, I have welcomed the distraction with the extra shifts. Clay hasn't touched on the subject regarding my "hookup" from the wedding, and I can't say how relieved I am.

I hear the front door open, and I hear a voice I've now come to miss since that night when lines got blurred. When I would usually find this interaction exhausting and always keep my guard up to ensure I take the final jab, I now realize how much I longed to see and hear her in my vicinity.

I look over my shoulder to see Kennedy striding in, a smile stretched out across her face. For the last month, I've been telling myself that I have been hyping this woman up, truly putting her on some fucking pedestal because I was horny and needed the release. But now, as I see her again, my thoughts realize two things: one—no, she really is that fucking gorgeous; and two, I've become consumed by her in the span of a few simple moments when my skin was near hers.

The moment she spots me in the kitchen, she stops cold in her tracks. She stares at me for a beat, frozen in place. Sammie looks at her and then swings her gaze at me, a questioning look taking over her features.

Kennedy must realize her misstep and recovers.

"Hey, Riv. I didn't expect to see you here today." For someone who usually sounds so sure of herself, she sounds quite reserved. We usually throw at least two jabs within the first few seconds of seeing one another, and so far, her words are soft in a tone she's never reserved for me in the past.

I see the thoughts going through that pretty head of Kennedy's before she must push them aside, and Sam walks up to her. "Let me take those from you. What did you bring?"

There's a box that looks like it might carry some baked goods inside. I see the grease stains on the side of the box, and I wonder if she grabbed them from that bakery next to the stadium.

"They're your favorite Danishes from Ginger's Bakery. Thought you'd like it with your coffee this afternoon." She smiles and continues to move further into the house, putting her purse down and removing her shoes near the couch.

Her eyes connect with mine one more time before moving beyond me to land on my best friend seated in front of me at the kitchen table.

"It's good to see you, Ash. Looks like that Hawaiian sun did you some good. You've got a helluva tan going." She smiles wide for Ashton, and a part of me is jealous that she didn't greet me with that beautiful smile.

I watch her move closer to us, hugging Ashton when she rounds the table, yet only giving me a quick verbal hello and moving further into the kitchen to help Sammie with the items she brought with her.

The women are talking in hushed voices, not sure why the secrecy. Hopefully, Kennedy didn't mention what happened that night because I have kept my mouth shut on my end. I do not need to open a can of worms with the endless questions I know I'll get from Ashton, especially if he's the last to know.

"When do you work again?" Ashton asks, picking up his phone when it chimes.

I sneak one more peek toward the kitchen, then move my focus back to my friend. "Tomorrow. It's finally getting back to normal. The firehouse got hit hard with that stomach bug."

"Yeah, Clay mentioned that. Did you have someone to watch Lola?"

Lola usually stays with Ash and Sammie when I do my shifts, but I had my neighbor stay with her while I had to work and my friends were off enjoying their honeymoon.

"Yeah, Sally watched her for me." I take another swig of my beer, noticing the glances Kennedy is swinging my way while she talks to her best friend.

"Oh man, that chick has it bad for you," Ashton says, and I quickly look at him, panic etched along my features.

"What?" I nearly yell, unease sliding down my spine that he sees right through me and Kennedy. Maybe I'm not doing as great a job hiding this attraction for Kennedy like I thought.

"Yeah. Sally has a major crush on you, dude. Don't tell me you didn't notice." Instant relieve courses through my veins at Ashton's words.

I wasn't clueless to my neighbor's attraction to me. Her cheeks pink up every single time I talk to her. She's a sweet woman, but I have zero chemistry when it comes to her.

She isn't my type, if I'm being completely honest. I'm attracted to strong women, those who can power a conversation and won't just succumb to whatever I want. I know many women like my neighbor Sally—molding their world to fit someone else's. That might be attractive to some, but I sort of enjoy the pushback in a relationship. I like a woman to speak her mind. It's becoming more apparent with these lingering thoughts about Kennedy that my attraction is to one woman, and she's merely standing a few feet away from me right now.

"Well, it's not something I'm pursuing," I say, hoping that if Kennedy caught any of that conversation, she understands nothing is going on there.

The ladies meet us at the table with a fresh coffee and a piece of the Danish split in two. Kennedy settles next to me, unease evident in the way she sits stiffly by my side.

"I didn't really talk to you much at breakfast the morning after. How did you enjoy the wedding?" Ashton asks, which causes Kennedy's spine to straighten even more as if this question caught her off guard.

"Um, the wedding was beautiful. Every detail was perfect." I see her swing her smile toward Sam, knowing most of the wedding was planned with so much detail Samara had envisioned. "I was exhausted afterward." She takes a sip of her coffee, shyness oozing off her, which is new for the usual ballbuster she tends to be.

"I'm surprised you slept through the sounds next door to you with this guy." Sammie says, and immediately, I snap my head up, shock evident in my expression.

Kennedy looks over to me with surprise in her gaze.

"Yeah, someone rocked his world that night." She snickers. Fucking hell, Samara. I didn't know she'd out me like this.

I scratch the back of my neck, unease creeping up my spine, and I can feel the heat in my cheeks as the discomfort doubles as I sit here.

"Oh really? Is that so, River?" Kennedy looks all too amused.

I simply shrug, not knowing how to proceed in this conversation. Little do I know, luck won't be on my side as Ashton, unbeknownst to him, is going to continue to shove his foot in his mouth.

"I guess that girl is long forgotten, huh, buddy?" Ashton laughs, his tone completely at ease while I feel the hairs stand on my arms, knowing this isn't going to end well for me.

"Oh, why's that?" Kennedy asks. I can hear the ice in her tone. This is not how I saw this going.

"Apparently, Rivie here just got back from a date. Too bad it was the date from hell. His vet tricked him into being a pawn in a little scheme to win back her true love at a coffee shop." Now Ashton is laughing, genuine tears forming in his eyes. Fucker. If he only knew the hole he's digging for me with his words.

Without looking to my side, I can feel Kennedy's gaze boring a hole in my skull. She's probably trying to kill me with her glare. Luckily, she's not that powerful.

When I sneak a peek toward Kennedy, I see what was a playful look just moments ago, now morphing into one of anger and disappointment.

"Looks like you're going to need a new vet, River." That's from Sammie, but without expanding further on this torturous coffee date that I just left, I decide to veer the conversation in a different direction, asking about their honeymoon.

"How was the luau?" That was part of my gift to them for their wedding. Instead of buying something they likely won't need, I gifted them something for them to do on their trip.

Samara's features soften as she reminisces about their honeymoon and how romantic the entire experience was. Hawaii must have lived up to their expectations and beyond.

The entire time we are getting a rundown of the adventures the new Mr. and Mrs. took on the tropical island, I notice how quiet Kennedy is by my side.

She finishes her coffee quickly, looking at her phone, which never pinged, stating an emergency has come up at the office and she has to run.

I can see the disappointment cross Samara's features, but she doesn't push her best friend, and soon enough, Kennedy is walking out the door. It didn't go unnoticed that she barely looked at me, nor did she say goodbye on her way out.

I look over to my friends, their gazes at their front door in bewilderment, wondering if something they said spurred her quick exit.

I can't leave things hanging like this with Kennedy, so I head out the door, stating I have to take Lola on a walk before the sun sets. It's nearing summer hours, and the sun stays out longer, something my friends reminded me of as I said my goodbyes, but I can't get that look of defeat on Kennedy's face out of my mind.

I need to fix this, even if it leads to nothing but a clear conscience for me. I realize that what she thinks of me matters now that we've crossed this imaginary line between us.

CHAPTER 8

Kennedy

HE WAS ON A DATE.

I'm paralyzed by the thought of River going out on dates while I'm still replaying that night in the hotel with him on repeat. I know River is not really boyfriend material, but something about this is just rubbing me wrong. Especially since he was rubbing something else on me not that long ago. Add to the fact I want a repeat of said rubbing yet again.

I don't have dibs on the man, but this is really throwing me off. The last month has been hell with the chaos waiting for me at work, topped with my fucking brain rearing back to that night in the hotel room.

I get that I didn't reach out after I sent that photo, but his silence was deafening. And the longer the silence stretched, the more I knew that what we did had to stay in the past. But knowing he brushed it off like it was nothing—like I was nothing—stings more the longer I sit here thinking about his mind moving onto someone new without even giving me a second thought.

I wanted to reach out to him, but each spare second on my end was filled with another fire that needed to be put out. The baseball season is in full swing, and this is my first year as president of the organization. I can't just put that part of my life on hold so I can explore things with River. Now I'm thankful I haven't because he obviously didn't think about me any longer than beyond that night.

Once I realized River was not going to text or call me, I decided to let what happened at the hotel stay in the past. As much as I wanted to see where it would go, another part of me knew it was probably a bad idea.

Thoughts of that night are now bombarding my mind while I think of River on endless dates, probably doing that and much more to women, while I am just a forgotten piece of ass in his book. He probably thinks it's not worth it in the end.

I continue to sit at the table, listening to stories about their honeymoon. Don't get me wrong, seeing my friends loving their married life brings me endless joy. But I can't shake what Sammie whispered to me when we were gathering our coffees and pastries.

"Apparently, River had a date right before coming here."

She had mischief in her eyes when she whispered it, assuming I would love this tidbit of information to pester him about. Little does she know, I feel like it's a punch to the gut having this knowledge.

I'm really trying to let it go, but I can't help letting my mind wander. I'm this strong, independent woman, yet the thought that River could dismiss what happened in my hotel room, especially knowing me for so many years, just leaves me feeling dirty.

I wasn't anything more than another naked body he looked at. I left the hotel that day feeling like I had the upper hand in some weird way. I thought we'd have a little fun. I didn't expect any strange tension after our encounter at breakfast felt like our usual banter.

Plus, I had no idea what he thought after I sent that photo, even if he choked on his coffee. However, his lack of response was all the answer I needed. I waited around a bit before checking out. When I didn't get anything back in our text thread, I walked myself out of that hotel with my head held high and no regrets. I had fun that night. I left it at that.

But hearing Sammie talk about River going on a date, no care in the world that I was sitting right here, really pisses me off. And I don't know if I am pissed at myself for caring so much or if I am just pissed because it's River, and everything he does makes me want to scream.

The words tumbling out of Ashton's and Samara's mouths are falling on deaf ears, so I scramble an excuse of needing to leave, always blaming work, and get myself out of their house.

The moment I step out of their front door, I feel like I can breathe again. This reaction seems a bit exaggerated, but I can't ignore the suffocation I felt as the minutes ticked, and I had to sit there, pretending nothing had shifted between River and me. I begin to take my steps quickly away from their apartment, grab my phone, and order myself a ride.

Since my parents died in a car accident, I haven't been able to build the nerve to get my driver's license. That might sound unbelievable as a busy executive with a position of power in a male-dominated industry. Going from New York to now a resident in Boston, not having a car isn't uncommon, so I haven't found a need to get my own car and have continued to use a service instead of learning. Boston is such a busy city, that it all seems to work seamlessly anyway.

I'm too distracted by the app to realize someone is calling my name. I only hear his voice the moment he reaches out to grab my arm.

"Fuck, Skipper. You could at least acknowledge me as I'm yelling for you," River says, acting as if this little run was that strenuous on him. He's a fucking firefighter, for god's sake.

"I didn't realize you needed to speak to me. I've been around. You could have texted me." Fucking hell. I'm letting him know how hurt I am, and I don't want to give him that power. The sooner I get myself back to our regular irritation between the two of us, the sooner I can go back to not caring about whatever it is we could be.

"Can you stop the prissy act, Kennedy? It's getting old." The audacity of this dick.

"Fuck you, River," I seethe, my molars grinding as I look up at him with fire in my eyes. "I don't remember agreeing we were on good terms. Why don't you go find yourself another date, and you can get her to comfort that bruised ego of yours."

The moment I say it, I close my eyes and inwardly groan. That green-eyed monster doesn't look good coming out of me.

A smile spreads across his face like he won this battle before it even started. Selfish prick.

"I'm sensing some jealousy there, Skip." He moves a little closer to me, gauging if I'm going to accept the proximity or if I'm going to knee him in the balls. Honestly, either possibility is a high probability right now.

"You wish I'd spend even a second jealous about your high-maintenance ass." I honestly don't know what he's hoping to do here. I mean, so he played with me using my vibrator—let's call it what it is—a glitch in the matrix.

"You don't mean that. I know you don't." I'm about to chime in, and he stops me. "The date meant nothing, Kennedy. I swear." I hear the sincerity in his voice, but it doesn't mean I completely let go of my anger.

However, I hate the way my shoulders sag a bit with his words. I don't want to feel relief knowing he didn't care about this person he went on a date with. It's never bothered me in the past, but now, it feels like a weight lifted off my chest, knowing this date was nothing to him. Maybe I'm hoping that if that means nothing, I mean something.

This is why I avoid situations like these. I hate this feeling of connection with someone. The moment my heart starts to expand, it will only hurt when it doesn't lead to more. If this whole experience with River last month and my emotional pull toward him now has taught me anything, it's that I just cannot handle something more with him or with anyone for that matter.

River must sense my mind doing this push and pull, so he leans into my personal space and cups my cheeks with his hands.

"Plus, I can't start something with someone else when I haven't gotten my fill of you yet." He leans in, his eyes searching mine, hoping I'll give him some sign that this proximity is okay with me.

Despite my desire to keep my distance, to keep my heart whole, the moment I feel his hands on my face, it feels like I have no power to push him away. It's like all those cracks that etched themselves into my heart years ago begin to find a means to stitch themselves back up.

I don't pull away, and that's all the permission he needs to bring his face closer and connect his lips with mine.

The moment I feel those soft lips touch mine, it feels like my world has stopped spinning. The sounds of the cars, the people walking past us on the sidewalk, the horns in the distance all dim. All I feel is River. My only sensation is this one, where we are connected, and it's like I'm soaring when he's this close to me. It feels like all the synapses in my body are reserved for this one spot, this one link, where we are finally bridging a gap after years of pushing each other apart.

I grip his biceps, my nails digging into his skin. I swallow his moan, and then he opens up to me, and I let him in. I feel the swipe of his tongue, and then the kiss deepens even more.

Fuck, this feels good. This kiss is all-encompassing, yet not enough of a bond. All these years I pushed River away only to find out that he was the one thing I was missing in my life.

As if I lived this life looking for something to make me feel whole again, yet he was the missing piece all along.

I don't know how long we stay connected, but after what feels like too soon, we come up for air, his eyes opening and connecting with mine.

"Shit, Kennedy." He swallows, vividly perplexed by the way that kiss tilted both our worlds on its side. For so long, we've fought each other, and now it feels like all I want to do is take back all the hateful jabs and replace them with moments like these.

"Shit is right." That's all my brain can process right now. I have no idea what this means. I am blanking on how to respond beyond being mesmerized by this unexpected connection with a man I've lived to hate for so long.

"There is no fucking way I'm walking away from this after that. No fucking way." I see the determination in his expression as he looks at me, almost like he's waiting for me to pull away.

He knows I don't hold on to people long, and, for the most part, he is all about the casual fling over commitment. Regarding my past, he knows what happened to my parents years ago, but the details are something I've always kept close to my chest. Whatever he's heard, it was from Samara or Ash. My story is vague, even to them, with little detail regarding the accident and how it transformed the trajectory of my life in ways I will never be able to fully comprehend.

I start to pull away, but his grip on my face holds me in place.

"I wasn't kidding when I said I have to get back to the office," I say, my voice just above a whisper.

"When can I see you?" I can see the sincerity in his expression. Gone is the River who throws sarcastic phrases my way. In his place is a man giving me a view of his softer side, something he's reserved for so many but never me. It's unnerving yet uplifting, all in one.

"If I said never, what would you say?" I throw back. I don't seem to have the strength to leave this here and walk away. I need to hear him tell me this might be a bad idea. I need him to walk away because, for the first time in my life, I can't simply let this lie.

"I would say I'll see you tonight and show up at your doorstep then." He smiles, his dimples making an appearance.

"Then I guess I'll see you on my doorstep after nine tonight." I use my fingers to pry his hands off my face and walk away. I see the Uber pull up that I had just ordered before River stopped me, and I walk toward it.

I look back and see a smile take over River's face. I guess I'm just throwing caution to the wind and letting this thing go wherever it's supposed to go. Maybe it's time I toss the rules to the side and see what happens. Something casual is all I can give, but I doubt River wants something deeper anyway.

CHAPTER 9

River

"MA, YOU HOME?" I walk into my childhood home with Lola, and I'm immediately pulled into comfort. Not much has changed with the layout of the house, something my mother takes complete pride in after years of people nagging her to move things around.

After my father passed away, there was a moment she thought she'd move us out and start a new life, keeping with the plans she and my dad had prior to his passing. But after many people around us told her to take a year and reflect on that after some time passed, she chose to stay put, knowing she could never really part with the last place my father called home.

I walk further into the house, Lola sniffing out where Grandma could be. I find my mom and brother sitting at the kitchen table.

"I didn't know you were coming over here today," I say, directing my comment to Clay as I walk toward my mother and wrap my arms around her.

She's much shorter than us, as we tower over her much like my father once did. She looks up at me, and I can see the pride in her eyes. Before I know what's happening, Lola is pawing at me to move so she can get her grandma cuddles in.

"Mom said she wanted to see her favorite child before you came over to ruin her afternoon," Clay says before I flip him off.

"Hey now, both of you stop. You know I find you both equally a pain in my ass." She chuckles and moves toward the coffee pot to grab a cup of coffee after giving my dog a few scratches under the chin.

My mother, despite years of pain after losing my father, never faltered in caring for us, even with a broken heart. I look at her now and see all the pain she carried on her shoulders for so long, bearing a lot of that pain for all three of us.

Once she's greeted me, she turns her attention to the golden retriever watching her every move.

"And you, Lola, did you miss Grandma? I know, Daddy didn't let you come stay with me. He made you stay with that neighbor of his." My mother is speaking to my dog like she's a baby, but her eyes dart over to me narrowed as if she's holding a grudge.

"Come on, don't do that. It was easier to leave her with the neighbor with the way I was coming and going to the firehouse. No hard feelings." I give her my sad eyes, and that makes her laugh.

Attempting to veer this conversation in another direction, I switch gears. "Ma, you were missed at the wedding," I say as I grab the hot mug out of her hands. "How was Shelby's red carpet event?"

Apparently, one of Shelby's best-sellers was picked up for a Hulu movie, and the big event was the same day as Ashton's wedding. She was conflicted about what to do, but she had confirmed the red carpet event before knowing the date of the wedding.

"Oh, Jasmine was so happy I was her plus one. Shelby was shining the entire night. It was really special to see. Let me show you pictures." She gets up to grab her phone off the counter.

"There were so many celebrities. I was starstruck, boys. Truly in awe of everyone I got to meet." Mom's smile beams at us as she opens her phone and starts going through what feels like a thousand photos.

"Geez, you almost have as many photos from one night on the red carpet as you do of the dog," Clay says, earning himself a smack across the shoulder.

"Don't start, Clay. Lola and I have a special bond, don't we, sweet girl?" She looks over at my dog, who's currently panting, her tongue wagging to one side, looking at my mom like she's her reason for living.

I roll my eyes and sip my coffee, feeling a bit surprised at all the accomplishments Shelby has attained throughout the years. She did apologize for her actions back at her high school prom, and we can now laugh about it, but I won't lie and say I'm not slightly scared of her imagination. I've read her books; she might be slightly unhinged. Luckily, I had the wedding as an excuse not to attend this event.

"Did you go to the memorial?" I ask. My mom takes in a breath and looks over at me, the pain of that day still close to the surface.

"I couldn't do it," she says, her mind on something distant.

Although we live in Boston, my father was out in New York for the week training with one of the firehouses out there. We were left back here packing up the house. Moving to New York had been a sure thing until everything changed, and our lives were forever altered.

Unfortunately, the week he went out there was the same week as the terrorist attacks of September 11. My mother watched in horror as she began to realize my father wasn't coming home to us. I remember bits and pieces of that day, but nothing is as cemented in my mind as my mother's sobs that took over the room as she watched everything unfold on the television.

"I'm thinking of going this year if you feel like going. I'm headed out to Ground Zero on the actual day. If you decide you want to go, just let me know." I grab her hand and kiss her knuckles.

"I'll let you know, sweetie." She returns a small smile at me, and I would bet all my money in the world she will stay behind. She tries to go every year to that part of New York, but she never can get herself near that portion of the city. Jasmine, Shelby's mother, asks every time my mother visits, and each time, my mom says she's not ready. I think she'll never be ready, and that's okay. We all handle grief in different ways.

"So, what's up with you and Kennedy?" Clay's curiosity wins out, and I school my expression to keep from showing how annoyed I am that he brought this up around our mother. Thanks to him, now she is going to hold onto that piece of information and pester me with it.

"Um, well," I move my hand along the back of my neck, "I'm seeing her tonight, actually." I should have lied. With the way I see my mom's face light up, I know this is going to bite me in the ass later.

"Finally, sweetie, you've opened your stubborn eyes." My mom looks like she's going to bounce out of her chair with excitement. "I knew you two would finally see things clearly. You've been fighting this for too long."

"No, we haven't. We've hated each other for a decade. Don't read so much into this." I omit the part that we are just keeping things physical. It's not anything deeper than that.

"No, ask your brother. From the moment I met Kennedy years ago, I saw she would be the right fit for you. She keeps you on your toes, and she doesn't sugarcoat anything. She's exactly what you need."

"That's interesting because she seems to have more of a

liking toward my twin than she does me," I say, a little more bitterness to my tone than I would like to have.

"Rightfully so. Fuck, I'm way more fun," my brother says, then gets a glare from our mother.

"Language, Clay!" she scolds, and I see my brother's cheeks pink. I chuckle to myself even though I know my mother could do the same to me, and I'd cower the same way my brother just did.

"Anyway, she doesn't like me more, Riv. She knows it gets under your skin, so we just play this little game. She and I aren't attracted to one another like that. She looks at you completely different than she looks at me. Isn't that weird that we're identical for the most part and people aren't attracted to both of us? Abby always mentioned how different we were in her eyes. I don't see it. I see myself as an extension of you."

"Way to get deep, brother. But yeah, I guess it's hard for us to understand. I mean, I never dated a twin to understand what people are talking about." I get up in search of something to eat.

Grabbing an apple, I move back toward the table and start eating. "I guess we'll just have our fill and move on."

"River Nichols, you will treat that girl with respect. I raised you better than that. I mean, there has not been one girl you've brought home who I've liked. The latest one, what's her name," my mother snaps her fingers, "Klarissa, right?"

"Karissa!" Clay and I both say aloud to correct her.

She waves us off and continues, "I wasn't a fan. She was only into dating you to hang out with your firefighter friends. I don't like that, son. Kennedy is the one to hold on to though. I love that girl." She pats my hand, followed by a little squeeze.

Mom gets up from the table, not giving me much room to explain that this thing with Kennedy is just an attraction.

"Is this the right time to clarify that 'dating' is a stretch for what you do with the women you hang around?" Clay whispers, and luckily, my mom's ears are nowhere near us to eavesdrop.

He's not wrong though. Kennedy and I are going to get this itch out, and then we'll probably be good. Even though that kiss earlier today was anything but simple. I have never felt that kind of connection from one kiss.

"I'm going to take a shower. Will you boys be around a bit longer?" Lola is already up and ready to follow when my mother looks back for an answer.

"Yeah, I'll stick around," I say, taking another bite of my apple.

"Same. I don't have much to do now that I cook for one most of the time," my brother replies, and I see the pain in his eyes when he says it.

Mom nods in understanding and begins her walk up the stairs. Lola's paws follow right behind her. They're two peas in a pod.

"So you're seeing Kennedy tonight? Going to dinner?" Clay asks, curiosity evident in his tone.

"You know it's not like that, Clay. I'm just going over there, and, I don't know, we'll see where things go." I shrug, unsure how I should approach this whole evening.

Of course, if it were up to me, I would get there, strip her out of her clothes, and show her exactly what I've been fantasizing about doing to her since that night at the hotel.

"Hmm, maybe bring take-out? Or some dessert? Unless she is the dessert." He's now wagging his eyebrows and showing me his sly grin while I laugh.

"Yeah, that's always a thought. Although, I have a feeling she's going to want to plan everything out. We need to make sure we aren't bringing feelings into this. You know that's not my thing, and it's sure as shit not hers. I just can't get her out of my head."

Clay's chewing his lip. "How is it that the two most relationship-phobic people are going to start something together?

Watch out, you're going to catch feelings. Just you wait." He laughs, and I roll my eyes.

The only truth in his statement is that Kennedy and I are allergic to relationships. I date here and there but keep things very much above the surface. The excitement usually fizzles out, and we just part ways. I know that this thing with Kennedy and me is simple: two people who want one thing—to get naked together.

"She's sort of not really into long-term relationships. It's the best of both worlds." At least, that's how I'm taking this.

"Oh man, brother, you're going to be head over heels for this chick in a few months and then crying on my shoulder," he teases. I decide the best response is with my middle finger.

Although she and I look at relationships with the same effort we do in picking our socks, I know we look at life differently. I think the way I live my life might actually piss Kennedy off. At least, that's how it feels when I talk about some of the adventures I've been on in the past. I remember telling stories of skydiving, scuba diving, and other things, and I could feel her judgment in the way she shot daggers with her stare.

I think she's someone who would thrive off a little thrill every now and then but finds it hard to turn that beautiful brain of hers off. She's constantly ready for the next step, and that can sometimes hinder people like her from discovering new passions in life.

"Yeah, she's a ballbuster. I can't wait to see this unravel." He holds his hands together and rubs them like he's an evil villain in a movie.

My brother isn't wrong about Kennedy being a ballbuster though. I will admit I'm a fairly confident person, but it's not always something I see in a lot of women. Many women I have met will act like things don't phase them, but when digging deeper, they're as insecure as the next. So seeing it in her is a definite turn-on.

"Well, if I can give some advice and you can do what you want with it," my brother starts as if he's really going to give me an option not to hear it. "Be mindful that she's going to be in your life forever. She's Sam's best friend. Ashton's your closest friend, besides me, of course. You don't want to fuck this up with Kennedy only to have it backfire in some way with Ash and Sammie."

I've been thinking with my dick because now that he says that, it feels like a weight has been dropped in my lap.

"Either this is going to be absolutely amazing or a fucking shit show. I'll be here either way, Riv," he says as he sits back in his chair.

Of course Clay chooses this moment to find that small piece of romance still left in his heart. Here I am, thinking what a nice setup I've got going here with Kennedy because we know each other so well. We can skip over all the awkwardness and get straight to what we both want. But here he is, planting seeds in my head about how this is going to be a bigger thing. Now I just need to see what page Kennedy is on, and hopefully, it's the same as me.

CHAPTER 10

Kennedy

I WALK THROUGH MY HOME, the feel of the carpet between my toes a soothing difference compared to the heels I had to wear all day.

Today was brutal and my mind has been either on work or my encounter with River. I just can't seem to shake this attraction we now have brewing between us.

My day started with drama after an article came out regarding the late-night antics of one of my star players. This player thinks it's part of his persona to go out, get drunk, and make a fool of himself any chance he gets. I got a call before the sun was up, and this issue is still wreaking havoc on my day.

I hate unresolved issues at work and although par for the course, this one seems to be following me each time I go into the office. This particular player's behavior is starting to weigh on my shoulders, and I think it's just the price one pays to be in the position I'm in. Brett Henry might be the league's best pitcher, but right now, he's becoming my biggest headache.

I only left the office because I knew River was coming over. And that brings me to the other part of my life that I can't seem to adjust to. I have never had thoughts pertaining to River in a sexual way, and now I can't get him out of my head. Ever since the wedding, my mind is constantly pulling in the direction of River.

I went over to Sam and Ashton's place because I needed a break from the issues at work. The moment I walked in, it felt like none of my problems stemming from work existed because River was all I saw.

Without trying, my brain seems to solely steer my thoughts back to that night in my hotel room. I can't even get myself off without his fucking face entering the picture. The fact that who I saw as enemy number one morphing into whatever this new version of him is, it's got me feeling off-kilter. I don't even know what could happen next between us that won't take us down a road we can't turn back from.

River and I have one, and only one, thing in common, and that's our stance on relationships. Have I been in them in the past? Yes. Do I long to be tied down right now? Absolutely not. And from the way I've seen him parade a new date to every event I go to where our friends are concerned, I can say he puts the same damn effort into staying unattached.

Pursuing even something sexual with River feels heavier than any date I would go on with a random person. I feel like we already have baggage, and we aren't even connected romantically. We push and pull to get a rise out of one another; no mental path I go on leads to a good outcome the way I see it.

The fact that we aren't starting from scratch with one another makes me nervous. It means there are already feelings there, even if those feelings were the result of years of irritation. We have a history, and one wrong move would not just leave my heart broken and our connection severed, but it might contribute to dismantling all I've built with Samara and Ashton. They're part of my family now, and I can't risk losing that as a result of my need to explore River's body with my tongue.Oh gosh, just the thought of that is causing me to sweat.

Is it hot in here?

I move around my kitchen, opening my fridge to see if Heidi left anything for me to eat. Although I'm known for my kick-ass persona in a boardroom, I'm a shitty cook. Heidi has been with me for a few years now, and I don't think I could see myself surviving if it weren't for her. She keeps my home life in order while I try to keep up in a professional world that society has deemed male dominated. So I fight this idea that because I'm a woman, failure is behind every corner.

I rub the space between my eyes, hoping to subdue the inevitable headache that's bound to erupt. My mind is going a mile a minute, and even if I try to think about something not relating to River, my thoughts go to work and all the stress that comes along with my position in the organization.

I look through the meals in my fridge and decide a glass of wine would probably hit the spot better than any high-protein meal. I'm reaching for a glass when the doorbell rings, causing my heart rate to skyrocket.

I get to my front door and pause with my hand on the handle. I close my eyes and take a deep breath. I can do this. I've dealt with more intense situations; I can handle a man I've spent a decade verbally sparring with. I've got this.

I swing the door open and realize I've got nothing. All those mental notes I made regarding how catastrophic this can be if it fails fall by the wayside because all I see is a man who has no right to look so good in jeans and a T-shirt. Does he look better now than he did a few hours ago? How is that even possible?

River is standing in my doorway, leaning against the doorframe, an easy smile gracing his features.

"Hey, Skipper. Miss me?" His confidence is palpable, and I'm just standing there, taking him in.

He's changed since I saw him at Sam and Ash's place.

He's got some dark denim pants on, a clean V-neck shirt, with a leather jacket. He has bad boy written all over him, and I have to stop from salivating.

I look down at my watch. "Not as much as you must have. Nine on the dot. Must be antsy to see me." Hoping I sound more confident than I feel.

He moves toward me, and out of instinct, I move back, not sure how to maneuver through this new path between us. I've spent years dodging his words and hoping none of them stuck. But now all I want is to stand in the way of all his words and feel them take over my body the way that orgasm did when we were in my hotel room.

"You didn't answer my question," he says, moving closer to my ear. The goosebumps that erupt along my arms are unstoppable and do not go unnoticed by either of us.

He's got me against a wall, my open door forgotten in the kitchen at this point, his eyes pinning me with his stare. I look straight at him, wondering what his next move is.

He slowly brings his right hand up my body, careful not to connect to any portion of me. Soon, his palm goes around my neck, not enough pressure to cut off my airway, nor does it feel threatening. The only feeling it does bring is heat to my core and a spike in my heart rate.

"By the feel of that pulse of yours, you're just as excited to see me, Kennedy. So tell me, did you miss me?" I feel his breath against my face, and all I want is for those plump lips of his to take over and kiss me already.

Knowing he's expecting words and not actions as a response, I decide to throw him off his game, even for a second. I grab his shirt and tug him so he's flush with me, and I plant my lips to his.

The moment we connect, the same feeling as this afternoon consumes my senses. It almost feels like all the moments I thought I was living a fulfilling life come crashing down. I know in this instant, each step forward will never be the same because I know what it's like to be consumed by River Nichols.

He brings both hands to hold my face, and he deepens the kiss, and I swear I see stars. He's only kissed me at this point, and all my big moments in life already feel insignificant compared to this one.

He puts his hands behind my thighs and hoists me up. I wrap my legs around his middle, and I feel his dick at my center, ready for attention. He's moving me through the house, never pulling away. My breath is his, and this control he has over my movements is his to take.

We're going into the hallway when I remember the mental pep talk I had before he arrived and find the strength to pull my lips off of his.

"River, hold up. Wait," I say, and he stops, keeping me in his arms but looking conflicted as his gaze meets mine.

"Scared?" We might be crossing into new territory together, but he reverts to his playful banter with me like we'd usually do.

"Honestly, yes. Aren't you?" I hear the seriousness in my tone, and I can't help the ice bucket this feels like I've doused over both of us.

I undo my legs from around him and let my feet connect to the ground again.

"I mean, I have no doubt what we'd do in there would be epic." I nudge my head toward my bedroom. "I mean, years of pent-up frustration coming together. I can guarantee it would be explosive. But I'm not sure I can handle ruining multiple friendships if this turns out to be a huge mistake between two people. We have Ashton and Samara to consider. If this blows up in our faces, we could potentially ruin four friendships, not just two." The moment I say it, he starts to walk off toward the couch, but I catch his hand and interlace my fingers. He pulls me with him toward the couch. He sits, pulling me onto his lap.

"River, I want to do this with you, but I'm scared about what this means. I think you and I can agree we like keeping things casual. But I'm well aware nothing about us together can be casual. We're always on the verge of destruction when we are in the same room. Plus, we aren't strangers who have just met. We have years of history, even if it's volatile."

It's true. My relationship with River, aside from what I have with Samara, is probably the most constant thing in my life. Although the word constant is more in the sense of wanting to rip each other's heads off, it's still something I've come to expect. I don't know if I put much weight on that fact until this very moment.

"The thing is, once we move from enemies to whatever this is, it has the potential of destroying everything," I say, fearing we may already be threatening this whole thing with what we've done.

"It also has the potential of being everything," he says immediately and brings his lips to kiss me right under my ear, a place I didn't know triggered so much heat within my body.

It's then I realize how comforting this side of River is for me. This side where I don't get his jagged edges and he doesn't get mine. I want that side of him to be mine more than I ever imagined.

I move my face away to give him more access to this part of my body, and he takes it. He begins to leave open-mouth kisses on my skin, and I feel like he's setting me on fire. When his lips reach mine, we deepen our connection with another searing kiss. I bring my arms around his neck, caressing that soft spot of hair on the back of his head.

Once we pull apart, he gives me his full attention.

"I get it, Kennedy. I know how you're feeling because for months now, I've been fighting this tug I've felt toward you." His confession catches me by surprise. "It's true. For the last few months, I've wanted to touch you, feel you squirm with my touch. I've wanted to explore this thing that seems to be simmering, and if I don't try with you, I may seriously boil over."

I can't help the laugh that escapes me.

"I can't pretend I know how this turns out. But I do know that I crave your presence instead of fighting it lately. I don't know what switched, but it's happening, and I think it would be a disservice to us both not to explore it further. If you tell me right now you can't do this without getting deeper feelings involved, I understand," he explains as he rubs his hands in circles over my hips. "Please don't mistake my need to be with you as taking all the other things that could happen lightly."

He continues, "I get it. You're scared, and you have every right to be." He moves a piece of hair behind my ear that fell out of my messy bun.

"So what should we do about it?"

"I think we explore this. We try it out and have some fun. We keep Ash and Sam out of it. That way, if things get messy, we walk away and avoid a huge ordeal involving our closest friends. I'm not asking you for your hand in marriage, Skip." He winks at me, keeping things light like he usually does. "I just think we could have a little fun together."

I chew on my lip as I think about what he's saying. Can I keep this from Sam? Would she be pissed if she found out I was dating River? Would Ashton be pissed?

I know this is going to eat at me, knowing I'm keeping this big secret from my best friend. But it's also exciting to have something that's just mine and River's, even if it's casual.

"Okay, so I guess we're doing this," I say, continuing the movement of my fingers through the back of his hair.

A cocky smile spreads across his face, his hazel eyes pulling me in like a vortex. "You ready for me to rock your world, Skipper?" He pulls my face to his and kisses me, this time starting slowly, and I feel it build in intensity.

I move myself so I'm straddling him, and start gyrating my hips. I need a release, and I'm hoping I get the opportunity to do so multiple times tonight.

River's hands move down my back, and he grabs onto my ass, squeezing me tight. I can't wait to feel his bare hands on my flesh, no clothes between us.

I begin to pull at the hem of his shirt, but he breaks apart from me.

"Nope, Skipper, we're not doing that tonight. I've got to keep you coming back for more." He smiles and winks at me.

"What the fuck, Riv? You're going to leave me like this?" I move my hips again for added effect.

He drops his head back and laughs. "I know I'm going to regret this tomorrow. But I think we should do this another night. I think if we're going to start something together, we do so when we haven't both had a long day."

"You've gotten me off with my vibrator and seen me naked. I have needs, River!" My voice is rising as I speak, irritation lacing my tone.

"Oh, I know you do, sweetheart, but I need to make sure I get you nice and antsy for me before I give you everything," he says as he peels me off of him and deposits me on the couch cushion next to him. "Gotta keep you coming back for me and all."

"That's the opposite of casual!" I complain. "River, you're going back to being a royal pain in my ass again." I cross my arms over my chest and make sure my scowl is prominent in my features.

He runs his hands through his hair, looking up toward the ceiling as if contemplating whether this was his wisest decision. Standing up, he straightens his shirt.

"Listen, I work a twenty-four-hour shift starting tomorrow, so I'll see you in two days. You around then?" I can see he's really having to hold back here, and that's bringing me some satisfaction, at least.

I look down at my nails, feigning indifference. "Yeah, I think I could fit you in."

He laughs, then comes back toward the couch, caging me in as his hands rest on the back, his body hovering over me. "Oh, sweetheart, I'll fit, but I know you'll have to get used to me once I'm there."

I swear my panties are even more drenched than they previously were at this thought.

Damn him and his taunting.

"Well, that magical dick of yours has a lot of competition with the silicone one that's in my drawer," I throw back at him.

A soft smile consumes his face. "That's okay. I'm not jealous." Then he does something I don't expect. He stands back up, and places my hand up to cup his dick. He's hard, and that rod is definitely one I'll feel the effects of for days after I finally get a taste of it.

My mouth goes dry, and I swear I'm going to have to burn this underwear because they're toast at this point. He chuckles, leans down again, and gives me a quick kiss.

"I'll see you in a few days." He winks and heads off toward the front door. I'm still sitting on my couch when I hear the elevator chime its arrival.

Fucking River, always getting the upper hand.

CHAPTER 11
River

I'M GASSED, and it's only twelve hours into my shift. The moment I stepped foot in the station, we were called out, and it's simply been call after call since. Luckily, each one was pretty manageable, but my body is tired, and my muscles are sore.

I move through the firehouse, ready to help with dinner, and I run into a good buddy of mine, Jamison, who just had a baby a few weeks back.

"Dude, welcome back!" I shake his hand and pull him into a hug. I won't tell him, but he looks exhausted.

"Thanks, man. I swear, that stomach flu was almost the death of me, then right when I was feeling human again, Tamara went into labor. I haven't slept for weeks now." He laughs, and I see that despite the lack of sleep, he's happier than I've ever seen him. "My first shift back is next week. Just came by to make sure everything was good before my return."

"How's baby Ivan? I would love to swing by and meet the little guy," I respond, truly excited to meet the newest member of the firefighter family.

"He's the best, Nichols. Honestly, I feel like my whole

world will never be the same." The love for his newborn son is palpable. "I think Tamara is going to swing by one day with him once I'm on shift. Being gone after having him around will be rough, so she said she'd come visit."

"Awesome. I can't wait to see the little guy." I start to move toward the kitchen, seeing what the probie has in mind for dinner.

The moment I walk in, I'm assaulted with the most delicious fragrances, from oregano to garlic. My mouth is watering already.

"What's for dinner?" That's from my brother, who's seated on the couch watching television.

"Something edible, I hope," my captain hollers from the corner of the room. He's engrossed in the latest crossword from the Sunday paper.

Apparently, our newest probie burned his first meal, and since then, he's been hounded on the regular even though it was a fluke, and he has only made incredible meals ever since. He attributed the disaster to nerves on his first day, and I can't blame him. It's intimidating coming into a house like this and feeling like you have to win everyone's affection and trust.

Clay had been living in a different part of Boston with Abby when he was married in hopes to expand their family, but once she asked for a divorce, he moved back to the city and quickly transferred to the same station and hasn't looked back.

Now that they're divorced, I'm glad he has us to lean on because when Abby left last year, he was in bad shape. Luckily, I think with the consistency of work and the support all of us can provide, he's finally seeing the light at the end of the dark tunnel of his divorce.

I grab a water and sit next to my brother. Soon, the kitchen is filling in, everyone ready for our next meal.

"So, you seeing Kennedy tomorrow?" My brother looks

too excited about the prospect of us getting together that I can't help but wonder why.

"You got a bet on us or something?" I know my answer the minute I ask, as he can't even look me in the eyes.

"Fuck you for betting on me. That's our thing with other people. Who are you taking this bet with?" I shouldn't have expected any less than this from Clay. We are known for doing this to others, but I guess I'm at the center of this for him now.

"I went in on that bet." This comes from Dario, who keeps his eyes on the television while interjecting himself into this conversation.

"Same here. Where we at in the saga?" That comes from another of the guys at the firehouse.

"What the fuck? You guys are all in on it?" Slowly but surely, I see everyone bobbing their heads; even my captain took part in this little deal.

"Great, so all of you are betting on my sex life?" I gape at all my brothers who I would literally walk through fire to protect.

"Well, yeah, man. I mean, have you seen her? She's fucking hot. If your brother hadn't told us you'd called dibs, I would have asked her out," Dario pipes up.

"Watch it!" I point to him, then direct my glare to my brother. "You've been busy getting everyone on board in the last few days." Right when I say it I see my brother cower lower into the couch.

"Clay, when did you start this bet with the guys?" He's avoiding my eyes again, and I know he's been up to something.

"Dude, everyone saw the way you eyed her when she stopped by a few months back. Remember, she came by on a mission to get you to try on that tux for the wedding because she said you were way behind, and Sam was going to come after you next?"

Kennedy did come to the firehouse, and she was fuming. She said I was wasting her only afternoon off with the mundane parts of the wedding details and that I had to get off my lazy ass and try on the tux. It didn't hurt that she caught me lifting weights with my shirt off. I saw her gawking, even though she was acting like I was a pain in her ass.

"Was that the blonde who came in here with those fuck-me heels? Yeah, I wouldn't mind getting more acquainted with her." Fucking Delarosa mouthing off, and I swear I see red.

My brother must sense my rising anger and tries to diffuse the situation. "Well, she's not someone's property, and she's got her eyes on a Nichols, not a Delarosa. Also, I told you my side of this bet was the way to go. Look at him—he's going to Hulk out on Deli over there." My brother laughs, and I feel the rage dampen a fraction.

"Fuck all of you for betting on my love life," I throw out and realize my mistake.

My brother does a double take and then stands up. "You said love! Oh my god. Mom's going to shit a brick when she hears this!"

"Don't you dare tell Mom, you fucker. And it's an expression. Plus, you already said too much the other day with her. Now she's going to hound me. Do not add fuel to that fire, man." I jump off the couch and start chasing my brother.

In the midst of all the chaos, as I chase my brother around the kitchen, I see our Cap shaking his head, although a smile graces his features.

* * *

I wake up to Lola's tongue on my cheek, licking me, most likely trying to get fed or go to the restroom.

"Good morning to you, pretty girl. You ready to go on a walk?" The moment she hears the W-word, she barks and starts to pace the room as I gather my things to get her outside. The weather is finally warming up later in the day, and I feel like summer is right around the corner.

Once Lola gets a few laps outside, we get ourselves back into the apartment, and I take her food out.

While Lola's inhaling her meal, I pick up my phone and start to solidify my plans with Kennedy.

> Hey Skip. We still good to meet at the restaurant at 5:30?

SKIPPER

> Yeah. That should still work. I have a few meetings throughout the day and hopefully no one stops me on the way out.

> Great. See you at Luigis soon.

I look down to find Lola watching me, clueless that I have to leave her a few more hours on her own. Hopefully, she's out of her vendetta phase. When I would leave her alone when she was still a puppy, she would go into my closet and chew one of my shoes. Of course she'd choose my favorite and most comfortable pair. I started closing the door, but the taller she got, the quicker she learned how to open the door. Back then, I'd come home, and she would be lying on the bed with my shoe and a torn pillow to boot.

She hasn't done that in some time, and I just hope she doesn't decide to grace me with that personality again.

"Alright, sweet girl of mine. We've got a little more time together, but then I'm headed out after my shower," I say as I scratch her under her chin. "But I won't be gone all night. I promise. I have to get Kennedy right where I want her. Don't worry; you're still my number one girl."

* * *

I stand outside of the restaurant, waiting on Kennedy. She's a few minutes late, but she texted that she was on her way. I stand just outside the entrance, as there is no wait for a table on a random weekday. The influx of tourists won't start until next month, so we are still a few weeks away from the chaos this city brings in the chaotic summer months.

Kennedy's Uber pulls up, and she steps out. I'm used to seeing Kennedy in some sort of business attire, as she's always running from work to whatever friend gathering we usually see one another at. But tonight, she's dressed in a flowing dress, something very reminiscent of summer, and I take her in a bit longer, realizing how naturally beautiful she is.

Her hair is pulled to the side into a long braid, a much more relaxed look for her than I was expecting. She isn't one to wear too much makeup, but she has a little bit on her eyes, and I'm not sure if the redness I see on her cheeks is her own flush or something she added. Either way, she is absolutely breathtaking.

"Hey Riv, sorry I'm late. I got pulled—" The moment she's close enough, I pull her in and kiss her. I have been thinking of her nonstop, and when I didn't have things going on at the station, my mind constantly drifted back to her. Now I can act on it when I'm around her, and I'm not wasting any time.

She closes her eyes and melts into my touch. I don't know how long we stand there, but someone walking on the sidewalk yells out, "Get a room," and I can't help the laugh that slips out. I pull away, and I see Kennedy's cheeks flush; this embarrassed side of her is new to me.

"It's good to see you," she says as I interlace my fingers with hers and pull her toward the entrance to the place. "So where are we going on this non-date?"

I laugh thinking about the back and forth exchange via text. When I told her we should grab a bite to eat, she kept arguing that we weren't dating and that this was the exact opposite of what we should be doing together.

I'll admit, we have a deal that we are just having some fun together, but it feels wrong not to at least grab food and talk to one another. We are usually at each other's throats, and finding neutral ground felt like the gentlemanly thing to do.

"Have you been here before?" I point at the restaurant behind me. My parents discovered this spot soon after moving into this neighborhood, and it's been a staple for my family and me.

"Maybe once years ago? I can't remember. The sign may have been different." She looks up and points at the sign inside that mirrors the sign hanging above the door outside as well.

"Yeah, Luigi is the father, and his son, Leonardo, decided to revamp the colors and bring more people in when business wasn't doing so well. I was here watching the entire thing unfold when the son broke the news to the dad. It was like I was watching an Italian movie with the father yelling and throwing his arms in the air. It was hard to look away."

"You seem to be quite invested in this place." She looks at me, sort of surprised I have this deep of a connection with a local restaurant.

"Yeah, they were sort of a big part of my upbringing after my dad passed. We would come here as a family when Clay and I were small, but then my mom couldn't come back into the restaurant for years, so they'd deliver to my mom's house until my brother and I were old enough to come by ourselves and pick up take out," I ramble, and I see Kennedy taking everything in, without seeming bored.

"River, hey, son. How are you?" Luigi's booming voice pulls my attention as we walk inside, and I look over to see the older of the Russo family coming toward Kennedy and me.

"Hey, Luigi." I shake his hand, and an easy smile takes over my face.

"And you brought a beautiful woman with you. Bellissima." He pushes me aside now that he has spotted Kennedy and pulls her hand up, kissing her knuckles. I see her blush and smile at the sweet man.

"It's a pleasure to meet you. I'm Kennedy," she introduces herself. I stand there and take her in. No matter if Kennedy is in her work attire or in a simple dress like she is now, she exudes strength. Her confidence is nothing but a turn-on for me, and I am taken in by her beauty.

"Come now, let me show you to our best table in the house." Luigi takes us to the back, where he has a whole setup with candles in the wine bottles like you see in the movies.

"I'll get you some carpaccio on the house for the beautiful lady. We love our River here, and now he finally brings a girl to my restaurant. I can't wait to tell Maria." He claps his hands together, and before we have a chance to thank him, he's already disappeared into the kitchen.

"Wow, so you really know this place well," she says as she pulls the menu open. "Also, this is screaming first date, Riv. I told you, what we're doing isn't dating."

I try not to let her reminder sting, but it does nonetheless. I get it; we're not coming together for anything other than the physical aspect, but it felt wrong not to take her out. Plus, I know how much Kennedy wants this between us, so I may as well have a little fun and draw this out as much as possible. May as well make her sweat a little bit, right?

"Um, yeah, we have been coming here for as long as I can remember. My brother and I eat here a few times a week when we are too tired to cook." I rub my hands down my jeans as I grab the menu in front of me, trying to act like I don't know what I want. I've had this menu memorized since I learned how to read. "And I'm not just going to use you,

Kennedy. I think we can at least hang out here and there without pulling our clothes off."

I can feel her eyes boring into me. When I look her way, I don't know if she's irritated I made us come out tonight or if she appreciates how I'm treating her. Kennedy stares for an extra beat, then brings her eyes down to the menu in front of her.

"What's good?" she asks after she looks over all the different items.

"You can't go wrong with anything, but their lasagna is one of my favorite dishes. The ricotta is fresh, and I swear you can never go back to store-bought or even ordering it from another restaurant after you eat this one. It's incredible." I solidify my statement with a chef's kiss, bringing my fingers to my lips and kissing them.

This draws a laugh out of Kennedy, and it seems to relax her a bit.

"I want to be honest with you. I was so nervous today. I thought coming out with you tonight would feel weird. Like whatever energy we were feeling the other times we were together would have fizzled. But, and I can't believe the words that are going to come out of my mouth right now, I'm really enjoying this side of you, River. I mean it." She beams a smile my way, and I know how much this is throwing her off. We went from clawing each other's eyes out to undressing each other with them instead.

"I know what you mean." And now it's my turn to bring her knuckles to my lips and kiss them.

"So what's the plan after this? You coming to my house, or are we going to yours." She sips her water and locks back at me.

"After this, we are headed to a movie. They're showing some old ones down the street at the Cinemake. I thought it would be fun to go there."

I swear her eyes double in size. "What is going on, River? I mean, I thought we were on the same page with this arrangement." Her irritation is evident in her tone.

"We could still have a little fun in the dark." I take a drink of my water this time and throw a wink her way. She's looking at me, and I know she sees right through me.

"You're going to make me squirm, aren't you?" I nod at her question, and she throws a napkin at me.

"Fucking jerk," she hisses.

"Well, soon enough, I'll be a jerk you want to fuck. It will be well worth it," I toss out at her. I know that I'm prolonging what we are planning on doing, but something about it makes me want to see her drool for that physical part with us. Okay, so maybe everything I said about making her squirm hasn't passed. I like seeing that fire in her eyes when I push her a bit further.

Even in the dim lighting of the restaurant, I see her cheeks deepen in color, and I know I've got her mind wondering when that night will come. It's taking everything in me to not throw this gentleman act out the door and run her back to her place.

"Well, let's hope next time we can skip to dessert then," she throws out, and the wheels are already turning about the next time we meet up. It's a marathon, not a sprint, and in the end, I'll get Kennedy, naked and ready for me, at the finish line. Hopefully, I'll get a little begging to boot.

CHAPTER 12

Kennedy

TEN DAYS. That's how long it's been that I've been going on fucking dates with River, and it's like I'm back in high school again. Every night that we hang out, he walks me to my door and rocks me with a mind-bending kiss, even grabbing me in a way I assume he'll lift me off my feet and take me to bed; he then pulls away and saunters off. And I know he wants more if that tent in his pants is any indication.

Tonight, I will not let this date end until I come. And it will be with River's dick. I swear.

I put a dress on that showcases my ass and my tits, hoping that will do the trick. I don't know what kind of willpower that man has, but it ends tonight. I am getting agitated at this point. And he's not fooling anyone. I know what he's doing. He's pushing me to my limits because he must get off on that. Not today, Satan.

Just looking at River, I get hot and bothered now. I think that was his plan all along. He purposely won't put out this fire that's seriously consuming my body at this point.

I take one last look in the mirror when I hear the doorbell ring. I came up with a plan of my own tonight. I asked him to pick me up, with plans of heading nowhere other than the bedroom. Enough of this shit.

I walk eagerly to the front door, swinging it open with more force than anticipated. The moment my eyes land on River, I swear I'm salivating.

With the warmer weather, I can see he's gotten a little more sun. His hair is still a little wet from his shower, and it just adds to his sex appeal. I want to move my fingers through it as he's between my legs.

"Hey, Skipper, I think you're drooling, sweetheart." He chuckles, then pulls me against him.

His kiss is all-consuming, and I moan as he slides his tongue in my mouth.

I shove the door closed, and I push him against it.

"Tonight, dessert comes first," I say, and then go back to devouring his mouth. I guess I have to take charge of this whole thing right now because he seems a little hesitant to do anything about my needs.

He pulls me away and looks at me. He's breathing heavily, much like me, and I can see desire swimming in those hazel irises.

"Oh yeah, you've made the executive decision?" he taunts, and I don't know if I want to yell at him or devour him. Probably both, if I'm being honest.

"Well, someone has to take charge," I say, and right then, I'm flipped so that my back is against the door, and River's gaze feels like a flame taking over every part of me he is inspecting.

"My sweet, sweet Kennedy, you should know by now I love playing games with you," he says, and the slyness to his tone confirms my suspicions; he wanted to get me agitated and horny.

"You prick. You set me up," I say, but there's no malice in my tone.

"No, I just made you want this," he says as he grabs my

hand and puts it directly over the bulge that's growing behind his zipper. "I needed to know you wanted me, and now I know."

Cocky bastard. "Well, now I don't know if I want you anymore." Liar! My subconscious screams back at me.

"Oh really," he says as he moves his hand along my neck, down my collarbone, sliding down my abdomen, then reaching down and pulling the skirt to my dress up. He slowly moves his fingers up my inner thigh until he reaches the juncture of my legs. He moves my panties to the side, then slowly moves his index finger through my folds.

"Someone is lying." He smiles as he moves that finger along my slit and brings it back up between us, the glistening evidence of my arousal.

"I think someone needs to eat her words." He moves his finger closer to my lips, and, on instinct, I open for him.

I don't know why I comply. I'm usually the one commanding my partners sexually, so this is a welcome change for me. It feels like I can finally let someone else take control, and I can let go a bit.

The moment I wrap my lips around his finger, I moan, swirling my tongue and tasting my musky scent, feeling my body ignite.

"All I picture are those red lips wrapped around my cock." He yanks his finger out of my mouth, and a pop is made from the suction I had around his finger.

He crashes his lips against mine again, this time picking me up, much like the last time we were mauling each other here, and starts carrying me to my room.

The moment we enter my bedroom, he puts me on my bed, hovering over me.

"Such a shame this gorgeous dress is going to be a waste." His words don't register until he's taking the front of it and ripping the fabric in two down my chest and torso.

"That's a brand new dress, Riv." I try to sound angry, but

there's no bite to my words because, fuck, if this is ever the turn-on. He's ravenous for me, and that's making my heart pound even harder. I'm surprised he can't hear it beneath my ribcage.

"Sweetheart, there's nothing gentle about me in the bedroom. Get used to it." With that, he finishes off the remainder of the dress, and I'm in nothing but my thong. His eyes flame as he sees me panting, my nipples pebbled with the air conditioning hitting my skin. He pulls his lower lip in with his teeth, and I can see he's taking in the sight of me naked beneath him.

All I see is need in his eyes, and I wonder how we went this long, ignoring this electric current that obviously exists around us at every turn. He's searing me with his gaze as he looks me up and down. I feel like each cell in my body is on fire, and I'm wiggling because the anticipation of what will come next is making the hairs on my body stand at attention.

"I don't know where to start with you, Kennedy. You're fucking perfect." He licks his lips, looking like a man preparing for his next meal.

"Maybe start by taking your clothes off," I say as I reach for the fabric of his shirt.

He brings his hands behind his head and pulls his shirt up and over. The movement only accentuates his muscles, and I see all that tanned skin on display.

His pants come off next, leaving him only in boxers.

"You're almost there, just one more piece of clothing," I taunt, moving my toes to try to pry the fabric off him.

"Ah, ah, Kennedy. Patience." He brings his hands to my stomach and then moves his thumbs under my lace panties, grazing the skin above the spot that I know would bring some relief. He knows what I want, but he's deliberately avoiding that one place between my legs. He holds that power, knowing all the right buttons to press along my body.

Without warning, he balls a side of my panties in his

hands and pulls, ruining yet another piece of fabric on my body.

"I'd tell you I will replace them, but I have no plan of doing that. Maybe I'll leave you without any panties so that each time you're with me, I know I can fuck you anywhere and anytime I want."

His dirty mouth is just fuel to this fire he's building within me. I can't help the way my hips move, trying to find friction, even if he's still in his boxers. I know I'm getting my wetness on those boxers, and something about that just makes me do it more.

"But then I wouldn't have underwear when you're not with me." I decide to play this little game back, hoping I'll get a rise out of him.

A growl escapes him, and he grabs my hair and pulls my head back, forcing me to look into his eyes. "No matter what, Kennedy, you're mine. You hear me, baby? This body, this pussy, is mine."

"Same goes for that dick. I'm the only one that can touch it." I bring my hand over his erection, squeezing a bit to make my point. "And don't think I share nicely either."

River lets go of my hair, stands up, and reaches down into his jeans that are thrown on the ground. He pulls out a foil packet and throws it next to me on the bed. Then, he pulls down his boxers, and that's when I finally see River, completely naked in front of me.

I gape at him as I take in his form. He is fucking hung. What. The. Actual. Fuck. I know my eyes double in size as I take in the extent of his fire hose in front of me. That will not fit comfortably. No fucking way.

"It's going to fit, baby," he says as if he's reading my mind.

I lift my gaze to meet his, not quite believing his words. My mouth has gone dry.

"I wish I could promise to go slow, but I need to fuck you

right now. I thought I would take my time, maybe fuck you with my tongue, then have you suck me off, but no way. I need to be inside you, right the fuck now."

He juts his chin toward the foil packet. I'm still staring at the biggest dick I've ever seen. It's long, thick and I swear it has its own zip code.

"Focus, Skipper." He snaps my attention back to his face and points to the condom sitting on my chest.

I get to work covering him, then lie back down, waiting to see how in the world I'm going to fit that thing inside me and still walk straight tomorrow.

Instead of laying his body back on me, River rounds the bed and lies down, putting his hands behind his head, making his erection stand at attention, and it looks even bigger now.

"Let's go, Kennedy. Sit on me and take control of how fast we go at first. Take my offer because next time, I'm not going to be so kind." Something about his promise causes an uptick in my pulse, and I crawl over to him.

I bring my leg over, and I'm straddling him, hovering over his cock, a little scared about how this is going to feel once I start.

"Don't worry, baby, just take it slow. You're in charge here. Go ahead and start to sit down." He has his hands on my hips, grabbing my ass to urge me on.

I line him up and begin to gradually move my pelvis down, his cock slowly penetrating me. The minute his mushroom head is inside me, I see him breathing through his nose. His hands remain on my hips, helping steady me.

He gets a few inches further, and I'm already feeling fuller than I've ever felt. The moment I'm fully seated on him, I moan, throwing my head back and pushing my chest out.

Before I start moving, I'm just letting myself adjust to his size. River sits up, bringing one of my nipples into his mouth, swirling his tongue around the sensitive bud. He then grazes his teeth on my nipple, and I can't help the sounds I'm making.

"Fuck, Kennedy, you're so fucking tight and perfect. Please, baby, move your hips for me. I need you to move."

I bring my lips down to kiss him and slowly begin moving my hips. The feeling of fullness continues, but the way my clit is rubbing against him, my movements get faster, and soon, I'm chasing my first orgasm.

At this point, River is lying back down, and my hands are on his pecs, his hands on my hips, the sounds bouncing off the walls as our bodies move together. The way we are positioned, my clit is hitting a part of his pelvis as he moves in and out of me.

Every part of me feels like it's been lit with a match as my climax begins to build again, and soon, I feel the explosion of a million little stars consume my sight. While I'm still coming off that high, I feel my body get moved, and I'm pulled onto my hands and knees.

In this new position, he feels even deeper. River wastes no time and starts to pound into me.

"Grab the headboard, baby. I need to fuck you harder," I hear him say between gritted teeth. I know he's trying to make this last longer, but it's like he can't hold back. This take-charge attitude he's showing in the bedroom only adds to his appeal.

I grab onto my headboard, and he starts to lose control as he chases his own release. The slapping of skin and our moans are overwhelming my senses. My last climax has dissipated, but I feel yet another one crash through me.

Right as I'm coming down, my body exhausted from the overexertion, River's movements only intensify as he grips my hips tighter. A guaranteed line of marks will be left behind tomorrow.

He begins yelling, "Shit, Kennedy. Oh fuck, yes, fuck,"

and he pumps one final time before exploding into the condom.

I can feel the sweat dripping down my chest as his hips slow, and he brings his lips to my back, kissing up a trail until he has his lips near my ear.

"Yeah, I'll need to eat my dinner before we have dessert again."

He nibbles my ear and then slaps my ass before he pulls out of me, running to the bathroom to clean himself up. I'm about to get off the bed to do the same when he brings me a washcloth to clean up.

Before I get to wipe myself off, he grabs my chin and gives me another punishing kiss.

"That was the most incredible sex I've ever had, Kennedy. Fuck baby, I can't wait to do that again, but next time, we're starting with you on your knees," he says, and a cocky smile paints his features again.

I try to hold back a smile, but I know I'm already counting the minutes until I get to see him succumbing to me as I take him in my mouth.

CHAPTER 13
River

THE LIGHT IS SHINING in as a new day warms the room. I blink my eyes open and realize I'm not in my bed. It's in that moment memories flood my mind of all the things I did with Kennedy. Hours I devoured every inch of her body.

I look over, not seeing her anywhere in her room. I get myself up, taking a few extra seconds to rub the sleep out of my eyes. I had mentally told myself I wasn't going to spend the night, keeping what we're doing as casual as possible. But I must have passed out after round four of our sexual escapades.

Once I'm done getting myself semi-presentable, I make my way out of her room and into the kitchen. The moment I get close enough to hear her, her voice carries. She's singing again, still the worst fucking voice I've ever heard, along with the sound of something frying in a pan.

I stand at the entrance to the kitchen and watch her move around, shaking her ass, that fucking hair curler contraption taking over her head, and moving the food along the pan. From what Ashton has told me, Kennedy can't cook worth shit. It's cute to see her try though.

"Morning, sunshine," I say, causing her to yelp at my surprise intrusion.

"Fuck, River. I didn't hear you!" She scowls as she points the spatula in my direction. From the little pieces of egg flying around, I assume she's making them scrambled.

I make my way over to her and wrap her up in a hug, pulling her lips to mine. It's going to take some getting used to that I can show some affection to the person who's been so prickly since the second I met her.

A soft smile grazes her face as she hums in satisfaction once I pull away.

"Good morning, Riv. How did you sleep?" She gives a cheeky smile in my direction and winks.

"Barely at all, yet I have absolutely zero complaints," I say as I smack her ass and turn toward the fridge.

It's then I see a cutout of the newspaper taped on the refrigerator door, with my face plastered on it.

"Fucking hell, no!" I snatch the photo of me in my fire gear, holding a little girl in my arms. This was taken in the middle of the night during my last shift, and I'm beyond irritated to see myself in black and white.

"I never thought a uniform could look so sexy on a man before. Maybe you should wear that one day when you come over," she says as she turns toward the stove, mixing the eggs a bit more.

"I appreciate the compliment, but I hate having my picture in the paper. Actually, all of us do. Damn it!" Annoyance oozes out of my tone.

"What's the big deal? I mean, you're doing something heroic. It's hot," she says as she looks my way, grabbing her lower lip. As much as I would love to grab that lip and carry her over my shoulder and have my way with her, I bring my attention back to the picture that's now in my hand.

"What's that look for? I mean, it's just a picture, River." If she only knew what a hassle it is to be photographed.

"Easy for you to say. Not only will the guys give me shit, I now have to make a batch of brownies before my next shift," I explain, rubbing the area between my eyes.

The last time my picture was in the paper, multiple copies were put up along the house, that one a lot more incriminating because I was holding a little kid's doll. The most comical part of it, I was holding it like an actual baby when they snapped the picture. I still find random copies throughout the firehouse just to fuck with me.

"They make you do it? Can't you get some from the market?"

"No, the guys take food very seriously. Nothing can be store bought. The rule is that if you end up with a picture in the paper or you appear on the news during a shift, you're in charge of bringing brownies on the next shift you work.

"When I was a probie, I went to the market and picked it up, ready-made, hoping to catch a few more hours of sleep before the shift, and they figured it out. The rule is it's home-made, or you're making brownies for a month straight. It's a nightmare." I roll my eyes as I ball up the photo, toss it into the trash, and open the fridge for a water bottle.

I grab what I need and make my way toward Kennedy, nuzzling her neck and breathing her in. She's intoxicating, even more so now that I know how my name sounds coming off her lips when she climaxes.

"Hold your horses, big guy. We need sustenance, then we can do what you've got in mind." She giggles as I move my scruff along the sensitive part of her neck.

"Yeah, not sure I can focus if you've got those things in your hair. Why does it look different this time? And how long have you been up?" I take a soft bite of her shoulder and move to open a cabinet in search of plates and mugs for coffee.

"Second one to the right," she juts her chin in that direction, "and I tried something new. It's a unicorn method. I got up early and had time to put the curler in so it would set before I have to head out. I worked out and showered already," she continues, as I stare at her in astonishment.

"You did all that while I slept in? You could have at least woken me up before the shower. I wouldn't have minded joining you," I say as I find the plates and grab a few utensils.

"No thanks. I've seen you after Ashton has woken you up. You're a bit crabby." She gives me an eye roll, and I can't help but take in how beautiful she is, even with the ridiculous contraption on her head.

I decide to ignore the "crabby" comment. "You get up early every day?" I mean, it's not that late right now, so she must have been up before the sun.

"I usually sleep like shit. Last night, I didn't sleep poorly, aside from going to bed late due to the endless orgasms, but my body is now used to the early rising schedule. No matter what time I go to bed, it's like my body is on autopilot." She's talking as she's dividing the eggs on the plate, along with some toast that's seen better days.

Without commenting on the state of the toast, which looks more burnt than not, I take a seat at her kitchen island.

"Why don't you sleep well?" I ask as I take a big forkful of eggs and shove them in my mouth. The moment I do, I want to gag. I honestly cannot swallow because this is not edible.

"Not good?" She makes a face, almost like she's not surprised.

"No, it's good if I were going for something as salty as the Atlantic. How much salt did you put in there?" I spit the food out and swallow a huge gulp of water.

"Sorry." She winces and then starts laughing. "You sure you don't want me to make the brownies for you? They'd be so shitty, they might excuse you from making them for a while." She beams, even after I just insulted her cooking.

I stand up and pull her into my arms. "You might be onto something, Skipper."

I grab behind her thighs and hoist her up, her legs locking behind me. I carry her to the couch and make sure the meal I just tried to consume isn't on either of our minds anymore.

The moment I lay her down on the couch, I open her robe to find she has nothing on underneath. I move toward the weird curler on her head and pull the scrunchies out, slowly pulling the entire thing free. The moment her hair fans out on the cushions, I take in the sight of her.

"You are mesmerizing. Every inch of you, Kennedy. You're flawless." My words make her blush, and I push my shorts, along with my boxers, off, and my erection springs free.

Kennedy takes me in with her gaze, licking her lips, then grabbing hold of her bottom lip with her teeth.

"If you keep doing that, I'd guess you want me to fuck your mouth." I give myself a few strokes, trying to tame the wild thoughts going through my head.

Without another thought, Kennedy is jumping off the couch and kneeling in front of me. She looks at my cock, then brings those beautiful blue-gold eyes up to look right at me.

"Your wish is my command," she says, a devilish smile taking over her face.

I watch her in utter disbelief as she licks her lips again and then, in one single movement, takes my dick all the way into her mouth, touching the back of her throat. The moment I feel the warmth of her mouth consume me, I can't help the moan I let out. My head falls back. "Fuck, that's perfection."

She begins to slowly bob her head, my cock moving in and out of her mouth, her slow strokes driving me crazy. Something comes over me, and I start to take charge, even though she's the one holding all the control.

I grab her hair and pull it back into a ponytail, looking down and continue watching her suck me off. "That's it, let me fuck that pretty mouth of yours."

My words spur her on, and she begins to move quicker. Then, I see her hand disappear between her thighs.

"Don't you dare come yet, Skipper. That's my job." She doesn't protest, but her groan vibrates along my shaft.

I grip her hair a little firmer and begin moving my hips, watching the tears come down her face and the drool drip out of the corners of her mouth.

"Oh fuck, Kennedy. I'm going to come. Fuck, that's right. You better move, or I'm coming down your throat." She grips my ass tighter, holding her mouth where it is, letting me thrust into her mouth while I seek my release. Soon, I'm coming down her throat, and I watch as she swallows everything I give her.

My hips slow, and she pulls her mouth off me, licking every last drop that she sees. Fuck, that was hot.

My vision starts to return, and I look down, seeing the flushed skin across her chest.

"How wet are you for me?" I need to see her, all of her.

She sits back up on the couch, opening her legs so I can see her glistening sex.

"Where's your vibrator?" I ask, needing to have a little more fun.

She seems stunned for a second, then proceeds to tell me it's in her bedside table.

I run to her room, and the moment I open the drawer, I find it and run back to the living room with it.

"When was the last time you used this?" I ask her as I settle between her legs. She's still on the couch, and I'm on the ground, her pussy in my direct line of sight.

"Two nights ago." She's looking at the vibrator then at me, wondering what I'm planning on doing to her.

"Oh yeah? What did you think about to get off?" I flip the silicone toy on and let the vibration touch her calf and start to move it up her leg. She watches, mesmerized, as my fingers move closer with the dildo in my hand.

"I thought about you," she says, her eyes now meeting mine. "I thought about how it would feel for it to be your dick instead of that." She moves her chin slightly toward the dildo that's inching closer to her center.

I reach the apex of her thighs and let the vibrator graze her clit. She nearly leaps off the couch, her senses heightened after what she just did to me.

"Mmmm, the fun we can have," I whisper, my breath close to her folds, allowing the air to add to the stimulation she's feeling.

I let the vibrator move through her wetness, glistening the silicone as I have a little fun. Once I feel it's lubed enough with her own arousal, I begin to push the head of the cock into her entrance.

We both watch as the dildo disappears inside her, the hum of the vibration hitting her at all the right spots.

She's on her elbows but lets her head drop back, opening her mouth and moaning loudly, her enjoyment palpable.

"You like that, baby?" I say as I keep moving the dildo in and out of her. As much as I may want to be the one inside her, I prolong that need to heighten the experience for both of us.

"Mmhm" is the only thing she can say while she's overly stimulated.

I keep pumping the vibrator in and out of her, then bring my mouth to her clit and start sucking hard.

I push her silicone dildo in her and leave it there, letting my tongue play with her clit while her hips move, enjoying the immense stimulation this is causing her.

I feel around the floor for the condom I had brought back from the room and sheathe myself. The moment I feel like she's close to climaxing, I pull the cock out of her and fill her with my own in one hard thrust.

The moment she realizes what I've done, she screams, grabbing the cushions behind her head in hopes it will be enough to hold on. I start to pump in and out of her, the slapping of skin overtaking the room. Our moans begin to increase in volume as we both chase our climax together. We fall off that cliff at the same time, stars shooting into my line of vision, clouding everything as I let my release consume me.

I try not to focus too much on the pull I feel toward this woman. As much as I went into this with no strings attached, I can already tell I'll be counting the days until we can come together like this again.

CHAPTER 14

River

THE MUSIC IS BLARING in the club Ashton and Sam dragged us to. Sam had an absolute freak-out apparently a few nights ago, saying that her freedom was going to plummet to the ground, so we needed a night out. She's now dancing with Kennedy and some other girlfriends, sipping her virgin daiquiri like she's going on house arrest pretty soon.

The beer in my hand is doing shit to cool my blood as it slowly comes to a boil with each man who puts his hands on my girl.

My girl? Where the fuck did that come from?

Kennedy and I are satisfying a need right now, and I'm indeed more than satisfied at the moment. We've been playing this little game for a few weeks now, and each time we're together, I don't know how to describe it other than it just feels better than the last. She's got this hold on me, my attention constantly drawn to her blonde locks and long, tanned legs.

Kennedy is shaking her ass, that fucking dress teasing me to the point where I may honestly commit a crime if one more guy ogles her. I can feel my hand tense around the bottle until I feel my brother attempting to pry it out of my hand.

We started the night at a nearby restaurant, and the moment she walked in, I nearly ran to the restroom to rub one out like a fucking teenager. Her dress is silver with sequins, and it's shorter than anything I've ever seen her wear around us.

I take a long pull from the beer bottle in my hand, and I feel my eyes locked on her every move.

"Bro, you're going to break this, and I don't need you cutting yourself before our next shift." He successfully pries it out of my grasp, then continues, "Plus, you're making it fucking obvious." I look over at him and see Ashton eyeing me funny from the other side of the table.

"You owe me one," my brother says, and before I can ask what the fuck for, he announces to the guys, "Hey, I can't let the women be the only ones showing off their moves."

Without asking, I'm being shoved along with Clay as we walk toward the rest of the crowd grinding against one another.

Clay gets right behind Kennedy and starts dancing with her. I love my brother, but right now, I want to pull him off her and claim her as my own. I take deep breaths through my nose, trying to remind myself he's doing this to keep the other guys off her right now.

I watch as he moves Kennedy's hips to the music, and she goes right for it, but her gaze finds mine, and she bites her bottom lip. Fuck, she teases me with each little movement of hers, and I know she's just trying to get under my skin.

I keep chanting to myself that my brother has no attraction to her, but I can't help the irritation that bubbles at the thought of his hands, actually any hands, on her. For the time being, she's mine, just like I'm hers. But she's playing into this game with my brother, and now I feel like I need to give her a taste of her own medicine.

It doesn't take me long to find a woman who's eyeing me on the dance floor, so I bring my attention to the woman with her dark eyes and pixie cut. I begin to move my hips to the music, and soon, I've got this chick's back to my front, and I let the music guide us. I wish I could say I get lost in the moves this girl's got as she bumps and grinds along my body, but I keep my gaze on Kennedy, seeing her temper rise.

My brother senses the shift in her body, and he looks over and lets a smirk cross his features. He knows what I'm doing, and I can't even apologize for how juvenile I'm being. But I want to get a rise out of her. Somewhere deep inside I need the reassurance that I drive her as crazy as she does me.

The woman I'm dancing with keeps moving herself along my body and starts getting pretty handsy with me. I shoot my brother a look, but when my gaze moves toward Kennedy, she seems to lose it.

Sure enough, she tells her girlfriends something, then moves off the dance floor. I watch her retreating figure through the crowd until she's gone toward the bar.

I grab my brother's attention as he's about to start dancing with someone else and move him closer to me. The girl dancing with me turns to look at me and realizes she's seeing double.

"There's two of you?" she asks, and I'm surprised she isn't seeing more than two of us in her intoxicated state. Her breath smells like a brewery.

"Yep, double the pleasure, double the fun," my brother answers. I roll my eyes because he always said shit like that when we were in college, and I nearly gag at how dumb that still sounds.

"Gotta take a leak," I tell my brother as I move off the dance floor.

"Sure you do," he says in my ear and starts laughing. He knew I wouldn't last the whole night without touching

Kennedy. Now I just have to hope Kennedy doesn't knee me in the balls for dancing with that woman.

I make my way through the crowd, still surprised this many people are out tonight. It's been a long week, and all I wanted to do was stay home with Kennedy. I had plans to fuck her on every surface of my place tonight, but then Ash called and told me they needed to get out of the house. The moment I heard, I already knew Kennedy had accepted the invite, knowing how much she loves to get out and dance.

I scan the table where my friends are standing, but there's a big enough crowd blocking their view of me in this far corner. I make my way closer to the bar, and I stand right behind Kennedy, close enough she can feel my breath along her shoulder. People are surrounding us, but no one seems to be paying too much attention to what I'm doing to her.

"May I buy you a drink?" I whisper, trying to keep myself from showing too much interest in case someone in our group walks by.

"Oh, I bet your little friend needs a refill after shaking her ass all over your dick with such vigor," she bites back, and I can't hide how much that turns me on.

I keep moving my gaze to our surroundings and see we are still in the clear. I decide to get a little bolder and move my hand up her thigh, under her short skirt, grazing her panties. I hear her breath hitch the moment I touch her center.

"Mmm, someone's wet," I say as I move my hand over the lacy fabric.

"Yeah, Clay really has moves on the dance floor," she replies, and I immediately move my pelvis into her backside, pinning her closer to the bar.

"Oh, Skipper, you and I both know it's my dick you crave. Don't act like you weren't thinking of all the ways I could fuck you on that dance floor and make you scream *my* name, not my brother's," I bite back because she has got balls acting like Clay makes her hot and bothered.

She may be pissed at me for pulling that little dancing stunt, but she still moves her ass into my growing erection.

"Fuck, Kennedy. This dress and those heels, you're killing me." I let my breath move along her skin so I can see her react with goosebumps moving down her arm.

"Too bad I'll be removing them alone tonight. It's a shame because I sure needed some help getting undressed." She pouts as if that option is off the table.

"Like fuck you're going to take any of this off without me there to watch you do it," I throw back at her, and she simply smiles. I see her reflection in the mirror behind the bar.

A squeal behind us causes me to push off the bar and off of her, hoping my erection isn't evident in the dim light.

"O. M. GEEEE. Kennedy, the hottest guy just asked for my number." Jessa comes barreling toward us. She's been getting over a breakup recently, and apparently, she's taking it out on the Jack Daniels she's been chugging all night.

"That's great, sweetie!" Kennedy tries to sound enthusiastic, but I can tell there's worry etched in her tone. Jessa is usually the composed one, and this breakup is hitting her hard.

"He has a friend too. I told him I'd bring you back to dance before the night is over. Come on! Let's go." She screams the last part and pulls at Kennedy's arm, giving her no option but to follow as they make their way back toward the dance floor.

Kennedy turns her head in my direction, and I can tell she's not at all excited about this turn of events.

I wink at her, hoping my disappointment isn't evident in my gaze. I decide I'll text her instead.

To be continued...

> Also, don't fucking dare take anything off tonight without me as your audience. That dress is getting peeled off by me and only me ;)

> Also, the heels stay on…

I see her look down at her watch, reading the text that just came through. She smiles at the message and then looks my way, winking in my direction with a sly smile on her lips.

"Whatcha doin'?" Ashton creeps up next to me and looks to be solving a puzzle.

"Nothing." I feign innocence, but I have a feeling I better be more careful, or this whole thing is going to be blown.

"Doesn't look like nothing," Ash continues, swinging his gaze from me to the dance floor. "Kennedy seems to be calling attention tonight, wouldn't you say?" He pushes, and I try to keep my response simple, much like I would have before all this started between her and me.

"I didn't notice," I respond, taking another swig of my beer and letting my gaze look around, trying hard not to look her way.

"I see," he says, then focuses on the bartender and asks for another IPA.

Luckily, my brother saves me yet again, although I know it will not go without a favor in the future. He's been watching me all night to make sure I don't make my fling with Kennedy too obvious.

"Well, boys, it's been fun, but I think Sam is about to take a nap in the middle of the dance floor if you don't go get her. She may not be drinking, but she still knows how to party. I think your baby mama needs to go home," Clay says, and Ashton wastes no time looking for his wife in the crowd.

"I guess I better call it a night. Fuck, I knew coming out was a bit much, but she's sort of scary while pregnant," he says, his body shuddering at the thought of her new angry persona.

My brother and I laugh as we watch our friend retrieve an exhausted Sam and nearly carry her out the door.

"I think I'm going to head out too, man," Clay says. I can't help but wish Clay would stay. I love Abby but a part of me wishes Clay would move on and start dating again. He needs to start getting himself out there. As much as he's trying to find happiness again, I see so much heartache in him still.

"You gonna be okay, Clay?" I ask because no matter how much time seems to pass, that wave of sadness has been a permanent fixture in his demeanor since Abby left.

"Yeah, just need to get up early tomorrow. I promised Mom I would take her to the farmer's market. You in?"

I look toward the dance floor and see Kennedy dancing, and the only plan I have in the near future is one where I watch that silver dress fall to the floor while those heels wrap around my middle.

A smile stretches over my face. "Naw, I think I've got plans in the morning."

I hear my brother chuckle and walk away. My eyes stay fixed on the blonde who is slowly captivating every second of my attention when she's around. I can't really ignore the fact that even if she's not around, my thoughts are slowly creeping toward her any chance they get.

CHAPTER 15

Kennedy

BOSTON, we've got a problem.

Tonight, when I saw that woman dancing with River, even with a full understanding of what he was doing, I felt pure jealous rage come over me. I swear, I saw red. I wanted to be the one openly touching him and feeling his muscular body against mine.

I won't lie, I was pissed, and I truly wanted to haul him into a corner and remind him who he woke up to between his legs a few mornings ago. I can't ignore the pull we feel toward one another whenever we are in close proximity. The moment our eyes connected at the restaurant tonight, the heat that doused my skin was instantaneous for me. It felt like he was undressing me with his stare.

Of course, I had to act like he did nothing to me as I said my hellos at the table, but the moment I got near him, I felt my fucking pussy fluttering at the thought that she might get some attention tonight.

Now, as I stand outside waiting for an Uber, trying to get Jessa situated in Ashton's car, I only hope I can jump into River's truck and have my way with him. I've never been this way, and yet, here I am, needing a release like my life depends on it.

Jessa is squealing as we get her situated in the car, her body having a hard time staying seated upright. She keeps laughing and falling over in the backseat. I keep myself from rolling my eyes, but I can't overlook the fact she is an absolute mess.

Before I close the passenger door, I hear River's voice carry over.

"Here, for the ride home." He runs over and hands a large disposable cup to Sam, who looks at him like he may have saved her life.

"You're a lifesaver, River. Thank you." She lays Jessa's head on Samara's lap. I think Jessa has gone from hysterically laughing to full-on passed out.

"You okay with her, Ash?" River asks, giving his best friend a look of pity, knowing he's going to have to transport a belligerent Jessa into his home.

"Yeah, she's going to sleep in the downstairs room tonight. I'll make sure Sam and I get her water and some ibuprofen on the nightstand. She won't be happy tomorrow," he says as he rolls the windows up and says his goodbyes.

River and I are waving until we see the SUV turn right at the street ahead.

The moment we are alone without our friends surrounding us, I look over at River, and it's like we can have an entire conversation with our eyes. The woman he allowed to grind all along his dick is long forgotten, and all we need is to get ourselves back to his place.

"My truck is out back," he says, and even with the pain these shoes are giving me after dancing for too long in them, we book it out of there. I nearly trip in one of the cracks in the asphalt as we approach his car.

The moment we're inside, River turns to me. "I'm not even going to touch you because if I do, I won't stop."

He turns the keys in the ignition, and I am relieved this club is only a ten-minute drive from his place.

We make it to the underground garage of his building in record time, and the moment he turns off the ignition, I can't help myself.

I pounce on him, pulling his lips to mine. I'm hungry for his touch, his lips, all of him. My moving limbs connect with the horn, and a loud beep pulls us apart.

"Let's get upstairs," he pants, and I shake my head.

"No, I need you now, in here," I say, my breaths coming in quickly as I move my hands to his belt and make quick work of unbuckling it.

He moves his seat further back to give us room, then slides his hands along my legs, up toward my hips. He lifts my dress so it's bunched at my hips, giving me more room to straddle him in this confined space.

I release his cock from his pants, and the moment it springs free, I swear I moan in gratitude.

"You know I don't have tinted windows up here, right?" he says.

I move my hands along his chest, and before I think through what I'm doing, I grab both sides of the button-down and rip it open.

The buttons go flying, and I yell, "I don't fucking care, River. I need you inside me. Now!" I'm hungry for him, and I cannot wait, audience be damned.

"Fuck you're hot when you're horny," River says, and he crashes his lips onto mine.

Each time we connect, it feels like my world aligns itself. All my troubles fall to the wayside, and all I see is him.

He moves his hands down my chest, squeezing my breasts through the fabric of my dress, then his hands trail further down until he reaches my panties. Without hesitation, he demolishes them with one pull. The sounds of our breaths and the cotton coming apart surround us, spurring us on further.

I move slightly to line myself up to him and slam myself down. The moment I feel him deep inside me, I moan, letting my chest move toward his face, and my head falls back.

River wastes no time and pushes my dress down, exposing my breasts. He takes one of my taut nipples into his mouth and uses his opposite hand to knead the other.

I feel like all my synapses are firing at the same time, this chemistry between us unreal.

I'm bouncing on him, feeling my release crash into me too soon.

The moment I fall off that ledge, River wastes no time, grabs my hips, and starts pumping into me, falling down his own cliff.

It doesn't take him long to be yelling out my name, his eyes squeezed shut, as I milk him until he slows down.

My face is in the crook of his neck, my breathing hard against his skin, trying to calm my racing heart. Everything is sensitive, my nipples still exposed and rubbing against his chest.

I catch my breath and pull myself off of him. It isn't until that very moment I feel his cum beginning to move down my inner thigh.

"Fuck, we didn't use protection," I say as River is still coming out of his euphoric state.

"Huh?" He's still catching his breath, not quite on the same page as me yet.

"We didn't use a condom. Shit," I say, disappointed in myself. I have never been this reckless.

"Fuck, no wonder that felt so amazing. I've never gone without protection. I promise, I'm clean. I got tested when we started this between us," he says, no concern laced in his tone.

"I'm clean too. I just got tested last year," I say, hoping he doesn't press me on how long ago last year.

"Okay, so we're good?" he asks, but it's like a lightbulb goes off. "Hold up, when last year did you get tested?" He pushes the hair off my face where the sweat kept it stuck to my skin.

"Um, like fifteen months ago?" I say, slightly embarrassed of my dry spell.

"Fuck, Kennedy. I didn't realize I was your first after that prick you dated. What was his name? Dennis?"

"Not a big deal, okay? I swore off men for a bit," I say as I climb off him. "We better, um, stick to condoms next time though." I make sure he knows this is a one-time thing without a condom, although I can't complain about how it felt just now.

"Yeah, of course. Also, that was fucking fantastic." He sits there, cock out and now starting to soften, as he moves his hands down his face.

"Yeah, no complaints from me either." I pull my dress down and move myself back to the passenger side. Not sure what I'll do when his cum drips down as we go up the elevator.

"I might have a sweatshirt back here," he says after pulling up his pants and zipping them up. The muscles along his chest and abdomen are just there for me to ogle, and I can't help the sweep my eyes do in appreciation of his physique.

He finds a BFD hoodie and hands it to me. I throw it over my head, allowing it to swallow me up in size. It will give at least an extra inch or so over my ass compared to this skimpy dress.

"By the way, that dress was sinful, Kennedy. Although, next time a warning would be nice. I was walking around with a stiffie most of the night." He pulls my lips to his one more time before pushing away and opening the door of the truck.

I sit there, looking out the door he just left through, unable to pull myself out of there. I can't help whatever it is that's starting to bubble inside me. It feels a lot like butterflies taking over my stomach.

River makes his way to my door and opens it for me. I'm expecting him to walk away, but he puts his hand out for me to take as I make my way out of the lifted cab.

He grabs my face and plants a soft kiss on my lips the moment I step out of the truck, and I do everything I can to keep my mind from taking off and overanalyzing the gesture for more than it is.

We make our way to the elevator and the moment we are inside, he presses me up against the wall.

"You're insatiable, Skipper. You know that? I literally can't get you out of my mind," he whispers into the shell of my ear.

Fuck, my mind has taken off, and I find myself wondering what it all means. Something that began as just a fling is slowly starting to blur those lines, and I'm having a hard time keeping myself from moving across territory that is going to get me into trouble.

But that's the thing with River—he's been trouble from the start. However, I allowed this to happen, and I know I'm not strong enough to walk away just yet. I haven't gotten my fill of him.

The moment the elevator doors open and he flashes me that dimpled smile, my heart does a little flip. Yep, I'm royally screwed.

CHAPTER 16

Kennedy

"SO, what movie do you want to watch?" I ask Sam while I'm at the microwave popping popcorn.

Ashton had to go on a trip, and Samara called and asked me to spend the night and keep her company. She has always hated when Ash travels for work, but now that she's pregnant, Ashton was more insistent that she not be alone while he's gone for the night.

"Let's watch *Serendipity*. I love that whole storyline." She sighs and points the remote toward the television to find where it's streaming.

The moment the snacks are ready, I'm carrying a tray full of food to tackle all her cravings. She asked for an interesting assortment: gummy worms, popcorn, pickles, crackers, mayo, and jam. I feel like throwing up thinking about what she's going to pair the mayo with, but I'm going to grab my bowl of popcorn and focus on that.

She finds the movie and is about to press play but then hesitates.

"Kenny, what's going on with you?" Her question completely throws me, and I can't help the quizzical look I give her in return.

"Come on, are you seeing someone or something?" she continues.

"What do you mean?" I stuff popcorn in my mouth in hopes it masks the heat I feel overcoming my cheeks right now.

"I barely see you anymore," she whines, and I want to laugh. She knows I work crazy hours, and I try to see her whenever I can.

"Sam, I work like a lunatic, remember? I mean, look how late I made it over here tonight when I was supposed to be done at a decent hour."

I was supposed to be over here three hours ago, but I ran two hours late because an impromptu meeting was put on my calendar thanks to Brett Henry once again. I swear that man is going to put me into cardiac arrest.

"Yeah, but there's something different about you." She eyes me like she's trying to see if something will pop up to give her a clue as to why I've been a bit more cagey than usual.

"I work, and when I get home, I'm wiped. That's all." My gut twists from lying to my best friend. But I can't handle letting what River and I are doing out into the open. That is the opposite of being causal. If we start telling people, we'll be in so much trouble when we finally decide to break things off in the future. Plus, who knows how our friends will take the news that I've been fooling around with the one man who has caused me to lose my shit more often than not.

"I don't know, Kennedy. You're up to something. My preggo senses are tingling." She narrows her eyes and looks at me for an extra second. But much like her cravings, she's quickly distracted when the trailer to the movie starts to automatically play.

She presses start and brings the tray full of food closer to her. She brings her hands in front of her, and like an evil villain, she gives a slightly scary laugh and begins to dig in. I can't say it's not a little horrifying to watch her take a bite of each thing without flinching because I can't imagine dipping a sour gummy worm into the mayo is any good. But here we are.

I pull my eyes away from the disgusting snacking tendencies of my bestie and focus on the love that is all-consuming between Kate Beckinsale and John Cusack. No matter how many times I've watched this one, I still feel my heart race a bit as the two try to time everything right between one another. And slowly, as the movie carries on, I find my thoughts drifting to a certain someone who seems to have softened me up after years of us getting the timing wrong.

* * *

"I think Sam is going to sniff this out of me," I blurt out when River rolls over after giving me another mind-blowing orgasm.

"What?" He's panting, exhausted after we just pushed each other to the brink several times without letting either of us climax. Finally, once we fell off that cliff, I can't lie and say it wasn't the most intense orgasm I've ever experienced.

"I swear the other night, Sam was pestering me, and even though she let it go, she knows I'm hiding something." I can't shake the way she looked at me, and I feel like she saw into my soul.

"I wouldn't really read into it. Just act like yourself, and she'll move on from it." I love how nonchalant men can be, but a woman's intuition is something that can't be shaken off. I doubt Sam will let this go, and she'll probably only keep pestering me until I break.

River gets out of bed and makes his way to grab his clothes. At first, I think he's putting things on the chair to clean up a bit, but I realize he's getting dressed.

"Um, what are you doing?" I can't help the irritation lacing my tone.

"I'm headed home," he says as if it's obvious.

Since we started this, River has spent the night a few times. I thought tonight would be no different, and I could coax him into a shower before we go to bed. I know I wouldn't mind continuing this little sex-fest we've started tonight. We were ravenous for one another after nearly a week apart. Work has been a beast lately, and he had shifts at the station. Our schedules aren't always lining up, so the sexual tension only mounted as the days moved forward.

"I thought I'd go home, and you could get some sleep. You mentioned having an early morning meeting." He's pulling his shirt over his head, running his hands through his thick hair. The more he moves his hands through it, the less you can tell I was pulling at the strands not that long ago as he slipped his tongue through my folds. Just the thought of that makes me hot all over, even though I don't have any clothes on right now.

"Oh, okay. Sounds good." I try to sound casual, much like this arrangement between the two of us. "So, I'll see you in a few days?" I'm grateful for the darkness surrounding me in my room right now because the shame I'm feeling is probably evident on my face. Something about him hurrying off makes this whole thing feel dirty.

Snap out of it, Kennedy. This is casual. This is the entire arrangement you made with him. No attachments, remember?

My subconscious is constantly having to rein me in when my thoughts start to move in the wrong direction. I've never had a hard time with casual hookups. But here I am, letting my emotions get the best of me.

"Hey, Skip, where did your thoughts go?" He crawls back onto the bed and brings his face into the crook of my neck and nibbles. The laugh that pours out of me is automatic, and I relax a bit at his gesture.

"Nowhere. Just have a lot on my mind with work." I hope I'm more convincing than I feel.

"See? You need to sleep and not have me disturbing you all night with my manly ways," he says as he kisses my cheek.

"You're right. Lucky me," I say, and River doesn't pick up any difference in my tone.

Making one last sweep of the room to make sure he didn't forget anything, he looks at me and smiles. As he's walking out, I stay in bed and he yells out, "I'll text you after my next shift."

This is casual, Kennedy. Grind that into your thick skull. River isn't thinking twice about what this is. This isn't a relationship. This is a hookup and nothing more.

Yeah, my subconscious can say this as a mantra every second of the day, but I can already feel the push and pull between my mind and my heart. I better keep myself focused on our arrangement because he isn't thinking twice about it on his end.

CHAPTER 17

River

I RUB my fingers across the name staring back at me, and I can't help the lump that has formed in my throat.

I don't come back to New York often, mostly because it harbors a lot of feelings for me and my family. But today is different, and I try to keep my thoughts focused on the man I came to pay tribute to. A man I had taken from me far too early in life. My brother comes up by my side, and it all feels too heavy.

I squeeze the hand that is holding mine, and I look over to see Kennedy next to me. I didn't think I would want anyone other than my brother to come with me on this trip, but spur of the moment, the request came out when I was leaving Kennedy's house last week. At first, I thought she was going to decline the offer, her hesitation lingering, but then she agreed to come along. I know she had to move a good amount of meetings around to be here today, so it feels special to have her next to me.

This thing with Kennedy is purely sexual, but no matter how I try to keep our relationship physical, we started off as more. We've been weaved as so much more before we started this physical relationship. And the intensity of this attraction is strong, that I started to set some boundaries and go home after we'd have our fun. I really thought I could separate the fun from the emotion. But then I found myself asking her on this trip and now here we are. And having her here feels right.

For so long, I've pushed her away from getting close to me, but the more time we spend together, the more I feel like her presence is comforting. I know this is all a casual thing between us, but once she accepted the invitation, I didn't feel it was wrong in any way. It felt right to have her here, and the reason behind that feeling isn't something I'm really trying to focus on at the moment.

My mom couldn't bear to come with us, much as I expected. She tried, telling me she would attempt to make it, but in the end, she felt overwhelmed with the thought, and I told her I wasn't judging her for keeping her distance.

I can't imagine what she feels. I know how it is to lose a parent, but to go through life, making this leap into the unknown with someone else by your side just to lose them in mere seconds, it feels soul-crushing to imagine.

Right after my father passed, my mom turned into a shell of herself for so long. I only remember portions of that time, knowing my brother and I had to be good because we didn't want to make Ma cry more. Our neighbors and some family would stay with us a lot in the beginning, always offering to take Clay and me to the zoo, ballgames, and even to the pool to swim the following summer. My mother always let us go because she couldn't handle being a single mother.

Her world was altered in a matter of seconds, and it seems a part of her never recovered. I've carried her sadness with me at times like this as I've gotten older. Now, standing here, with so many who suffered much like us that day, it's overwhelming.

The sound of the reflecting pools brings a sort of calm amidst the dust that hasn't settled in this area of New York.

It's like the souls that were lost cling to the pieces of the city that were left behind.

The World Trade Center is flooded with people paying their condolences today, and I can still see the way grief takes its toll on so many, even all these years later. I know that my pain is shared with countless others, but I also know from what I was told that the world changed in a way I will never fully comprehend. The innocence that was lost that day was felt across continents, and the ripples of that pain are still causing significant suffering throughout the people affected by the devastation.

I touch my father's name once again, sending a silent prayer above to the one man I will always wish I had had more time to get to know.

Clay, Kennedy, and I start walking away, silence consuming us. My brother is the first to speak. "You think we should stop by the firehouse Dad was at?" We've only seen the firehouse through photos from the days leading up to his death.

Although our father was here for a training prior to our move to the city, he knew a good number of the guys due to his connection to one of his firehouse buddies. My mom always tells us that even though he was only here a few days, he had told her he already felt at home with the group he got to hang out with.

I look at Kennedy. "You down to do that?" She immediately nods, and I can't help how whole I feel when I'm around her.

We begin to walk, the weather a perfect mix of late summer to early fall. As we make our way through the busy city streets, Kennedy points out places she frequented when she was young. I always forget Kennedy is originally from New York, so she has roots here beyond anything my brother and I ever had.

We make it in front of the fire station and are immediately

taken aback by the mural they've put in place since my father was here. It takes up the entire right side of the station, and it's hard to keep my eyes from roaming every detail.

The American flag is painted on as if it's flying through the breeze, each name of the firefighter lost from this station written in script in the sky behind it. My father's name is included, and it's just another piece of him that I can connect to in a city that has a profound feeling of loss for me and my family.

We move closer, and I run my fingers along each name, recognizing some from stories my mother told.

"Would you like me to take a photo of you two in front of it?" Kennedy asks, and I immediately nod my head. I look over to my brother, who is mimicking the gesture.

We came in our BFD shirts to show we continue my father's fight, even if in another city.

We don't hide the somber expression, but I bring my brother in, and in that moment, the three of us Nichols men feel connected in the only way we ever will.

The minute Kennedy is done snapping a photo, I hear a voice behind her. "May I help you?"

The sun is shining right in my line of sight, and I have to squint and use my hand to block the sun. The moment I do, I recognize the face in front of me.

"Scottie, is that you?" He's gotten older through the years, but his eyes haven't changed.

"River, Clay, what in the world?" He makes his way over, pulling both of us into a tight hug.

Scottie is my father's friend who had recruited him to New York prior to the attacks. He knew my dad from college, and I still remember the sadness in his expression when he came to see us at home after the funeral service. As much as I forgot a lot of my childhood memories at that time, his saddened face is etched into my mind, and I don't think I'll ever unsee it.

He has a smile across his face now, but it's noticeable that it doesn't reach his eyes when he looks over my brother and me.

"Damn, you boys are no longer little. Shit, you look so much like your father, it's blowing my mind."

My brother and I look over at one another, and bewilderment must cross both our faces when we look back at Scottie.

"If you say so. We've been told we look a lot like our mother," Clay says.

"Well, that you do, but you've got his height and his smile, that's for sure. The rest of your features are definitely Mary's, but I see you followed in your father's footsteps." He points to our shirts, and his smile widens in pride as he takes us in.

The moment he looks behind me, I see him change completely. "And who might this beauty be?" he asks, extending his hand and bringing Kennedy's knuckles to his lips.

I see her blush immediately as I answer, "This is our friend, Kennedy. She's actually from New York herself."

It feels weird in that instant, introducing Kennedy because I don't know what label we should put on one another. Girlfriend isn't right, but putting any other name to it seems demeaning. Hopefully, she isn't mad I didn't elaborate further than friendship.

"Well, you're breathtaking, Miss Kennedy." Scottie pulls out all the charm for her. I roll my eyes and chuckle while Clay just watches the exchange. I can tell my brother wants to say something, but he holds back.

We decide to follow Scottie back in to take a look at the firehouse. I haven't been here before, never really spending more time down this way than I had to. But as I walk the halls of the station, touching the walls and the lockers, it makes me wonder what my father touched as he walked these same steps. There's a connection for me when I get to do things my father did. I feel like I'm getting to walk alongside him, even if he hasn't stepped foot in here since that horrible day. No matter what, I feel like pieces of him are embedded in parts of the fixtures that make this firehouse what it is today.

I feel Kennedy bring her hand into mine and squeeze. I can't help but squeeze back. I look down at her, and in her gaze, I see kindness and empathy for the feelings that are swirling inside me right now. It feels like a deeper connection than I expected to this woman I've been feuding with for a decade. But something about her being here with me feels right, and I'm going to hold on to that for now.

CHAPTER 18

Kennedy

"AND YOU THINK that nearly shoving his dick up that girl's skirt on the dance floor looks like a great way to represent the team?" I could literally breathe fire at this point.

I woke up to headlines across every tabloid talking about Brett Henry's sexual escapades from last night and I've been putting out fires all day dealing with his mess.

"He's a star athlete, on top of the fact he's good-looking. What do you expect out of him? He's not the first athlete to act this way, and I promise you he's not the last," Jerry, the manager of the team, pipes back.

"Here's the thing, Jerry, this is going to bite us in the ass someday. Do you not see how this could snowball into something bigger? Indecent exposure, possibly having a woman come forward saying negative things about him, fuck, I don't know. Add in endorsements going down the drain for him and possibly the franchise if this gets beyond our control. Think of a shitty situation, then multiply it by ten, and that's how out of hand this guy will get if we don't nip this in the bud now," I say, exasperated that I have to have this conversation in such detail.

If I, or any woman for that matter, did something like this

while holding a position like Brett, we'd be persecuted. We'd be put out for society to throw every accusatory word our way. I get that this seems simple enough right now, but give it time, and Brett Henry will be in deep shit.

I've already heard talks of companies cracking down on players who are not putting their best foot forward when it comes to the media spotlight. They're trying to endorse players who are not just performing well in the sport they're in but also someone who people can look up to. This behavior of drunken nights and groping women on a dance floor does not bode well for him, nor does it reflect well on us as an organization.

"Listen, I'll talk to him." Jerry sounds exasperated by this conversation. Tough shit, he better start managing, or I'm taking the reins.

"You have a week to show me that Brett Henry can get his shit together. I do not want to wake up with another news story splashed across my desk before I've even had my morning coffee. This ends today." I lean my head back and exhale the breath I feel like I have kept in for the entirety of this call.

"Yes, ma'am." In typical Jerry fashion, the line goes dead. I swear it's taking everything in me not to chuck this phone across the room.

"UGH," I let out, staring at my phone while I try to calm myself down.

"Well, Skip, looks like your day needs to be redirected." I hear River's voice behind me, and I swivel my chair to face the door.

I see that easy smile across his face, and he makes his way into my office. I stand and walk a few paces before he swallows me in a hug. He kisses the top of my head, and I pull my gaze up to meet his.

"It's good to see you," I say as I breathe in his woodsy scent that instantly calms my nerves. I haven't seen him in a week. Work has been shit, and each night I have been free, he's been at the station.

"You're working late again. I was down the street having a beer with Ashton, and after I got your text, I thought I'd swing by and see if you needed some company." He pushes a piece of hair back behind my ear, looking deeply into my eyes, and it feels like all my frustrations fall to the wayside the moment he pulls me into his arms.

I'm so entrapped in everything River, I don't notice he's got a bag in one hand. The moment he holds it up into view, I see the logo of the restaurant, and I wiggle in excitement.

"I thought a little break and Costello's Deli would do the trick." He beams like he's found a way to solve all my problems in one simple gesture. He might not be able to handle Brett Henry's party animal ways, but he sure knows the way to my heart. Food and orgasms are always a win.

"Good to know," he says with a chuckle.

"Shit, did I say that out loud?" I look at him, and I can feel my cheeks heat up.

"You did, and I've made a mental note for the future." He sends a wink my way, and I feel it down to my core.

We make our way to the couch in my office, and I kick my shoes off and sit with the bag of food in my lap. Things with River feel comfortable, which is something I never thought possible. Had someone said a few months ago this would be my interaction with him, I would have laughed in their face. In no way had I predicted this would be the outcome of all those fights over the last decade.

"Tell me what that was all about," he inquires. I still find myself surprised by this side of River. He shows me this sensitive part of him that I never had a window into before.

I groan, thinking about everything I've had to deal with today. "It's been a bit hellish with the whole thing that came up with Brett this morning in the paper, but it's looking up." I smile as I take a bite of my sandwich.

The moment I feel the blast of flavor hit my taste buds, I moan, closing my eyes and relishing the taste. I skipped lunch due to the endless meetings today, and this feels like the best damn thing I've ever eaten.

As I continue to devour the sandwich, River tells me about his last few nights at the firehouse, going through stories about the newest addition to the team, the probie as they refer to him, who seems to be coming into his own. Watching him talk about the people at the firehouse really does depict a family versus a group of co-workers.

The sandwiches at this deli are gigantic, and I'm halfway done with this one. With each bite, I moan as the flavors just keep getting better.

"Fuck, Skipper, keep that up, and you're only going to get one more bite of that." River's body is now so close to me that I feel his breath against the side of my face. Despite my hunger, I feel that tightening in my belly, and my panties are on their way to soaking.

"Maybe that's my plan," I say with a mouthful of food, and I know there's nothing sexy about my response.

"You know it's a choking hazard to speak with your mouth full, right? I would hate to have to do CPR on you," he says as he slowly drops kisses down my neck, making my skin break out in goosebumps.

It doesn't take long for my sandwich to be forgotten, and he's pulling me down to the floor, consuming me in a kiss that takes my breath away.

"You know," kiss, "I should," kiss, "probably let you," kiss, "finish your," kiss, "meal."

Each connection feels like a burn mark on my skin. I begin clawing at his clothes, successfully lifting his shirt over his head, then making quick work of the buckle of his belt. I push his pants down, letting his boxers slide along with them.

Soon, he's naked in front of me, his erection greeting me at eye level.

He gives himself a few strokes. "You know, Kennedy, I didn't bring dinner over and a show. You better get undressed because dessert is already on its way."

He doesn't have to tell me twice. I start to unbutton my blouse, and then I fiddle with my skirt, pulling the zipper down. Finally, I'm standing in just my lace panty and bra set. Red was the choice of the day today, along with my thigh-high nylons. The moment I start to mess with the buckle of my heel, River protests.

"Absolutely the fuck not, Skipper. Those stay on. Actually, everything stays on below your underwear."

"Demanding tonight, are we?" I tease.

"Oh, you have no idea. I've been deprived of you for too long, and I need this release." He's still stroking himself, and it's mesmerizing.

I make quick work of my bra and panties, tossing them aside, ready to feel him inside me.

River nearly topples me when he pounces forward, pushing me toward the office window. My office has a view of the baseball field. Luckily, no one can see into these offices, but the uptick of my pulse is instant thinking of how dirty this is.

"You ready to scream my name so that everyone knows whose dick you're riding?" he says into my ear, only making me wetter the more I imagine it.

A hushed "Yes" comes out of my mouth, then I feel him move his dick through my folds. Every touch is enough to drive me wild.

"Fuck. Hold on." River pulls away slightly, moving toward his pants. He pulls out a condom like he won the lottery and rips it open. The moment he sheathes himself, he's back to pinning me against the window.

"Good thing you came prepared." I smile right before he kisses me again.

"Always," he says right before he lines himself up to me

and thrusts in to the hilt.

The moment I feel full with him, I let out a loud moan, entranced by this man that once only got on my nerves. I'm the last one left in the office, so I'm not concerned anyone will hear me.

He begins a punishing pace, and I swear I'm already on the brink of seeing stars. His dick is hitting me in that one spot that makes me wild, and I'm about to jump off that cliff, my climax hitting me faster than I expected.

"That's it, Skipper, let go. Fucking come for me, Kennedy." He's moving fast, like he's in as much of a rush to orgasm as I am. His movements are confirmation he missed this as much as I did.

The moment I feel my vision return, he's back to that fast pace, this time seeking his own release. He's pushing me harder against the window, and I know he's close.

He buries his face in my neck, his pumps becoming erratic. As much as I know River wants to drag this out, we've been deprived of one another for too long. It's like our bodies crave one another, and for each day we've been apart, we make up for it two-fold when we're together.

It doesn't take long before he's yelling, "Shit, I'm coming." He comes with so much force that I feel another orgasm consume my body as I fall off that cliff with him.

It feels like we've just finished running a marathon. The moment he stills, it's like every part of me is sensitive. His breath on my neck begins to tickle, and I can't help the giggle that escapes. He takes a little nibble of my earlobe and pulls away, his smile serene.

We move about the room, running over to my en-suite bathroom and cleaning ourselves up. I'm putting my clothes back on, slowly bending over to retrieve my underwear. I look over my shoulder and see River's eyes on me.

The fact that I still hold his attention after seeing me naked at least a dozen times makes me bold. I do a little shake of my ass, and he seems mesmerized.

"How about you finish your dinner, and I take you home?" he asks as he slaps my ass.

I simply nod my head, realizing that in just a short amount of time of seeing River in this new light, I like his use of home instead of saying my home. Something about that brings a flutter to my heart, and I'm opening my eyes to the fact this guy is climbing over those walls I've built, and I'm not sure I'm mad about it. Honestly, I may not be strong enough to keep this from becoming deeper.

CHAPTER 19

Kennedy

"WHY HAVEN'T I seen you in these yet?" River says, tossing the skimpy lingerie at me, hoping to get me out of my sour mood.

River and I have been doing whatever River and I are doing for a few months now. I thought this casual sex of ours would have run its course by now, but here we are, still finding ways to get together whenever we can.

"Okay, crotchless panties? Are you fucking with me now?" he gripes, still sifting through my drawers.

"Do you mind, River? Why are you even going through my things?" I ask, not even remembering how we got to this point where he's going through my things.

"Because you said you wanted to relax in the community hot tub. You pointed at your dresser to grab something for you to put on, and now I can't even focus anymore. There's lace everywhere in here. What the fuck, Skipper? You're holding out on me!" He continues his complaints while I had already forgotten about the hot tub request.

Honestly, my mind is mush right now. My issues with Brett Henry have only gotten worse. I've held off, hoping those below me would take care of it, but now the more I see things unfolding, it will soon be my shit to clean up.

I rub my temples, hoping it dissolves some of the tension I'm feeling. River chooses that exact moment to look over and catches me trying to absolve myself of this stress.

"Hey, get out of your head. You're supposed to be getting ready to go sit in a hot tub and let me rub your muscles… maybe rub a couple of other things." He waggles his eyebrows, and I can't help the chuckle that escapes.

"I know, I know. I'm shit company tonight though. I would need a million hot tubs to rid me of the crap mood that this player is putting me in right now. Ugh!"

I let my body fall back onto my bed, the frustration not dissipating even after so much work trying to make this problem go away. So far, no matter what I say to the people surrounding the great Brett Henry, no one is slapping this nonsense behavior out of him.

All of a sudden, I open my eyes and sit straight up. "I got it! Wanna get away?"

A gleam of mischief crosses his face, and I already know he's down to do something outside the city with me.

* * *

River blasts the music in his truck as we make our way up to Maine. It's my favorite impromptu getaway, and luckily, River was game to join me. We both have the weekend off; well, I'm never fully unplugged as the president of a baseball franchise, but I can do my work remotely for the next forty-eight hours. The team is on a string of away games, so I don't need to be physically there to watch any games at the stadium.

This is exactly what I need. I let my hand move through the air as we speed down the highway. It reminds me of the summers I would spend with my aunt and uncle, driving our way up through the States, feeling like time was standing still and my heart was soaring.

I will admit that this happiness running through me is unexpected, especially after going back to New York a few weeks back. There is so much pain I buried there that risked resurfacing, yet I didn't bolt in the opposite direction when he asked me on that trip with him.

If I'm being completely transparent, River is unexpected. I've always been aware that River is up for an adventure, but I've gotten a window into this softer side of him. And that side is finding ways of latching onto my heart, and it's getting harder to turn a blind eye toward it.

We've been on opposite sides of the playing field for so long that for years, I thought that's all I'd see of River. I thought that was the only side he would grant me. Obviously, I did the same, giving him the pieces of me that were tough and rigid. But when I spend more time with him, I see myself thawing that icy exterior just to let him get a little closer.

Part of me has to keep reminding myself that this isn't forever. This isn't part of the deal, where we move toward something deeper together.

But sometimes, much like the moments we are sharing together now, I feel like our connection runs deeper. But it feels like the lines are blurring, the pen bleeding through the paper, and I'm not too sure I'm upset about it. I sort of like whatever we've got going on.

I like feeling my smile grow as his brightens when we see one another in a room. I welcome the interaction, not just from being attracted to this man but because he brings out a side of me that feels good and free. I feel like I'm whole when he's with me, and all the things that keep me prickly around the edges simply disappear the longer we keep finding ways to connect on this new level we've discovered together.

He moves his hand off the wheel to touch my knee. I feel myself react to his touch, and he squeezes my thigh, almost like he can sense his touch turns me on, even with such simplicity.

"Where's your mind at, Skip?" He turns to me and throws that sexy smile my way.

"It's at peace, that's where it is, Riv." I continue to move my hand through the air, making waves with the way my hand glides with the force.

"I get that. I truly get that, Kennedy," he says, and right then, it feels like we have this force bringing us together that's deeper than anything we ever expected.

We arrive at our destination; one I've visited many times in the years prior: a quaint bed and breakfast right on the water. I used to stay here years ago, and I was surprised it was still functioning at the same capacity as a bed and breakfast. They had one cancellation, and I felt like it was meant to be that we came up here today.

I think I needed the getaway, not only to detach from this Brett situation, but to also feel like I wasn't hiding whatever I was doing with River. We can't really go out together in the city. Even if what we're doing is for fun and between one another, it's something we have chosen to keep secret. Walking freely in our neighborhoods, getting a bite to eat, showing any type of affection, isn't something we can do without running the risk of getting caught. Being here gives us some openness to our behavior and I can't help but feel a little more free.

We get out of the car, and I'm immediately engulfed in memories of my childhood. The way my feet crunch under the pebbles on the ground, the view of the sun reflecting off the water, and the wrap-around porch that feels the same yet so different from when we stayed here so many years ago.

River comes around and pulls me to him. He moves his

lips to my temple, then brings his lips to the shell of my ear. "I can't wait to fuck you against the window so this whole place knows you're mine."

My cheeks flame even as I elbow him, but somewhere deep down, the fact he's so adamant that I turn him on makes my stomach flip a bit. I know his words have an expiration date, but there's a part deep inside me, that wants a little part of those words to hold some truth. That thought scares yet thrills me at the same time.

We've spent months secretly touching one another, hoping to keep this a secret between us. But out here, we don't have the threat of running into someone we know, opening up the possibility of us being ourselves on a whole new level.

I pull his hand into mine as I march us up the steps and into the cottage. We walk into the lobby, and it's all so serene. I instantly feel better from the stress of the city being left behind. The woman behind the desk has a welcoming smile on her face, and I give her our information to check in.

I'm lucky I could get out of Boston this weekend. This break is a must right now with the chaos of the team and the stress off the field. The job is still something I love, but these last few weeks have been absolute hell. As much as I knew the uphill battle my job would be because I'm a female in a male-dominated industry, it doesn't mean the stress weighs any less with that expectation. Hopefully, this getaway is the recharge I need to mentally attack whatever comes next.

"Room 202, which is up the stairs and to the left. You'll have a view of the water from your balcony, along with an en-suite restroom that has bay windows as well. The best room in the house."

The older woman smiles as we make our way through the lobby, and I nod my appreciation. We begin our ascent toward the room, our bags minimal for such a short stay. The moment we open the door, we're both taken aback. This room is breathtaking. It's what Hallmark movies base their storylines on with the floral wallpaper, along with the accents of beach decor sprinkled throughout the bedding and furniture.

We step further in and within seconds, River is jumping onto the bed.

"Holy fuck, this bed is like a cloud!" he declares, then starts rolling around.

"You act like you don't have a bed at home, Riv." I can't help the eye roll.

"Try it, Kennedy. I swear this thing is what dreams are made of." He pats the spot next to him. I pretend I'm going to walk off, but then I throw my bags to the side and take a leap onto the fluffy bedding.

The moment my body connects to the mattress, I realize River wasn't exaggerating.

"Damn, that's nice." I move my arms and legs as if there's a potential of forming a snow angel. My mattress at home is comfortable, but this one is next level.

"It really is," he says, and when I turn my head, I see he's looking right at me. More like devouring me with his gaze.

I smile at him, and he inches closer.

"You know what I kept thinking while we were driving up here?" he asks, moving his hand onto my bare legs.

"What's that?" I mutter, my focus being pulled to the circles he's drawing up my thigh.

"The fact that those tiny shorts you're wearing are leaving little to the imagination," he says, and I turn toward him, letting the roaming hand cover my ass as I move my thigh over his hip. I feel a zap of energy move through me as he grabs my butt through my denim shorts.

"What exactly were you thinking of doing about it?" I tease, loving this surge of electricity I get right before he strips me out of my clothes.

"I was thinking about this top." He moves his hand up my side and pulls a strap down. "I was thinking about these tits and how I want to devour them one by one," he adds, bringing his lips to my breast and nibbling each of my nipples.

"Mmmm." My words are failing to form, and he hasn't done much yet.

"Feeling your skin against my lips feels like the ultimate dream, Kennedy," he says as he trails kisses down my abdomen and nears my center.

I look down to see him unfastening the button to my shorts and slowly inching the material past my hips and down my legs. He leaves my underwear on and returns all his focus to my center, his gaze trailing up my body until our eyes connect.

It's then I feel it—that attention he gives me in a way that makes the rest of the world melt away. It feels like time stops, and all my synapses are firing at the same time.

He begins to trail kisses along my chest, down my navel until his nose reaches the fabric of the lace thong I'm wearing. The wetness seeps through my underwear, and his nose grazes my clit.

I can't help my reaction, pushing my chest out and letting my head fall back. My knees fall open a little wider, hoping he'll ease that tension I'm feeling.

"Where do you want me first, Kennedy?" he asks as he moves his nose back down and then up again along the fabric, grazing that sensitive bud for a second time.

"You want me here?" He licks me over the fabric, and I'm so turned on that even with the thin layer of my panties in the way, it feels like enough to set me off.

He moves his body up mine, then brings his lips back to my nipples. "Or should I focus on this here?" he asks, trailing his fingers up my abdomen and grabbing my breasts.

His body comes up, caging me in and hovering over me, his face inches away from mine.

"Or should I really slow things down and just kiss you

until you are writhing beneath me to fuck you?" His words push me a little further into this euphoric abyss.

"I want you everywhere," I say because I do. I want a piece of him in all the places he's touched.

"Mmm, I like that answer," he says before he slams his lips against mine, stealing my next breath.

I move my hands under his shirt and up his back, feeling his ripped muscles beneath my touch. His hard body tightens under my palm, and I know he feels this connection between us beyond just the physical. He feels my touch the same way I react to his.

He takes the back of his shirt and moves it over his head. I make quick work of his belt and start to unbuckle his jeans. I use my feet to push the material further down his legs until he pulls away and stands facing me.

He pushes the pants all the way down and kicks them to the side. I look at him, his erection trying to force itself out of his boxers, while the V leading down to heaven is causing me to salivate.

I can't stop staring; his erection, even behind that stretch of fabric, is still intimidating each time I see it. He's fucking hung, and he knows how to use every inch of that beast.

"Hey, Skip, my eyes are up here," he snaps, but I keep my focus where it was.

Without saying a word, I move myself off the bed and down onto my knees. The minute he registers what I'm about to do, he pulls me up and tosses me back on the bed.

"I have a better idea," he says with a gleam of mischief crossing his face.

Before I know what's coming, he jumps onto the bed, lying prone, and brings me on top of him. But this time, he turns me so that my face is in line with his dick, and my center is in his face.

Just the thought of being in such a promiscuous position with him is dirty and enticing all in one.

We're both still wearing our underwear, but that doesn't seem like a deterrent.

"Take my cock, Kennedy," he demands, and something about that is beyond sexy.

I move his boxers down slightly and grasp his dick in my hand. Then I stick my tongue out and lick from base to tip. Without warning, I take him into my mouth and let his tip hit the back of my throat.

I gag, and my eyes instantly water. I begin to move, and I hear a moan slip out of his mouth.

"Fuck, that mouth of yours is perfect," he says as he kneads my ass. He gives me a little tap, and then he's ripping yet another pair of my underwear and brings his lips to my center.

I pop off him with a moan. Shit, that feels better knowing we're in this dirty position right now.

I begin to move my hips uncontrollably, and somehow find it in me to continue pushing his dick in my mouth and start moving.

I feel my orgasm pushing to the forefront of my mind as I'm riding his face, feeling myself lose control while my body falls so deep down that orgasmic abyss, my body goes limp once I climax.

He moves from under me and then gets behind me. I feel him removing his boxers and then grabbing a condom and slipping it on.

Before I have time to recover from my first orgasm, he's slamming into me, pushing me closer to another release.

"You grip my cock so well, baby. Fuck, feel how hard you make me. Your body is constantly on my mind, and fucking you is not ever enough of a release." His words alone are getting me back to my breaking point.

I start to moan louder, moving my hand to touch myself.

"Right there, Kennedy. Yes, get yourself off and let me feel you strangle me," he says, and I swear it takes one soft touch to my center to feel myself completely let go again.

I start to feel him move faster while I let go, his thrusts getting stronger, and his movements reach that punishing pace.

Soon, he's yelling my name, and I feel the moment his body lets go.

His movements slow as he starts to come down off that high, and we both collapse onto the bed.

He pulls my back against his chest, the sweat intermixed as we both catch our breath.

"Shit, Kennedy, how is this even possible? All these years and we missed out on this fun. We're fucking idiots." He laughs, and I smile to myself.

He's right, we were idiots. But right now, I'm feeling like the biggest idiot to think this is going to lead to me not catching feelings because I can already tell my part of the deal is starting to dissolve. But with that comes fear that this will soon be coming to an end.

River

After grabbing lunch, we're enjoying some ice cream while the sun is still shining. The warmth is sticking around a bit longer, but the bite of cold hits the moment the sun sets. With each lick of her cone, Kennedy closes her eyes, truly enjoying her treat as we walk hand in hand. She looks adorable, even with a smear of chocolate on her nose.

"You've got—"

"Oh my gosh, River, they've got face painting! Remember when Samara guilted you to get yours painted that year at the fair, and you had that massive dragon from Mulan painted across your entire face?" She starts laughing as she points ahead of us to the kids with butterflies on their cheeks.

"Yeah, she cried her eyes out. How was I supposed to know she could cry on demand!" Samara apparently knows how to turn on the waterworks, and that happened the summer after I had met her, so I wasn't quite aware she was so devious. She conned me, and I spent the better part of four hours walking around the fair with a cartoon dragon painted on my face. Some kids even asked to take their picture with me because it was so detailed.

"I should have had them paint something on your face so you could have been as embarrassed as me," I toss back at Kennedy.

She takes another lick of her ice cream. "Oh, please. I don't embarrass that easily." As she says this, she gets even more chocolate on her face, this time landing on the right side of her cheek. How does she not feel it on her face?

"Oh really? You're telling me you wouldn't get even a bit red in the face with kids pointing at you and laughing?" I find that absolutely hard to believe.

"No, River. I have no problem with a little attention. My ego can take it. It's not a big deal."

She's so full of shit. I have no problem proving my point, so instead of being the bigger person right now, I decide to play the long game on this. We continue our walk, and sure enough, she keeps licking that ice cream like a four-year-old. It's sort of a miracle to watch how sophisticated she can be in so many areas of life, yet she's simply a mess when it comes to this moment. But it's working in my favor.

I'm mesmerized yet flabbergasted all at once.

People are staring as we walk by, and I see Kennedy take note of the glances she's getting. At first, I think she's flattered, but with each added stare, she's starting to grow self-conscious, and it's hard to hold the laughter.

Luckily, the bed and breakfast isn't like a hotel lobby with mirrors everywhere, and we get back to our room without Kennedy catching a glimpse of herself in a reflection throughout the lobby or corridor leading up to our room.

The moment we walk in, she rushes to the restroom to wash her hands, needing to get the stickiness washed off.

She closes the door, and the moment she turns the light on, all I hear on the other side of the door causes me to roar with laughter.

"You're a motherfucker, River!"

CHAPTER 20

River

A GROUP of us were invited over for a gender reveal for Sam and Ash's baby. It's crazy to think in a few months, there will be a little one running around amongst the friends.

Clay is covering a shift at the station today, so I told him I'd let him know the big news once it's revealed. Kennedy and I also had to devise a plan, seeing as we are going behind everyone's back and having to play off our usual banter. I had to swear my entire firehouse to secrecy in case they run into Ashton or Sam and decide to open their big fucking mouths.

As much as we are keeping what we're doing under wraps, the guys at the station don't usually mingle with our outside friends. It's hard to keep things from my firehouse family because we pretty much live together when on shift. Not much gets past them when it comes to day-to-day life.

The moment I enter Ashton and Samara's house, I know something's up. I walk in and when I spot Samara, she looks to be scheming while Ash is hiding behind his wife, not making eye contact with me. We haven't even made it past the foyer, and I already know I should have mentally prepared before showing up here today. I was naive to think this would simply be a big gender reveal when, in fact, I'll be subject to one of Samara's little plans.

"Finally, you're here, River," Sam says as she pulls me into a big hug. "I'm so excited." She wastes no time pulling my hand through her house and into their little backyard.

The moment I see the tall brunette look my way, I know exactly what Sam is up to. I get confirmation when Ashton stands by my side and whispers, "I tried to stop her." Then he scurries to the side of the deck. Fucking coward.

"Willa, look who showed up!" Samara's acting like my attendance was optional.

The woman Sam is introducing me to would usually pique my interest if it weren't for a blue-eyed blonde who has recently taken hold of my thoughts.

Willa has bright blue eyes and long, wavy brown hair, with a figure I'd usually drool over. But the only thing I am really doing is looking at her and mentally comparing her to Kennedy, which is a red flag in more ways than one. Too bad Kennedy and I discussed how we'd approach dating while at this party, and we both agreed it would just lead to more questions if we said we were dating *someone*. Knowing Sam, she would sniff it out of one of us before the night was over.

I'm holding the potato salad I was instructed to bring to Samara and extend my hand out. The woman smiles brightly. "It seems Samara finally got us in the same room. It's nice to meet you, River."

I try to plaster the kindest smile I can and return the greeting. "I'm glad one of us is in the know. Sam here is great with surprises."

Sam snorts and it's a bigger reaction than I expect from her. I look over at my best friend's wife while she composes herself, who bats her eyes like she's some sort of matchmaker for the stars.

"I can already see the sparks flying." She claps her hands together and rushes off before I can protest.

"So, this is probably awkward," Willa says, although she keeps looking at me like I'm her next meal. Willa is quite bold because immediately following her long perusal of my body, she rubs her hand up my forearm and bicep, squeezing my muscles in appreciation. Kennedy is not going to like this.

As if my thoughts conjured her up, I hear a squeal behind me. I already know it's Kennedy because she makes the same sound when I catch her off guard and carry her to the bedroom. I look over to find the best friends embracing, then see Kennedy's eyes find mine once she's pulling apart from Samara. I see when her gaze jumps to the hand grazing my bicep and watch her face turn to stone. She covers it up quickly by reaching to touch Samara's belly.

Sam must be filling Kennedy in because while I have my eye on her, that blue-gold gaze shoots back up to mine as she sizes up the woman next to me. While I'm sure Kennedy is putting a spell on either me or Willa, Ashton, clueless to the facial assault Kennedy is subjecting me to, hands me a beer and starts making conversation, probably realizing the awkwardness of setting me up at his baby's gender reveal.

I finally pull my gaze away from the woman I was just inside two hours ago and try to engage myself in the conversation happening around me.

Turns out Willa is studying to be a lawyer, which is hard to find any similarity to as most of my experience with lawyers comes in the form of ambulance chasers.

"So, where are you going to law school?" I ask, hoping to keep the conversation casual, keeping my distance without making Willa too uncomfortable with the fact that I am not interested in that way. At least she's taken back her hand, not before doing one more squeeze of my muscles and telling me how fit I am. I internally roll my eyes at her attempted advances.

She's about to answer when she looks over my shoulder, and her expression changes from intrigue to confusion.

"Hey, I wanted to come by and introduce myself. I'm Kennedy, Sam's best friend." She plasters a smile across her face, and it doesn't take a genius to see she's being completely fake.

"Oh, hi, I'm Willa. I met Sam at the supermarket a few months back, and we've become fast friends," Willa answers, having no idea Kennedy is going to eat her alive.

"Isn't that sweet." Her gaze swinging my way is anything but sweet.

Ash must sense the tension and steps away, brows reaching his hairline. I wish I could join him.

"Yeah, Willa was just telling me about law school." I take a nervous sip of my beer, hoping this nightmare ends soon.

"How cute is this? Don't you two make the cutest pair," Kennedy seethes through her teeth. She's fucking pissed, and I sort of like it. Jealous Kennedy might be my new favorite. Maybe we can fuck the jealousy out of her later.

My smile grows, and I decide to piss her off a little more, probably because I have a death wish, and I reach my beer over to Willa's glass and clink in cheers.

Kennedy watches my movements, and then something snaps in her.

"It was nice meeting you, Willa. River, always a pain in my ass." She flips her hair over her shoulder and turns toward the rest of the guests. Then, in a not-so-subtle attempt to make me overhear, she yells over to Sam, "Didn't you say Brad was coming to this thing tonight?"

A tight smile takes over my features as I feel my blood boil. My plan backfired, and I'm not sure I'll last without being a dick to Brad. I already know who the guy is. He's some bigwig exec from Samara's building who she's tried to set Kennedy up with for the longest time. For so long, I couldn't care less, but now, it's making my eye twitch.

Willa, probably sensing something's off, pulls my attention back to her. "So I hear you're a firefighter. How do you like that?"

"I love it," I say, taking a long swig of my beer and letting my eyes roam the backyard, searching for Brad in the crowd.

The moment my eyes connect with Douchebag Brad's blond hair, I see Kennedy embrace him. I swear I see him close his eyes and move his face inward to get a smell of Kennedy. She's mine, fucknut. It's taking every muscle in my body to stay put.

"How long have you been a firefighter?" I can tell Willa is really trying to get my focus to return to her, but I honestly don't think I can look away. I pushed Kennedy with my little charade, even if it was minimal, and if I know her at all, she's going to milk this for as long as she can.

Sure enough, the moment she pulls away from Brad, a huge smile that I thought she only reserved for me is being given to that dick noodle. Then she swings her gaze my way and winks. Fucking winks. I'll make her pay for that later.

"I'm sorry, Willa. Do you mind if we take this conversation over to that area over there to sit?" I point to an area closer to where Kennedy is standing.

"There's a couch right here—" she starts, but I'm already grabbing her hand and moving us further into the backyard. At one point, I move my hand to the small of her back, and when Kennedy sees that, I swear she's going to throw her wine glass at me.

Two can play this game, sweetheart.

"What were you asking me earlier?" I bring my focus over to Willa again, not quite feeling awful that I'm using this situation to make the girl I'm fucking jealous.

"Oh, I asked how long you've been a firefighter for?"

I'm interrupted before I can answer.

"Hasn't it been about six years, Riv?" Kennedy pipes in, bringing herself closer to my conversation with Willa, yet pulling Brad by the hand for him to follow.

"Yep, that's right. Weird that you remember. Obsessed much?" I take a sip of my beer, narrowing my gaze at her. What's her angle?

"Yeah, I remember because the day you graduated from the academy, you had that questionable rash you kept telling us about. You know, in your nether regions." For added effect, she moves her hand around her bottom half as if her words weren't descriptive enough.

Of course, the moment she says that, Brad and Willa nearly projectile spit their drinks out. Fucking Kennedy.

Before I can even throw something back, Willa must feel the discomfort between Kennedy and me and decides now would be a good time to excuse herself. "I think I'm going to top off this drink." And she scurries off to the kitchen.

I see Sam in the distance make a face and follow her, and I know this will bite me in the ass later. Oh well, worth it if I can hopefully get Brad to beat it and leave me be with Kennedy.

He seems to sense the tension and excuses himself too; however, he seems to make a promise that he'll chat with Kennedy later. Over my dead fucking body, pal.

A satisfied smile takes over Kennedy's face, and as much as I want to give her shit, I can't help but laugh at what just happened.

"Way to keep it real, Skip," I say as I take a seat, then tap the spot next to me, hoping she'll risk sitting near me.

She's reluctant at first, then decides the hell with it and makes her way over. She keeps a distance, and I'm fighting the desire to pull her on my lap and claim her as mine. Fuck Brad, Willa, and the rest of our audience.

We both open our mouths to say something when a seething Samara comes stomping over. "You fuckers. You couldn't be nice to one another for one party, my party."

Right then, Ashton yells, "Our party," as Sam ignores his protest.

"And for once," she continues, "you couldn't just let your-selves explore something with people I think would work for you two? Why are you two like this? It's so childish!"

Right then, to drive the point home, Kennedy and I point to each other, Kennedy saying, "He did it," while I exclaim, "She started it!"

"Ugh! Don't talk to me for the next twenty minutes," she demands, and Ashton gives me a look like I should have done better for his sake.

"She's still pretty testy. I guess it wasn't a first-trimester thing," I say when I feel an ice cube hit my arm. "What the hell, Sam!"

"Don't fuck with me, River!" she whisper-yells at me, and I can't help the laugh that escapes.

Ashton once again throws me a look like, *What the fuck?*, and I just shrug my shoulders.

Once the two of them are off to the other end of the back-yard and no one is too close to hear my conversation, I turn to Kennedy.

"I hope you know you're getting spanked later after you let that guy put his hands on you." I point the bottleneck of my beer in her direction.

"Oh, look who's talking. She was groping your arm when I got here. Then you grab her hand and move her along the backyard. Who got handsy first, Riv?" Kennedy has this way of sounding calm, but she has this uncanny ability to shut you up quite quickly. She's not wrong; I one hundred percent pushed to see her react.

The afternoon turns into evening, and the anticipation is now full throttle to find out this baby's gender. We've played guessing games, recorded a video for the baby with a message, and we even wear pins with a color to depict our prediction.

I went with girl, and Kennedy went with boy. We both just want a healthy baby like everyone else at this party; however, deep down, I'm a little scared if Sam doesn't get her girl. She's been pointing to her belly and calling the baby a girl from the moment she told us, so I'm a little worried her anger issues will only grow if she doesn't get her way.

They bring a large balloon out and hold it above their heads. They're about to pop it when her work colleague walks out with an identical balloon.

What the hell is happening?

I look over to Kennedy, and she has tears coming down her face. She moves closer to me and whispers in my ear, "They're twins!"

"Surprise everyone! We're not just having one baby, but we're having two!" Samara announces, and her smile is goddam infectious.

Everyone screams with excitement, and I can see a little fear come over my friend Ashton. Obviously, he knew there were two prior to the party today, but I can't imagine it's an easy pill to swallow.

My mom always said as fun as it was to have two little kids growing up together, the amount of mischief we put my mother through was pretty crazy. Now that I'm older and can reflect on our behavior, I'm surprised she didn't have more gray hair at an earlier age.

Once we've settled our hoots and hollering, we begin the countdown. They're each going to pop a balloon. It feels like everyone has a phone out, but I just want to soak up this moment, this feeling, when everything is going to change for our friends.

"Three... two... one..." POP!

Everyone is going wild, and I reach my hand out and squeeze Kennedy's hand while everyone is distracted. She's fully crying now, and as much as I'm soaking up this big moment for my friends, my eyes keep looking over at her, enthralled by the love she holds for these amazing friends of ours.

CHAPTER 21

River

"I CAN'T BELIEVE they're having one of each," Kennedy says as we lie in bed later that evening. She's moving her fingers along my chest, her head resting in the crook of my arm.

I wasn't wrong; the moment we got back to my place, we were pulling at each other's clothes. I have never moved so quickly to get inside her, and I swear, we were letting off a lot of pent-up aggression tonight. It felt like each hour that ticked at that party was an added layer of foreplay between us.

"Yeah, they'll have their hands full, that's for sure." I smile at the thought of two little ones to spoil.

"At least you and Clay can give them some tips," she says, endless loops being circled along my skin with her fingernail.

"I think Clay and I would likely give more advice to the kids on how to torment Ash and Sam than we can really give on parenting itself."

Kennedy moves to rest her chin on my chest. "How was it growing up with someone who knew you so well? I mean, it must have been so cool." Her gaze looks genuinely interested.

"Yeah, it was cool. I mean, many siblings argue or are jealous, but we never felt that way toward one another. We never felt like we lacked in some way because we had to share everything with each other. It's like a built-in best friend. It's hard to dislike someone who's pretty much genetically identical to you, you know?"

Kennedy has returned to her cheek resting on me, growing silent all of a sudden.

"Hey, what just happened?" I can't help but feel the shift that just occurred.

"I was supposed to be a big sister. I was supposed to have something similar to what you have with Clay." Her confession surprises me. I never knew this.

"I had no idea, Kennedy. I'm so sorry. Sam never mentioned it." I don't know much about Kennedy's life, especially about some of the harder times she faced, so this is news to me.

"Sam doesn't know," she whispers, and I'm stunned for a moment. The fact she's trusting me with this information feels like a big moment. But the fact she never told Sam makes me wonder what else she's held onto in her grief.

"Why is that?"

"I don't talk too much about my parents and the day they died. I just sort of put it behind me," she says softly, as if she speaks about it too loudly into the space between us, she'll be transported back to that day.

"Do you want to talk about it with me?" I ask, hoping she'll lean on me.

"The day before my parents passed, I got to go to the doctor with them, and that's where I found out my mom was pregnant. I was so excited. All I wanted to be was a big sister. And my wish was finally coming true." Her voice gets thick with emotion, but I don't interrupt her, and I simply caress her back.

"The next day, on my way to school, both my parents decided to take me. We were talking about the baby, and I remember feeling like everything was perfect. It was the clearest day after a cloudy day before. It felt like I was living a dream, and then, in the next moment, everything became a nightmare. It still does," she says, and I feel the moisture on my skin of what I assume are her tears.

Lola must sense the emotion swirling in the room and decides to jump on the bed and lie next to Kennedy. Kennedy brings her hand to pet Lola's head, and my pup leans into the touch.

"I'm sorry you experienced that. I can't imagine that is an easy memory to live with." I really mean those words. My dad passed away in the most awful way I can imagine, but I wasn't there to see it happen in front of me. I know many did, but I will say I'm glad I didn't see him pass in front of my eyes. I don't know how I would have dealt with that.

"I know you understand the feeling of losing a parent. I know it's different how it happened, but the pain is the same. The loss is the same," she says so quietly I feel her own heartbreak inside my chest.

"That's true. But to live through that, to feel the pain along with recovering from the accident, could not have been easy." I can't help but differentiate her pain from mine.

"We aren't that different with the pain though," she says, not really saying more.

"Can you elaborate?" I push, feeling there's more to this story she isn't telling me.

"My parents died about an hour or so before the first plane hit the North Tower." She pulls her gaze to look at me, probably to gauge my reaction.

I'm stunned for a second as I look at her. All these years, and our parents died on the same day. I've met people who lost family members in those towers, but I don't think I've met one who passed away in a manner not related to the horrific events of that terrorist attack yet on the same day.

I stare at her, my eyes locked on hers. One lone tear falls down her cheek, and I grab it with my thumb.

"I never wanted to tell you," she confesses.

"Why not?" Why wouldn't she want to feel a connection with me where I could at least feel her pain in a deeper way?

"I mean, for so long, we just pushed one another to the point of anger. I never wanted you to think I was trying to take away from your pain. I never tell people what day my parents passed. Obviously, my family knows, but it feels like the moment the horrific nature of that day continued, the details of how my parents died were swallowed in the sadness of the country. I mean, one minute, the pain of losing my parents was only mine, but then the world shifted, and everyone felt some sort of pain that day, especially in New York.

"I started to keep it to myself because the day they died doesn't really matter. It doesn't change the outcome of their fate. They died, much like thousands of others. My pain is not more important than someone else's," she says, and I can feel the pain she still harbors is such a huge part of the armor she holds against her chest; she is trying to keep people at a distance.

"Kennedy, your story isn't less than just because it happened on the same day so many other lives changed so drastically though. You deserve to know your pain is valid and recognize that it happened to you." I push her hair off her face and keep my eyes on hers.

"It was easy for me to just lump my pain with the pain others were feeling. I never really had a reason to confess when they passed. So I keep it to myself, even now," she whispers, and my heart hurts for her.

"But when we went to the memorial, you didn't say a thing. Clay and I made it all about our dad, and you were grieving the anniversary just the same as us." I feel the guilt creep in that her loss was amplified that day, and none of us knew.

"I, um, you know that moment I left you and Clay at the

hotel for a bit?" I nod, and she continues, "I went to their grave to leave some flowers. I wasn't there long. I used to go every anniversary with my grandparents until they passed a few years ago. I hadn't been back much since, but I just had my time talking to my parents and updating them on my life. I don't feel like I need to be there each year though. That's not how I view my loss of them, especially now that I live far away and can't just hop in a car or subway to visit."

This is a new side of Kennedy, quiet and reserved. She's always so fiery and ready to battle with whoever throws verbal punches that I haven't seen her cower in any way toward any part of life. But this is different. And this side of her is something I haven't gotten to witness until today.

"I think you're brave, and I am so glad you told me." I move so that she's now below me, and I'm caging her in. I press my lips to hers and try to give her as much of my tenderness as I'm capable of sharing with another human. There's nothing sexual about my connection with her in this moment. My lips simply kiss her softly to show that she isn't alone.

For so many years, I misjudged Kennedy. And I assume my actions, my words, didn't really make her want to open up to me. I can't help but feel like I pushed her further into this version of herself where she felt she had to shield herself from others, including me.

"Just know you can grieve without feeling guilty, if that's even the emotion you're feeling," I tell her, my lips close enough to kiss her again but just hovering over her lips.

She moves her hands up and through my hair. I close my eyes at the feeling, leaning in much like Lola did with Kennedy's caress.

"Thanks for letting me tell you. Thanks for not feeling like I was trying to take your pain and make it about me. I just needed to let that out."

I lean down and kiss her softly again. I bury my face in

her neck and breathe her in. If this were another time, I'd have the ability to pull her in with me, to open my heart in a way where we were talking about our next steps in this relationship. But for now, this is as close as our hearts can give to one another, and I'll savor this space we've made for each other.

Too bad it's just that, a temporary space to savor and not one to stay and hold on to. That wasn't the pact we made when we started this weeks ago. I can't go changing the rules now.

* * *

The next morning, I make sure to wake up earlier than Kennedy. She rarely sleeps in, but last night must have wiped her out. She's still turned on her side, her frown lines evident as she dreams about something serious.

Lola and I move through the room quietly, and once we close the bedroom door, Lola starts moving in circles as I grab her leash. I keep shushing her, hoping she'll keep the morning madness to a minimum.

Once Lola has done a quick stroll in the neighborhood and checked the morning newspaper—sniffing the bushes in the surrounding block—we make our way back home. The moment we return, I get Lola fed, and then I start to evaluate my fridge for something to cook up. My work schedule has been so chaotic that I haven't restocked in some time.

I know Kennedy has attempted eggs, but I think maybe a little French toast will do the trick. The things Kennedy confessed last night felt like she was letting go of a heavy weight from her chest, making me feel a little closer to her. Having this little window into her life, one that she doesn't let others see, makes me feel like I'm holding onto something special that I don't have to share with anyone else.

I'm in the middle of mixing the eggs when my bedroom door opens, and a sleepy-faced Kennedy emerges.

"Hey, sleepyhead," I say, and she smiles. She reaches over and wraps her arms around my waist. I took my shirt off to avoid getting it splattered with food while I cooked, so she soaks up that fact by kissing my back, right along my spine.

"There's really nothing sexier than waking up to this view in the kitchen." I feel her smile against me. "These muscles, River, are simply everything." Then she bites me, and I flinch in surprise.

"Did you just bite me?" I turn my head slightly to sneak a peek at her.

"Yes, of course I did. I've never been with a man who has muscles on top of muscles. Is that even normal?" she asks, and I throw the fork I am mixing the eggs with and turn to face her.

"I don't think we should be talking about other men you've been with while you're touching me. It's an instant boner-kill, baby." I grab her cheeks and kiss her. She leans into my touch, and I can't stop myself from opening up and sliding my tongue in her mouth to intertwine with hers.

She moans into me, and I instantly feel my cock wake up.

"No, none of that. We need to eat. Go grab a coffee while I make you a proper breakfast without the added sodium you seem to like." I smack her ass, and she yelps.

"I'm going to learn to cook you some mean scrambled eggs, don't you worry!" she says as she pours herself a cup of coffee and stations herself on a stool at the island.

"Um, River?" Her voice is small, and it causes me to look back at her.

"Yeah?" Concern laces through me with her tone.

"Thanks for last night. You know, for listening," she says, and she seems small as she says it.

I place the fork down again and take my strides over to rest between her legs.

"Kennedy, you can count on me. I know we are just scratching an itch, but know that whatever you tell me, I won't repeat it."

For a second, it seems like hurt crosses her features, but she quickly recovers and nods slightly. I give her a quick kiss on the forehead and move back to my chef station.

"You good with French toast?" I ask, keeping my eyes on the toast as I move it through the eggs.

"Yep," she responds, her answer clipped. I bet talking about everything last night and then having to digest how all that feels today is a lot for her.

I continue to make our breakfast, a little quieter than I expected for how our morning started with her touching me from the moment she saw me in the kitchen. But after the emotional toll last night must have settled on her shoulders, I let her have her space. An hour later, she's rushing out the door, telling me she has to get to an impromptu meeting at the stadium.

The moment I close the door, and she's gone, I can't help but feel like something was off as she left my apartment.

CHAPTER 22

Kennedy

I KNOW *we're just scratching an itch...*

Talk about a bucket of water being thrown over my head. The moment River said those words, it felt as if ice was moving along my veins. Especially after I confessed something so close to my heart the night before.

It was a good reminder that what we are doing is simply surface level. There's no depth to our relationship. There's no forever, no possibility of something more. What we are doing is just meeting each other's needs.

I think if my reaction to his words and my inability to stay a minute longer in that house was any indication, it's that this thing between us needs to end. It's reached that point where I feel things, bigger emotions, coming into play, and he's just not on the same page as me.

Don't get me wrong, I'm the one changing the script here. He's exactly where we agreed we should stay. He's managed to stay in his lane, but I've deviated. I'm seeking more from something that doesn't exist.

I move quickly through the streets, opting out of an Uber and apparently subjecting myself to a walk of shame. That's what this feels like. Do the kids even call it that anymore? I have no idea, but this is how I feel—like a person who feels absolute shame for feelings I shouldn't be having for a man who is much like me—afraid of commitment.

The moment I cross the threshold of my penthouse, I begin throwing my clothes haphazardly and move myself toward my bathroom. I just need to submerge myself under a stream of hot water and hopefully wash this feeling of disappointment and embarrassment off.

I move through my morning routine on autopilot. The heatless curlers aren't an option this morning because time isn't on my side, so I decide to revert to my old ways and curl them with a hot tool. I've been good about caring for my hair this year, but right now, I just don't have the bandwidth to deal with that nonsense.

I'm putting my heels on when I get a text from River:

RIVER

Let me know what time you're off tonight.
Maybe I'll meet you at your place and we can
grab a bite and I'll be your dessert ;)

Sounds fun, but I'll have to ask for a
raincheck for tonight. I have meetings all day
and I'll be wiped.

I feel the annoyance seeping into my system right now. Much like stages of grief, stages of pulling away from someone feel eerily similar. Right now, I'm in a bitter phase. And I guess a bit of embarrassment. Maybe those aren't stages of grief—more like stages of humiliation. And I'm currently in the thick of those feelings.

I see the dots appear, but I don't stick around looking at my phone to see what he responds with. I can't tell if River noticed the shift in my mood this morning, and I honestly can't really fault him if he didn't. I'm the one realizing I'm in too deep. And for the sake of self-preservation, I think pulling away from this, whatever we've made of ourselves together, needs to happen.

Is it the mature thing to do? No, but who really acts maturely when they're embarrassed? I guess not me, the nearly thirty-year-old who decided to have a fling with a guy as against attachment as me. That's who.

The moment I get to the office, I'm pulled in multiple directions. The issues with Brett Henry haven't gotten better. They were quiet initially after I spoke to the general manager, but then he was back to his usual antics, and now I have to tackle this head-on. He's on my calendar for a lunch meeting; therefore, my meal will be ruined by his presence and most likely his excuses that he will be throwing my way for his behavior. This man is not that much younger than me, yet I have to scold a professional baseball player like he's a horny teen. Why can't he keep it in his pants when he's out in public? Fucking athletes!

The moment Brett walks into the office, I notice all the women and some men looking his way, drool visible even from this distance. I can't help the eye roll I let take over my face before he enters the conference room.

"Hey, boss. You know, we could have done this at a nice restaurant downtown." He throws his perfect smile my way, and I feel absolutely nothing toward the gesture. I guess he's appealing to some, but for me, he's my employee, and I hired him to do a job. He might be good at the sport, but everything outside of this stadium is fucked due to his behavior.

"Hi, Brett. Good to see you. Please sit down." I motion to the chair across from me and keep the small talk to a minimum.

Lunch was already delivered, and the buffet has been set up. His agent follows behind him, and luckily, he's one I have not had a bad experience with. From the bags under his eyes, his client might be causing more sleepless nights than he'd rather deal with as well.

"Grab a plate before we chat." I don't give much room to argue and stand up, walking toward the table set up in the back of the conference room. The way my morning has gone so far, none of this food looks appealing, but for show, I spoon a few items onto my plate.

"So, how you liking your new gig?" Brett is all calm and ease. I can tell he's used to getting his way, and that's about to end right now.

"Funny you should ask, Brett. You see, I'd like my 'gig' a lot more if I didn't have your face in headlines on my desk every morning." My features are stone as I look at him, taking in his reaction.

Of course, his laid-back smile takes over his features, and I have to control the urge to scream at the top of my lungs. Today is not the day to mess with me.

"Come on, not you too!" he says, then swings his gaze to his agent. Much like me, his agent looks like he's about to slap his own client across the face.

"Let's stop with the show, Brett. I get it. You're good at your job. But guess what, Brett? I'm good at mine too. I'm the one who signs that paycheck. I'm the one who ensures my organization is being represented appropriately. I'm the one who sees that the Gaels have a future in five, ten, fifteen years. I don't need some arrogant athlete to come in here and act like he owns the place. Because that job is already taken. By me." I make sure to smile at the end, something my uncle always said makes people uncomfortable.

Brett sits there, not sure if he's more stunned at my bluntness or by the fact a woman just put him in his place, but I'm ready for whatever fight he wants to throw my way.

"Last time I checked, the one who owns this joint is uncle dearest, not you," he says. The fucker has the nerve to act like he's the big guy on campus.

This is exactly why when my uncle offered to sit in on this meeting, I asked that he stay far from the office. I can handle my shit, which is precisely why I got his job. He had other candidates putting in their resumes, trying to convince him I was the weaker choice. But when it comes to me and the things I love, like this team, I won't fight harder for anything to succeed more.

"Let me make it real easy for you, Brett. You don't intimidate me. Your abilities as an athlete don't intimidate me. You think you're irreplaceable? Think again. I promise, even if you're the one to have on a team right now, next year, there will be someone better. You want to be someone else's headache? Go right ahead. I have enough on my plate, with or without you. What is it going to be?" I stand up and lean over my plate. "Oh, and just a little tip for you. When addressing the president of this organization, Ms. Sparen or President Sparen will suffice. My uncle might own this team but don't forget who steers this ship. It's me and no one else."

I throw my napkin on the table. "I'll let you chat with your agent, and you can call me when you're ready to listen. It seems your ears are a little plugged." I move around the table and out the door without even glancing back.

Pretentious men have been in my orbit my entire life. Going to private school and schmoozing with my uncle's "friends" has given me the best lesson on how to handle a man who thinks he walks on water.

My walk is quickly interrupted when Luke, Brett's agent, comes running toward me.

"Ken—I mean Ms. Sparen, please come back to the conference room. Brett would like to have a word with you." He looks absolutely wrecked. That didn't take long. I thought I'd at least make it back to my office before Brett called me with his tail between his legs.

I make it back, ready to hear something along the lines of

how he's still the big guy on campus and that he'll only comply with my request until his contract is up.

Instead, something is finally going a little easier this morning when Brett opens his mouth. "I apologize for my arrogance earlier, Ms. Sparen. I feel lucky to be here, pitching for the Gaels. This is the team I've always wanted to be on, wearing the green and white colors holds a lot of meaning for me. I would love to continue wearing them, ma'am."

I look up at him and then move my gaze over to Luke. I can see him pleading with his stare, and I finally relent.

"Great to hear, Brett. I'll see you on the field, and I hope I see less of your antics off of it. Is that understood?" He nods, and I continue, "And when that itch comes where you think I'm not really watching anymore, just remember, I've got my ear to the ground at all times. Represent those green and white colors with pride on and off the field. Got it?"

He nods again, and I feel like my job here is done. For now.

"Listen, I want you to stay and enjoy the food." I look down at my watch. "I'm going to head out and take my next meeting, maybe a little earlier than expected." Meaning on time. I shake both their hands and make my way to my office.

In there, I close the blinds and take a moment to rest my eyes as I sit in my large chair behind my desk.

I hear some commotion outside my door, and the moment I open my eyes and stand to see what it's all about, my door opens.

"Don't worry, she won't mind I showed up," River says, without even looking over at her. He keeps his gaze on me, and I give Daphne a small nod.

"I'm so sorry, Ms. Sparen. He just barged right in here." Daphne, my assistant, looks at me, probably concerned her job is at stake. Then she cuts her glare over to the man in question, who's paying no attention to her.

Before she closes the door, I let her know, "Daphne, please

grab me when it's time to head to the next meeting." She acknowledges my request and closes the door.

"What's up, River? I have a busy day." I hear the coldness in my tone, but I can't shake my feelings from this morning.

"So that's it, Skip? You're just casting me aside?" He's cold when he speaks, and his tone just makes me stand up taller and pull those walls higher.

CHAPTER 23

River

THE ENTIRE DRIVE over to Kennedy's office, my irritation kept escalating. That text from her felt cold, much like the old Kennedy was with me before we started whatever it is we are now.

Fuck! I know something changed this morning; I just don't know where things got lost between us. I mean, what did I say that could have pissed her off? I can't read minds, so I'm fucking lost.

I stomp through the lobby and make my way up. Kennedy has me as an authorized visitor, so there's no need to call up. I know her assistant is going to give me hell for barging in, but fuck it. I can't just sit at home and let my mind wander. I need to understand what happened in my kitchen this morning.

As expected, Dori or Daloris—what the fuck is her name? She fights me on letting me in the office, but luckily, I get around her and open Kennedy's door.

The moment I see her face, I know she's holding herself at a distance. This feels like the old Kennedy versus the new version of her that I saw last night. She's got a withdrawn expression written all over her face.

"Daphne, please grab me when it's time to head to the next meeting."

Daphne! I was close.

The moment the door closes, I forget about the pleasantries. I just want to run to her and kiss her. Even with the hurt in her features, I want to wipe it away and fix whatever happened hours ago.

"What's up, River? I have a busy day," she says, and her tone is enough to cause a cold front in this summer heat.

I take her in for an extra beat. She changed since she was at my house this morning. Which means she had time to stay longer, but opted to get away from me. A weight settles in my gut.

"So that's it, Skip? You're just casting me aside?" I feel like we're reverting to our old ways together. The uneasiness that crawls up my spine is hard to ignore. I thought we were past this.

"Casting you aside? Ha. That's rich. I think the only person getting cast aside is me, which you made evident this morning. I got the message loud and clear, Riv. We're scratching an itch. Well, don't worry; my itch is no longer needing to be scratched. I'm good." She's ice cold now. I feel it with the way she's looking at me, anger swirling around in those eyes of hers.

"Excuse me, but am I off here? I mean, isn't that what we agreed to? Hello? We are literally in agreement this was not about feelings. It was about us being together in a sexual way. What the fuck, Kennedy?" My voice is escalating, but I can't help the irritation I'm feeling right now the more I talk to her. I know if I don't watch it, it's going to turn into a yelling match.

"You're right, River. And now I'm telling you I want out. I don't want to do this anymore." She crosses her arms over her chest, much like I'd imagine three-year-old Kennedy doing when she didn't get her way.

"Oh really? So you call the shots, and I just have to accept it? I have no say?" I throw back.

"River, you can't force me to be with you just because you don't want to accept it. It is what it is. We had some fun for a while, and now the fun is over." I feel like I'm being slapped across the face.

"Are you fucking kidding me? From last night to right now, you've just gotten your fill?" What the hell? I mean, I thought we connected last night on a deeper level. "What am I missing here?"

"What are you missing? What are you MISSING? Open your eyes, River. Things aren't where they were before. I feel like I'm coloring outside the lines now. This isn't working out between us. That's it. Done. How else do you want me to spell it out for you?" She's looking at me with such an exasperated expression while I'm playing catch-up.

"Are you saying you have feelings for me? You like me?" I ask in a surprised tone.

"You know what, Riv, I don't need this right now. I don't need you making fun of me. I'm doing exactly what we agreed on. I see this getting too deep, and I'm alone in that feeling, so I am doing the mature thing. I'm throwing in the towel."

"What if I don't accept? Don't I get to have a say?" I throw my hands in the air.

"Not if I'm standing here alone. Are you saying you feel the same as me? You see a potential future with me beyond fucking me?" I flinch at her crass words. I know we were only hooking up, but even I can see it was deeper than that. The problem is I'm struggling to find words. I didn't expect this when I made my way over to her office.

"Exactly. Your silence is answer enough. Please leave, River." She motions with her hands like she's directing me out of her office, even though she is nowhere near me. She's behind her desk, and I'm still on the other side.

I'm just standing here, shocked in place. My hesitation in answering isn't coming from a place of confusion. It's simply coming from a place of needing a minute to catch up and process her admission. I'm still spiraling when I hear the door open behind me.

"Ms. Sparen, it's about time to go. Your driver is downstairs," Daphne says, and I still feel cemented in place.

"Thanks, Daphne. Can you see Mr. Nichols out, please. He's going to need a minute. He's rebooting." She motions toward me, her tone lacking the comedic tilt.

I see her moving along her desk, grabbing things, and finally passing me.

She gives me a soft kiss on the cheek, and I simply look at her, utterly speechless. I have no clue what to say. She stares an extra beat—I'm not sure if to just take in the proximity for a second longer or to see if I at least say something, but I continue my statuesque form, letting her walk out the door without a fight.

I don't know how long I stand there, long after Kennedy has left, when Daphne makes her way around the office, this time facing me.

"Um, Mr. Nichols, are you ready to head out? Please follow me." She doesn't wait for my response, and I begin to follow her. I walk the entirety of her floor, then down the elevator and out of the building, feeling like a piece of me was left behind.

* * *

I handled being in my apartment for about ten minutes, pacing, before I decided taking Lola for a walk would be the best course of action. Of course, I pulled my brother out of his place because I need someone to talk to. I have no clue how my day got so off-course.

"So let me get this straight: she just ended things out of

nowhere?" My brother looks as perplexed as me. I nod, looking ahead, feeling the muscles in my back tensing up the more I revisit what happened today.

"I don't get it. Why don't you tell me what happened word for word in your apartment this morning?" My brother is trying to dissect the information from the chopped version I regurgitated.

"I already told you, man. We were fine, talking about how she could talk to me and trust I would keep her secrets, even though we were just hooking up," I say, pulling Lola away from some food someone dropped on the ground.

"Hold up, wait." Clay stops abruptly. He pulls on my shoulder, forcing me to look at him.

"You said what?" he says, and I just stare at him, wondering what he needs me to repeat now.

"What? I told her she could talk to me." I don't get what I'm saying that's throwing him off now.

"No, no. That's not what you said. You just said that she could talk to you even though you were only hooking up." He gawks at me like I am the biggest idiot.

"Yeah, so? We were just hooking up. That was the deal." I start to turn to continue walking, but my brother stops me.

"You are the biggest fucking idiot, man. You deserve to have her walk away from this little thing she had with you." The disappointment is taking over Clay's features as he walks off ahead of me, leaving me scratching my head.

"What's the big fucking deal, Clay? How am I in the wrong?" I'm really lost and apparently an idiot at the same time.

"Dude, she likes you, don't you get that? And you pretty much said, 'Hey, confide in me because I like to fuck around with you, but that's it.' I don't think I want to be related to you right now." He scoffs, truly upset at me.

"Hey, that's a bit harsh. I didn't mean it like that. I like being around Kennedy. I really enjoy her company, and she's the only one I can spar with and have fun while doing it. She gets me, which is fun too," I say while my brother stops walking and simply stares at me.

"Are you fucking high, Riv? Seriously, are you this dense? I mean, what you just said is the epitome of liking someone. Mom must have dropped you on your head." He walks off, and I'm stunned in place.

"So I'm wrong for stating the obvious?"

"If what you're stating is going to pretty much degrade someone to feeling like they're nothing but a good lay, yes," he says in an exasperated tone.

He must have some sympathy for me because he softens his tone and continues, "Look, River, I know you have not really given this whole dating world a try for a long time. I know you thought you and Kennedy were just keeping things casual. But that's hard to do. You are both attracted to one another, you both have similar ways of coping with relationships in the past, and you both run in the same friend groups. What did you think was going to happen?" my brother questions, and I just look at him, wondering how things got so complicated with her when all we wanted was a physical connection.

"Come on, try to see it through her eyes. Whatever she was confiding in you with, it took guts to do it. She gave you a piece of her past, and as much as you welcomed it, you also made your connection with one another worth nothing. How do you think she'd feel?" I know, without looking at my brother now, he's disappointed in me, and I'm starting to see why.

"So what do I do? Run back to her and tell her I want more? I don't want her to think I'm just saying that so I can get in her pants again." I don't know why this is so foreign to me. I should know what to do, but I need some guidance, and I'm limited on who to talk to because it was all a big secret between Kennedy and me.

"Is that what you want?" he throws back.

"I mean, I'm a man. Of course I want to get back in her pants," I say, and it earns me a smack on the back of my head.

"You're killing me right now. Look, if you like her, you go grovel. But before you do anything, figure your shit out, man. It sounds like you're a bit confused about how you're feeling. Maybe she was right. She felt more than you did, and she did the right thing, the mature thing, by leaving you." I see him give a slight shake of the head, maybe realizing that the romantic gene really did only fall on him.

It's not that I don't like Kennedy. I mean, I enjoy spending time with her. We laugh together, push each other's buttons, and are quite compatible with one another. But is this something that won't fizzle out in time if we move further into the relationship? It's hard to tell. I think my brother's right: I need to figure out what I want before I go back to Kennedy, blurting demands.

The rest of our walk remains quiet, my brother oozing his disappointment for me in each long exhale he gives and me chewing on all the morsels of information I have to digest.

First things first: I need to decide if what Kennedy and I shared is worth going after. But based on how I feel right now, I'm gutted with the thought that I've pretty much burned a bridge that I wasn't ready to walk away from.

CHAPTER 24

Kennedy

IT'S BEEN a week since River stood in my office and pretty much confirmed what I was thinking: he can't make this more than what it already is. Pretty much, pursuing anything further with me wasn't in the cards in his eyes. The sting that comes with that realization isn't an easy pill to swallow.

Too bad life doesn't give me the reprieve to wallow in this pit of sadness that I want to throw myself in. Instead of sitting at home, wearing comfy sweats and letting the crumbs fall on my clothes while I eat my feelings, I have to sit in this box seat at the stadium and plaster a smile on my face.

Don't get me wrong, on a normal day, I live and breathe baseball. I love the Gaels and soak the love from the fans screaming them on. And I absolutely love seeing them bask in the glory of their winning streak.

Since that fateful day that I had to see River's stunned face as I walked out of my office, on the other side of the building, Brett Henry was turning a new leaf. And that leaf has led to fewer articles of his sexual exploits and more headlines focused on what he was hired to do—win baseball games.

The stadium is full of green-and-white-donned fans cheering for their favorite Boston team. They're screaming, following the lyrics across the teleprompter, where they sing the fight song to root their beloved Gaels to victory yet again.

The smell of baseball games—peanuts, hot dogs, cheap beer—seems to excite everyone who's out here tonight, using their hard-earned money to celebrate with the city they love.

As much of a slump as my personal life is in, I'm trying to put it behind me as I let my gaze sweep the stadium to take in the fans who are showing such pride in this sport.

I'm sitting next to my uncle, who looks tan after his trip to the Caribbean with my aunt. I'm glad I've been able to take on more responsibility, hopefully granting him some much-needed time off to enjoy quality time with Aunt Gennie.

"I love the way the team is playing, Kenny. They're doing great." My uncle pulls me into a half embrace. He is the spitting image of my dad. They were only a year apart, Irish twins, which is fitting due to the fact that my great-grandparents immigrated from Ireland when they first got married. Top that with his now white hair, which was once blond like mine, somehow adds to his handsome features.

He looks over at me and beams that smile my way, and I feel like I'm accomplishing something quite extraordinary.

We look on as the minutes turn to seconds, and soon, we are celebrating yet another W for our beloved baseball team. My aunt and uncle join me as we jump and cheer for the players while they make their way through the tunnel to their locker rooms.

I'm gathering my things when I look down at my phone to see a text from Ashton. I hate to admit it, but I've kept my distance this past week, too caught up in all the things that happened between River and me. I just needed a moment to recalibrate after that whole thing blew up in my face.

It was naive to think we could fool around and leave it at that. I'm disappointed in myself that I pretty much thought with my vagina instead of my head on this one. I learned something—a dick is never just a dick.

I pull myself from my thoughts and open the text, only to feel my heart fall when I read the message:

ASHTON

Hey, Kennedy. I'm so sorry to text this, Sam said you'd be at the game tonight. We are at the hospital. Had a bit of a scare with some cramping. She thought she was going into early labor, but everything is ok. The twins are fine and Sam is now on modified bedrest. I thought I'd let you know. We have to stay the night and then we'll be back home tomorrow.

I put my hand over my heart, trying to calm it down as I read his text a few times over. The guilt is clawing at me because I let what happened between River and me seep into my relationship with my closest friends.

I'm so sorry she had to go through that. I will swing by tomorrow with some food once you're home. Does that work for you?

ASHTON

That would be great. Thanks, Kennedy. I'll keep you updated on how she and the babies are doing and on what time we'll be home. See you tomorrow.

Of course. Let Sam know to text me if she wants me to bring anything particular she may be craving. Also, give those babies a pep talk from Aunt Kenny to be good for their mama. 😊

ASHTON

Will do. 😊

I click the phone off and grab my purse. I start to make my way through the suite, saying my goodbyes to all the people who hang out in the box seats to schmooze my uncle and me.

Once I get into the hall, I take a deep breath, composing myself for the whirlwind that the media circus outside will be like. Sure enough, the moment I step off the elevator, the vultures are waiting.

"Ms. Sparen, what do you think is going on that the Gaels are now on this seven-game winning streak?" *Maybe Brett not getting his dick wet every night makes a difference.*

"Do you think it will last?" *I obviously hope so.*

Of course I keep my answers cordial as I make my way through the crowd. I give a quick thank you to everyone for watching the game and for their constant support. I drop some kind words to our fans, and I'm off, moving quickly to get to the car that's waiting for me outside the stadium.

The moment I'm safely in the backseat, I let my head fall back and close my eyes. I'm exhausted, and all I want to do is take a hot shower and let today, no this week, wash off down the drain.

I walk into my house, and I'm already assaulted by the loneliness that stares back at me. It's strange that in such a short time, I got used to River's and Lola's presence. Something about having them here made my life feel more significant, mostly due to the fact I could share my day with someone.

Now, this is what my life has been turned into: something solitary and quiet. I think for so long, I imagined this was what I wanted for myself. Coming home to a quiet, clean house with no responsibilities outside of the office. Even if I was dating someone casually, they didn't bring such a presence with them like River did. He brought a lightness to my day when I'd felt consumed by stress and work, but the moment I saw him, it felt like so much of the day was left at the door. By getting a opening myself up and getting a glimpse of what the possibility would be like to share my life with someone would be like, I'm now seeing how lonely I really am.

I think, despite the mess that unfolded afterward, my time with River gave me clarity. I now see the closed-off life I thought I was thriving in was, in reality, me existing. I think I see now, with a clear sense of what I want, that life is more than work. It's more than control.

Maybe that's what I failed to see once my parents passed away. I know they wanted to see me live my life; they wanted to see my sibling born and add to their family. But even until that moment when life truly crashed into us, they would say they were happy. They didn't hold back due to fear. They simply grabbed life, the good and the bad, and lived. And here I am, letting life pass by as if tomorrow is guaranteed.

Maybe River didn't want a life with me, but I got to see that my life was lacking in some way. I might not find exactly what I want immediately, but I can put myself out there more. I can start to push the envelope a bit to see what's inside.

I feel a new determination take over my movements as I walk into the restroom. I take my shower, already thinking about how I can make some changes to try and meet new people. I deserve a chance at happiness, even if it took me this long to figure it out.

I get out of the shower, wrap myself in my fluffy robe, and pull my phone out of my purse. I sit on my bed and decide to pull up the latest dating app and make a profile. Might as well try this out—even though, from what Jessa has told me, these apps are simply made for hookups. That being said, I will probably gain some fun stories from them.

Finding a photo and getting my profile set up, I see I'm all set to submit and start this.

The moment I click save, it generates my profile, and I feel the uptick in my heart rate. I laugh at my reaction to a dating app. Imagine the actual dating part—with complete strangers.

After I take some time to familiarize myself with the app and its features, I toss my phone aside and make my way back to my bathroom to dry my hair. Once I finish with that, I grab my heatless curlers and wrap my hair to prepare for my long day of meetings tomorrow. The moment I finish putting the last scrunchie in place, I can't help but feel a pang of sadness that River isn't here to make jokes about my ridiculous hairstyle.

I decide some trashy television might do the trick. As emotionally draining this past week has been, I'm not feeling the sleep come over me the way I imagined.

Grabbing a water from the fridge and plopping myself in front of the TV, I put on the latest of this ridiculous dating show I seem drawn to and relax on the couch with a big blanket.

I doze off, only to be awakened by a knock on my door. It takes me a minute to figure out if that's a true knock or if I'm dreaming.

The sound carries again, this time louder, and I look down at the phone. It's after midnight, and I jump up, fear lacing my movements as I imagine nothing good comes from a knock at this hour.

I look through the peephole only to find the one man I've tried to avoid all week. His silence all week was deafening, and the hurt that carried each day that passed seems to dissipate the moment I realize he's on the other side of this door.

I shake my hands at my side like I'm gearing up to join a fight in the ring. I take a few deep breaths and then open the door, hoping I hold my ground and not cave to something physical again with this man.

The moment I open the door, I see him look up at me, and it takes everything in me not to jump into his arms.

CHAPTER 25

River

I MISS KENNEDY. Plain and fucking simple. What have I done about it? Bitch and whine to my brother and Lola. Can dogs roll their eyes? I think so because I swear I've caught her doing it about three times this week.

"Just fucking call her! You're bumming me out, and that's my job. Remember, I actually had my wife leave me." My brother pushes me when he passes me as we walk out of the firehouse.

"I can't just call her! I mean, I could, but it doesn't feel big enough of a gesture," I say, again I realize the whining persists, even now.

"I don't like heartbroken River. He's sort of a drag." That's from Rios, who hasn't been on the same shift as me for some time.

Heartbroken is exactly how I'm feeling these days. At first, even though I was hesitant, I quickly learned Kennedy left morsels of herself scattered on my heart. And the moment she walked away, it felt like everything in me dried up. She took all the good with her and left me scrambling to pick up what was left, which lacked the warmth her touch and her gaze surrounded me with.

"I haven't talked to her all week. Maybe my window of time is closed," I say back, mentally calculating how I can talk to her and say my piece.

"It's been a week, dude. She'll talk to you. She has to. If not, I'll grab a couple of the guys and go chat with her. I mean, I cannot go another shift with you wallowing all over the station. That was brutal," Dario complains, and I can't even argue with him or any of the others nodding in agreement. I'm an absolute mess.

"Try living in the same building as him," my brother pipes in, and again, I can't even push back because he's not wrong.

"Listen, let's go grab a few beers, talk this out, and get a game plan going. That way, we know you're all set, and we can all sleep better tonight knowing you're not broken inside." Rios smacks me on the shoulder and pulls me into his side.

* * *

A few hours later, the guys are doing a good job keeping my mind occupied and my phone out of my hand. Let's just say, that after my second beer, my confidence level in winning Kennedy back was growing. The guys kept telling me it was the beer talking, and at one point, Clay took it upon himself to hold onto my phone.

We stopped at our local bar called *Jenson's*. We've spent many hours on our nights off at this place in the past, and it's our go-to when we feel like hanging out together after our shift. The bartender, Tommy, is a retired firefighter who left our station after he injured his knee. He thought this was the closest he could feel to the firehouse after leaving his brothers behind.

He tends bar and lets us stay as long as we want. It feels like an extension of the station, and that's exactly what he was hoping to do with a place like this. I look around and take in the exposed brick, along with old photos from his time in uniform, along with other paraphernalia that pertains to his time as a fireman.

"Feeling any better?" Clay whispers in my direction while the guys are in the middle of another conversation about *Love is Blind*. It's funny to watch these big guys who run toward danger one minute, while the next, they argue about who ended up with who after the season ends.

"Not sure if I feel better, but I'm not feeling as anxious. I just want to see her and tell her I was an idiot."

"You're not wrong there. I remember when—" Right then, his eyes move toward the door, and his face goes pale. At first, I think by some cosmic fate, Kennedy walked through the door, but the moment I turn my head, the reason for my brother's stunned expression makes more sense.

Even the guys at the table stop their chatter as they take in the person, or shall I say people, who just walked into the bar.

I take in what's unfolding in front of me. Abby is standing there, my ex-sister-in-law, much to my bewilderment, with what looks to be a date. I've seen him before, yet I can't place where.

What the hell is she doing back in town? I thought she had moved back to California. I'm about to ask my brother, but Rios pipes up with questions of his own.

"Is that Malloy with your girl, Clay?" Rios asks, and right then, I see my brother stand up, and a rigidity takes over his body that I've never seen in him. He's about to move toward them, but I stop him, my hand on his shoulder, hoping to keep this from escalating.

I see the tick of his jaw as his eyes lock in on Abby. I see she's uncomfortable as she moves through the bar. You've got to be dumb and blind not to know who she is and who her ex-husband is. Malloy is asking for trouble.

Tucker Malloy is a firefighter from Dover, about twenty miles away. We've run into him in random trainings and some of the memorials throughout the years. He's standing there, smug and smiling as if his girl at his side is just that— his.

The moment Abby and her date make it close enough, I see her stunned expression, as if our presence in the bar is a surprise to her. She should have known this would blow up in her face.

I've always liked Abby, so seeing her do such a hurtful thing, especially to my brother, is below the belt. I know they've gone through some difficult times, but this feels like a huge betrayal. It's hard to keep an open mind when all I see is her pushing the knife a little deeper.

Through gritted teeth, my brother jumps straight to the point. "What are you doing here with my wife, Malloy?"

The moment he refers to Abby as his wife, I can hear her gasp in surprise.

"Last I checked, she no longer wears your ring on her finger." Malloy pushes back, and that does it.

My brother begins to move closer, but Tommy makes his way over from behind the bar, ready to intervene where needed.

"Hey, Abby, why don't you and your date head some-where else. Let's not cause any trouble right now, yeah?" Abby looks over at Tommy who won't take his eyes off Malloy, concerned a fight might break out in his bar.

She gives a slight nod, then moves her attention to Malloy, her hand rubbing his forearm, and I swear I see my brother grinding his molars from the tightness in his jaw. His eyes won't leave their connection, and I know for a fact his heart is breaking even more than either of us thought possible.

Her voice is just above a whisper. "I told you this wasn't a good spot. Let's grab some ice cream at that place we just passed." I can tell she's pleading with Malloy to accept her offer, pain etched in her expression.

My brother's breaths are short and labored as I see his

nostrils flare and his skin redden from his anger nearly bubbling over.

"That's a great idea. Why don't you listen to her," I say, hoping to diffuse the ticking time bomb that is this entire fucked up situation.

Malloy stares at my brother a few more beats, then turns away, agreeing to leave. He grabs Abby's hand, and my brother's eyes dart to where they're joined once again.

Abby looks at me, then my brother, and mouths, I'm sorry. I want to believe her, but a part of me can't help but feel the same betrayal my twin is feeling right now. She was once my family, someone I laughed with and loved like an actual sister. Seeing her cause this kind of pain to the one person who is an extension of me is gutting me, so I can't imagine my brother doesn't feel it tenfold.

Clay watches them stride out of the bar, and I know she's walking out with yet another piece of his heart. Any calm we were feeling prior has vanished, and the tension in the entire place feels suffocating. My brother sits back in his seat, but his demeanor is completely different. I see his spine straighten and his face harden. His mood is somber and the opposite of the free-loving guy he once was, living the dream with the woman he once loved. I guess, from his reaction, that love remains strong.

We grab one more round of beers, letting another hour pass, when Rios picks up his phone, a whispered fuck falling off his lips. I think nothing of it until his eyes fall on me, and my skin stands at attention.

"Dude, it's not your night either. I'm so sorry," he says, then turns his phone to face me. My brain takes a moment to connect the dots, but then I realize it's a picture of Kennedy staring back at me. At first, I'm confused, unsure how he got a photo of her. It's only when I pull my gaze off her beautiful face that I see he's on a dating app.

"What the fuck is that?" I stand, livid for the second time in a short span of time.

"It's a dating app. I just started using it. I swear, I wasn't seeking her. It matched us. It's her, right?" He seems hopeful that I'll tell him it's just a doppelgänger, but that's Kennedy. I know for certain because I took that photo at the gender reveal party not long ago.

Damnit. She's moving on. She's moving on from what we had, and it's only been a week. I see the pain etched across all the guys' faces. The Nichols brothers are real fun tonight. One is sulking because his wife is actually seeing someone else, and here I am, knowing the girl I want is moving on using a dating app.

As if someone slaps me to finally wake the fuck up, I realize I might still be able to rectify this situation. I need to talk to her. I need to make sure she knows everything I'm feeling. She told me how she was feeling, how her feelings were changing, and I just let her walk away. I pretty much gave her the green light, and now I have a choice to let this be and accept seeing her with another man on her arm, or I can fight for her before it's too late.

I stand abruptly and throw some cash on the table.

"Where the fuck are you going?" my brother asks, concern evident in his features.

"I can't just sit around and let her move on. I can't just watch something, someone, who makes me happy, find happiness with someone else. I was a fucking fool. I'm going to win her back," I tell the table, and then I'm off.

The moment I step outside, I get myself a ride and make my way to Kennedy's building.

In record time, I'm standing in front of Kennedy's door. I was hoping my name was still on her permanent list, and luckily, she hasn't removed it. The minute I am in the elevator making my way up, I feel the nerves kick in. My heart is pounding against my ribcage. It's only now that I realize she can easily kick me out of here and ask me to never return. But I have decided that losing her forever is not an option. She has to hear me out. Right? I take a few moments to compose myself.

The moment I knock, I look down at my phone and realize the time. Fuck, it's late. But I'm here, so it's now or never.

I knock, but no one comes to the door. I fear she might be sleeping, which means I might be sleeping outside her door because there is no way I'm letting her leave her place without talking to me. I can't just let this go anymore. I was dumb enough to let her walk away once. But I'm not stupid enough to let it happen again.

I knock again, this time hearing movement on the other side. I can hear her footsteps approach the door, and it's almost like my body reacts to her proximity, even with a wall between us. Her steps falter before she answers, and I know she looked through the peephole to see who was visiting at such an hour.

I hear the clicking of the locks, and soon enough, the door starts to open. Kennedy stands there in her heatless curlers and that thin-ass robe. I can see every curve of her body, and it's taking all my control to keep myself from reaching out and pulling her body to mine.

I just keep looking at her, stunned and speechless. I took her for granted all that time we were together. I took each look, each touch, each kiss for granted. Had I known the last time I touched her would be exactly that, my last, I would have memorized it better. I would have savored her feel under my fingertips. I would have kissed her a little longer. I would have given her all the words that made her smile brighter instead of causing this pain within her that is evident in her features now.

From what I see in her expression now, she looks just as beautiful, but I see the exhaustion marring her features with the bags under her red-rimmed eyes. My heart hurts knowing I did this to her. I also know I can try and take this pain away.

I must stand for too long, taking her in, when she finally speaks, "Yes, River? Did you forget we aren't seeing each other anymore?"

The old Kennedy is back, the one who held anger and annoyance at the center of our interactions. I'm the cause of that because I made her believe I didn't care about what we had. I made her think I didn't value what we had started.

"I'm sorry." My voice comes out hoarse as I start with a simple apology, hoping that's enough to get her icy demeanor to thaw.

She crosses her arms and stands, irritation lacing her mannerisms. Well, I guess that didn't quite work.

"Okay, well, thanks for the apology," she says and starts to close her door. I jut my foot out and hold it open, causing her to throw me a look that would make most men cower.

"Please don't date anyone else. I want to date you. I want to be the one you swipe right for," I say, and her look goes from annoyance to confusion.

"What the fuck have you been drinking, Riv? You make no sense," she throws my way and I continue.

"I saw you joined that dating app. The guys and I were grabbing drinks, and your profile matched with one of them. He showed me the notification when I was sitting at the table with him. Please, Kennedy, please give me another chance. I was an idiot. I miss you. I miss us." I can hear the desperation in my voice, and I'm not embarrassed for pleading my case. I know this is what I want, and I can't walk away without trying.

"So let me get this straight. You went from indifference when it came to us, letting me walk away after I told you things had changed for me, to now you're wanting me back because I have found a way to possibly move on? You want me because you don't want anyone else to have me? Like I'm someone to hold onto now that your ego is being compromised?" Her anger is seeping off of every word she's throwing my way.

"No, that's not how it is. I was already wanting to talk to you. I was going to talk to you tomorrow after I slept off the beers and my exhaustion from my shift," I say, noting how much I'm begging more than talking.

"River, you've had all week. You've had more than enough time to figure out what you want out of this thing we had going on. You made me feel like I was nothing but a good lay. And you know what, that's understandable because that's what we were supposed to be to one another. But I realized something tonight. I realized that I deserve what Ash and Sam have. I deserve more than feeling a physical connection with someone.

"I've lived too long on my own. I've been waiting for the other shoe to drop since my parents died. I took a chance last week and told you how I felt. I told you what was going through my mind, and you disregarded it. I don't want to be a choice for you because you feel threatened. I want to be your choice because you can't see life the same when I'm not by your side."

She takes a breath while she looks up toward the ceiling. "I want you to choose me because you don't see your world the same without me by your side. I want you to reach for me at night because, without my warmth by you, you're lost without me. I don't want you to come crawling back, professing this need for me because I'm someone you simply feel a physical release with. I want more. I deserve more." Her words have a resolution to them, and it's hard not to react to them.

I let her talk, and I listen because I know she's right. I was given a chance to speak up sooner, and I just let time pass. I was confused, and I didn't know how to look at this properly.

I wanted more with her, yet I hadn't let my head catch up to my heart. But I'm here now, and I want to try this… together.

"I messed up. I'm sorry." Defeat carries through in my voice, and I can't help the hurt it holds. I feel absolutely broken for letting this slip between my fingers. She deserved more, and I failed to realize what I had when I had it in my grasp. "I should have known things were shifting."

She shakes her head. "That's the thing, River. I didn't really put much weight on my feelings until you said we were simply scratching an itch. That's when it dawned on me that things are different for me now."

She walks toward me, her warmth right in my grasp. She brings her hand to my cheek, and it feels like everything I've been missing these last few days is all coming back to me. Her touch sparks life in it, and I don't even know how I went these last seven days without it.

My eyes connect with her, and it isn't until she utters her next confession that I feel my heart completely break for my stupidity.

"River, it was then I realized I was not scratching an itch the entire time we were together. I was giving you pieces of my heart because I am starting to fall in love with you."

CHAPTER 26

Kennedy

I CAN FEEL the tears threatening to break free, but somehow, I hold them back. I do not need to stand here, confess what I can undoubtedly admit is love to this man, then break down as an added bonus.

I relish my hand touching his warm skin and wish I could stay here forever. Seeing him standing at my door right now, wishing we could rewind to a few weeks back when everything felt much easier and less complex. But I'm the first to admit to myself that it wasn't easier. I was just not really putting much weight on the fact that I feel love for this man who stands at my door. It was the first emotion I felt at the sight of him.

Maybe I'm being unfair to him to go from a booty call to falling in love, but the heart wants what it wants. And I think I've ignored enough of my emotional needs throughout my life to not be honest in this moment. I think it's time to own up to the fact that I've tried to avoid feeling things for people, keeping me from opening up in a way I deserve with the people around me and leaving me scared that it will only hurt more.

If there's one thing I learned late in life, it's that life hurts.

Love can hurt too, much like it does for me in this moment, as I stare at the only man I've ever felt this type of connection to. But at the same time, I'm starting to realize that with my words, love is also freeing. Love is simultaneously beautiful and ugly. And I sort of welcome it now. I sort of long for it.

I take an extra beat to savor the feel of the stubble along his jaw, the warmth of his face in my hand. It takes a lot of effort, but I finally move away from him. I turn, knowing I'll have to mend my broken heart, but I know I'll be okay. We'll both be okay.

I'm about to push my door all the way open for me to cross the threshold when I feel him tug on my hand, forcing me to turn back around and face him.

"Maybe I don't want to be okay," he says, and that's when I realize that last part wasn't said in my head. I said that out loud.

I don't register what's happening until I feel his lips crash into mine. All the hurt is instantly evaporated, all the heartbreak I was going to continue to soothe in the days to come feels like a distant thought. Everything in this moment brings stillness to my heart and mind. It brings me a peace I didn't know I needed, yet I welcome all the same.

He pulls away too fast for my liking.

"Kennedy, I could walk away from you and do exactly that, be okay. I could wake up tomorrow and continue on. But I don't want that. I got a taste of that this last week, and I was miserable. I was hurting. I was lost. Things changed, and I finally saw what I needed to do. I was too stubborn and stuck in my old ways to pay attention to it until you walked away from me.

"But with each touch, each movement we made together, we inched closer to something unknown for me, and I ignored it. And that's on me. I was scared, but I didn't know it. I pride myself on living in the moment, though I think I took it too far. I lived so deeply in each moment that I took you for granted as a result."

I move my hands through his hair, unsure how we move past this speed bump without losing that connection we had.

"Please don't give up on me. Let me catch up. Let me find the pieces of crumbs you've left for me along the way. Don't leave me behind. I could move on, but I just don't want to. You're the missing piece, and I think I never had to think about it because, for the last ten years, you've been there, pushing me, berating me, caring for me in your own prickly way. I don't want you, Kennedy. I need you. I need you like I need warmth on a cold Boston night."

On a shaky breath, I speak. "You promise this isn't a reaction to seeing me on that app?" A morsel of doubt lingers regarding his intentions.

"Seeing you on that app stung, I won't sugarcoat it. I didn't hesitate when I saw you had put yourself out there. I ran here with no plan in mind except to plead with you that you don't need to look elsewhere. You've found your forever in me, Kennedy. I promise. No more stupidity from me." He moves his hands to my cheeks, and I relish the feel on my skin.

"First of all, I can promise you this won't be the last time you do something stupid, River." She rolls her eyes as I laugh. "Are you sure you want to try this? It could blow up in our faces even bigger next time."

"No, I don't want to try. I want to see us move past trying and live. I want to take my steps with you, no end date in sight. That's what I want." His big hazel eyes, more green than brown tonight, hold so much in them, and it's hard to say no to that.

I nod and smile at him, my words lodged in my throat behind the frog that's taken up space in there. I plant little kisses along his lips and on his cheeks. He brings me close and nuzzles me, and I feel him take a deep inhale, like he needs to take my scent in to believe this is happening and not a dream he's engulfed in.

He mumbles something into my neck, and his stubble tickles me in return.

"What are you mumbling?" I can't help but ask.

He pulls his face away and looks at me, seriousness taking over his features. "Can we at least acknowledge I just said I wanted everything with you while you have that weird thing on your head?"

This man is ridiculous, and yet the laugh that escapes me holds so much relief that it's hard not to let a few happy tears slip out while I nod and pull him close to me.

"Yes, you're the real hero in all of this, Riv. You really are." I hold him close to me, feeling his warmth against my body after thinking I wouldn't get this again.

* * *

River and I have been making out on the couch like two teenagers. He moves his hands along my body, touching me over my clothes, making me want more. But each time I try to push him a little further, he stops and shakes his head. Finally, my frustration gets the best of me.

"River, what the fuck? Why aren't you going past second base?"

He's got his nose nuzzled in the crook of my neck, dropping feather-light kisses along my skin.

"You're so impatient, Skipper." His breath tickles me, and the goosebumps are near impossible to avoid.

"Yeah, but I've also been deprived for a week. I have needs, Riv." I say with a whine. I mean, he's just scratching the surface at this point.

He nips at my skin, making me crave that rougher side of him a little more.

"You want me to take control, is that it, baby?" he asks, and I can't help the heat that stirs deep down in my belly.

"Do you need me to spell it out for you?" I decide to throw back.

He chuckles, fucking chuckles like this is all too much fun. "Yeah, why don't you do that?"

"Fuck me now, River, or let me out so I can go get the job done myself." I let some of that sass I usually held for him in our past come back to the surface. I see his eyes darken in need, and I know I've hit the jackpot.

He pulls my hands into his own and pushes my wrists above my head, keeping me pinned on the couch.

"Oh, so you think that purple dildo can do the trick better than me?" he says, playfulness etching his words.

"Well, if the shoe fits," I taunt, hoping to get a rise out of him.

My plan works as he keeps my hands pinned above my head, then pulls the tie to my robe undone, pushing it open and leaving me completely exposed under him. The moment he sees me completely bare to him, he lets out a moan.

"Fuck, I've missed you, Skip. I'm an idiot for wasting any time sitting at home being a jackass." He moves his head down and captures my nipple. I can't stop my body's reaction of arching my back and pushing my breasts further into his face.

"Well, at least you came to your senses," I say with a moan.

He nips and sucks, letting that current rush down my body. I moan and writhe as he moves his tongue across my lips to only capture the other nipple in his mouth.

He pulls his head to look up at me. "Keep those hands up there, or I'll tie you up. Got it?" I take his command, nodding while I keep my eyes on him as his head begins its descent.

I feel each movement of his tongue like a match trying to light a flame. My body needs a release, and he is moving at a snail's pace. From the small smile I see across his face, I know he's doing it on purpose.

He peels my panties off my body, and all I want is for that tongue of his to reach that juncture between my legs. It's taking all my strength not to bring my hands down and pull his face toward me.

"A bit impatient, Kennedy. Look how wet you are for me, though, baby." His sneaky smile grows as I whine in frustration.

"River, please." I pant.

"Please, what, sweetness?" he throws back, and I know he's just trying to get me more riled up.

"Touch me," I say, hoping he'll stop this little game.

He brings his lips to the inner portion of my thigh. "But I am touching you, baby." He then proceeds to bite me on my sensitive skin, so close yet so far from that one place I need him to be.

I don't even have it in me anymore to say anything else, so I growl, literally growl my frustrations, and he finally relents and gives me what I want.

The moment his tongue swipes my sensitive core, I swear my hips lift off the couch. Fuck, I've missed him.

"You know how perfect you are, Kennedy? The best part? This pussy is mine and only mine." His possessive words regarding my body light me on fire even more. I am his, just as much as he is mine.

I can't form words and just relish his touch as he strokes me with his tongue, then adds a finger so I can feel just a fraction of relief. I'm climbing further up that mountain, ready to fall off. The moment I'm about to take that leap, he pulls away, and the strangled sound that escapes me is of utter frustration and anger.

"Nooo, no, no, no, River. I'm almost there," I beg yet again.

"There's no way you're coming without me inside you. I

want to feel you strangle my cock while I fall off that ledge with you," he says as he quickly makes a move to remove his pants.

We're so desperate for one another, he doesn't even pull his shirt off all the way before he's sheathing himself and thrusting into me. The moment we are connected in that way, I feel myself chasing that euphoria with him.

He begins to move, and I'm meeting him, thrust per thrust, loving the sounds that this connection is bringing out of him just as much. Seeing him lost in our movements turns me on even more, and I look down to see him moving in and out of me.

Fuck, he is so hot, and this link between us feels like my heart is soaring now. Before, I believed we could separate and live our lives independently. Now that I see us, this spark we ignite when we're together, I realize I was in complete denial. He doesn't complete me, but he certainly makes me see pieces of myself coming to life more than they ever would on my own.

His movements only push me closer to the edge, and soon, I can't control the fall I take into that blissful state that makes me see stars clouding my vision. I feel like my skin is on fire, and it's a heat I never want to see extinguished when it comes to us.

River is pumping in and out of me, his movements becoming erratic and his moans getting louder. He's holding my hips as he moves, and I swear I can already see the marks etching themselves into my skin. Tomorrow, I'll look down and know that this man has claimed me, body and soul, and I will never be able to turn away from it.

"Fuck, Kennedy, fuck, I'm coming. Fucking take it, shit," he keeps yelling, and he throws his head back, eyes closed as he comes. A sense of ease takes over his features as his thrusts slow until they stop.

He drops his body next to mine, bringing me closer to

nuzzle his neck. I kiss him slowly under his ear and down his neck.

I feel his hand caressing my hair, his nose breathing me in.

"I didn't know it could be this way. I didn't know I could feel this type of completion with someone. Not until you," he tells me, and it feels like, for the first time, my life has exactly what it lacked: River Nichols holding my heart.

CHAPTER 27

River

"SO, should I just tell them you finally fell for my charms?" I still hope to get a rise out of Kennedy where I can.

"Sure, I'm the one who finally fell for your charms? Is it opposites day or something because I think you're the one who broke into my hotel room and fucked me with my dildo." She smiles, batting her eyes at me, feigning sweetness and innocence.

We're trying to figure out how we break the news to Ash and Sam later today. Samara was in the hospital, and she's going home in the next hour. To make their night a little easier, we're swinging by in the afternoon to leave some dinner for them. Of course, Kennedy said she'd buy something, but I decided something homemade would be best.

"Seriously though, what should we do? Do you think this will upset Sam more and cause more stress on her and the babies?" I don't know what to expect as a reaction from our friends. This will be out of left field for them, and I don't want to upset either of them. However, I already know I can't walk away from this with Kennedy.

"Honestly, who knows? Pregnant Sam is a whole other

creature." She laughs, looking over my shoulder to see what I'm doing.

"How did you get so good at cooking?" She seems absolutely perplexed by anything regarding food prep.

"Well, after my dad passed, my brother and I took on one night of cooking a week to help around the house. Of course, we were young when he died, so it was many peanut butter and jelly sandwiches, but then we graduated to using the stove and oven. We just tried different things. Burned many things. Drove my mom crazy at first, but we got the hang of it."

"Well, I'm really good at microwaving, so if this recipe requires that kind of help, I'm here," she says, utterly proud of her accomplishment of using something in her kitchen.

"I will definitely let you know." I give her a kiss on the nose and get back to layering this lasagna.

"So, back to our news. What if you and I show up together? That's at least a foot in the door, no pun intended." She makes her way over to the stool and sits down, her eyes seemingly mesmerized by what I'm doing.

"Okay, then what? Just come in, drop off food, then hold hands? Or should I grab your ass in front of them and yell, 'Mine!'" I'm so lost on how to go about doing this. I may have dated women, but none who meant something to me.

"Ha! I dare you to do that and see how it goes from there." She rolls her eyes and takes a swig of her water. "I guess we sit down and just tell them. I mean, how the hell do I know? I'm the female version of you with relationships." She shrugs her shoulders.

"I guess it's the blind leading the blind." I say as the last layer is placed on the lasagna.

* * *

The unusually warm fall breeze is doing nothing to calm

my nerves now that we stand at Sam and Ashton's front door. I don't know why I'm so nervous to tell them Kennedy and I are dating.

"Hey guys!" Ashton looks exhausted after a night in the hospital, but his smile is genuine, and I can see he's happy to have some support. The fact Kennedy and I are standing at his doorway together doesn't seem to phase him in the least.

He ushers us inside, and I make my way through to the kitchen. Kennedy is walking quietly behind me, probably letting her nerves get the best of her too. It's still strange to see someone usually so composed let something like our newfound relationship ruffle her feathers in such a way.

Once I set the food in their oven and get it turned on, I make my way back and sit on the couch. Kennedy could not be any farther away, but at this rate, I think we need to start slow with our little announcement.

Sam comes down the stairs, and the moment she sees Kennedy, her face lights up.

"Yay! There's Auntie Kenny and Uncle River!" Sam waddles her way over, her belly seeming to have popped overnight. I swear her stomach was half that size a little over a week ago.

Kennedy stands up to greet her friend and then sits back down, this time fiddling with the ring on her finger.

"I didn't know you were coming over right now, River." She makes her way over to me, and I meet her halfway, knowing that although bedrest is modified, she shouldn't be doing much.

"Shouldn't you be sitting in bed?" I say, wondering why she's walking around the house.

"I'm allowed one stroll around the house once per day, and I haven't done that yet since we got home. I've been resting for a few hours now."

I look over at Ashton, and I can see the concern etched across his face.

"We're quickly learning Sam makes a horrible patient." He sighs, and that wins him a look that could kill from his wife. He quickly brings his arms up. "You know it's the truth, babe."

She shrugs and goes to sit down on the couch.

"So, what's new?" Such a simple question, yet it causes me to pause, an uptick of my pulse evident as the blood is now swooshing in my ears. Why is this so nerve-wracking?

"Um..." My gaze darts over to Kennedy, and she looks at me in a panic.

"What's going on? Everything okay?" Ashton speaks up, and I can tell from his expression he's worried now.

"Oh yeah, fine, but..." Kennedy attempts to say, and I feel like if we don't just say it, it will just be the two of us walking in circles all night.

"Are you fucking kidding me?" Sam yells, and now I'm not just nervous, but I'm scared. My gaze swings her way, and I'm not sure if she's stunned or pissed.

"Fuck you, Ashton. Go get my wallet!" she yells at her husband.

He throws his fist in the air and punches it. Utter confusion is the only emotion I feel right now.

"I knew it! I fucking knew it!" Ashton yells from the other room, and Sam just keeps huffing in her corner of the couch.

"What the fuck is happening?" I ask, hoping they can explain themselves.

"You two are fucking each other!" Sam points at both of us, and I still can't read if she's pissed or happy about this turn of events.

"Geez, Sam, so crass," Kennedy says as she rolls her eyes, and my mouth hits the floor.

"You knew?" I say, looking over at Ashton, baffled by this reaction. Right as the pieces are coming together, Sam retrieves her wallet and pulls out a fifty-dollar bill, handing it over to her husband, begrudgingly, might I add.

"Did you fucking bet on us?" I ask. My jaw would be hitting the floor again, but it hasn't left that spot yet.

"Well, 'knew' is a bit presumptuous, but did I guess it was happening? Yes," Ash confesses.

"How? We were discrete. We tried to keep up charades whenever we saw you," Kennedy pipes up, just as baffled as I am.

"Ha!" Ashton yells. "I saw you put your hand on her leg at the gender reveal. I thought you were just trying to piss her off at first, but then she didn't punch you like she usually would, so I knew something was up. I ran to Sam to tell her, and she thought I was crazy. So I made it interesting—for me, that is," he confesses, no shame in his antics.

"So you made money while you were at it? You're hanging out with Clay too much!" I throw back. Why is everyone betting on me and my sex life lately?

"You dirty girl," Sam says, a sly smile taking over her features.

Right then, Kennedy's cheeks flush, and it's hard not to enjoy her reaction.

"Yeah, well, he grew on me," Kennedy says.

"Yeah, I bet he did!" Sam snorts as Ashton throws a look in her direction. "What? Remember that time I walked into the gym locker room by accident, and he was changing? I saw things, hun." Now her gaze swings back to Kennedy. "Congrats, sis." Her wink is exaggerated, and now I'm blushing.

Samara is usually shy and reserved, but those pregnancy hormones are making her loose-lipped, and it's sort of funny to see from her.

Her husband decides not to open that can of worms and looks at us. "How long has it been going on?" Ashton asks.

"Since the wedding, pretty much," I say, not really thinking much about it.

"Months? Fucking months you've kept this from me,

Kenny?" Sam says to Kennedy. Now I think the hormone shift is making her angry.

"Well, sort of? I mean, it was just a hookup at first, but yeah, it all started at the wedding," she says.

"Wow! So it's serious then?" Sam asks. I can't help but look at Kennedy and take her in. I think if I had been asked this same question before everything that transpired this past week, I'd say no. I would have confidently gone along with the fact that this was just a fling, thinking nothing more would come of it. But being away from her has taught me that I can't go a minute knowing she's not mine.

"Yeah, it is." I decide I should answer, if anything, to prove to Kennedy I mean it when I say I'm in this with her.

"River finally has a girlfriend," Ashton says, a completely innocent comment.

The moment I say "Yeah," I hear Kennedy comment with, "We haven't put labels on us."

Her response makes me pause.

"What do you mean *labels*?" I say to her, wondering what the actual fuck that means.

"River, we haven't talked about that. I think now isn't the time." Her eyes go wide like this is a discussion we should save for later when it's just us.

"This is the perfect time. Kennedy, I don't share. I told you that. There's no waiting around to see if that's the case. It's fact." I make sure the finality of the conversation is understood with my tone.

"Oh, is that right? Like you have some sort of power over this relationship or something? So you're my boyfriend, and we don't even have a conversation about it?" I can see this is riling her up, and I'm okay with it. I thought this was decided already. I mean, wasn't what happened not even a day ago exactly what this was about? She wanted commitment and I'm giving it to her.

"I damn well better be your boyfriend. Change your social

media profiles and everything. Taken! That's final. There's no question about it!" I stand up, moving closer to her.

I see her inch back a bit in her seat like that's going to keep her at a distance from me. I pull her by the hands to stand and crash my lips to hers. A faint "Fuck yeah" from Ashton can be heard while I hear a clap that I can only assume is coming from Sam.

Our lips part, and I look her in the eyes. "Is that enough of a confirmation for you, Skip?"

Her eyes are slowly opening to meet mine, and I know from this point on, they're the only eyes I ever want to see staring back at me.

Her voice is slightly above a whisper. "Yes."

I smack her ass, no care in the world who our audience is. "Mine!"

I turn toward our friends and clap my hands together. "Who wants lasagna?"

CHAPTER 28

Kennedy

WE'RE up by one right now; however, all bases are loaded, and Andrews is at bat for the opposing team. The New Jersey Stars have been the team to beat, and this game is a nail-biter.

Brett is getting ready to pitch, and I can see him take a breath to calm his nerves. We are in the beginning of playoffs, and every win counts.

I look over to find River at the other end of the box, talking to my uncle, their eyebrows drawn in concentration. As much as we fought for years leading up to this point, it's hard to look back at my life and not think of River and me together in this way now. Almost like each touch we've shared has erased the memory of the snarky comments and irritation we felt toward one another.

I feel a nudge at my side and look over to see my aunt smiling up at me. The moment my aunt learned of my dating River, she was smitten. She and my uncle have met him in passing through Sam and Ash, and my aunt always commented on how handsome he is, but now, it seems this whole romance has unleashed another side to her.

"You know, your uncle used to look at me the same way River looks at you." She sighs.

"Ew, gross. Not information I needed, thank you." I can't help the gag that follows.

"Oh, stop it! Your uncle was quite the romantic one when we met. And after everything we went through trying to grow our family, he never lost it. He always took the time to tell me that he loves me and that I was all he needed in his life."

The love they share is something I've always admired, second to my parents. They always seem to have this unspoken love for one another. Despite having the means to enjoy all the luxuries of this life, they never let that get the best of them and their relationship. They're always putting their relationship first, and it's something I never took for granted.

"It's something to admire, that's for sure," I say, meaning each word.

"River looks at you with so much love in his eyes. I'm so happy for you, Kennedy," she says, and my stomach does a little flip when I hear that four-letter word.

I can't think of what to say, so I smile back, feeling like I can't wait until we say those words to one another. As much as what I said in my doorway when we reconnected was confessions of love, I haven't actually said those three little words together. I've nearly let it slip about twenty times since we decided to go all-in for this relationship.

I've thought of being the first to say it plenty of times, yet I keep stopping myself. And the longer I wait, the more I'm holding back because after everything that did go on between us, a part of me wants to hear him say it first. Is it childish? Probably. Do I care? Apparently not.

If I know River the way I think I do, he's waiting for me to cave and say it first. It's just the way we work. I can feel it in the way he looks at me, the way he steals glances much like he's doing tonight, and his eyes tell me he feels the same way my heart does—full of love.

I hear the cheers in the background, and it pulls my focus back to the players on the field. We need Brett to strike Andrews out, and we will need a miracle to pull this off. Andrews is the Stars' best player, and he has shown up with a vengeance at every game this season; tonight is no different.

The moment Brett begins his windup and releases the ball, I can tell all of us are holding our breath. The pitch is delivered, and Andrews takes a swing at the pitch and misses. The cheers are instantaneous, and I mentally tell myself just two more strikes. That's all we need to get us that win.

Brett throws a fastball, and we see another strike cause an eruption in the crowd. I'm holding onto my aunt's hand, probably cutting off circulation.

Brett shakes his head at his catcher, probably not liking whatever sign is being tossed at him. Finally, he gives an assuring nod, and I see the determination in his glare. Right then, I bring my hands together in front of me, letting a little prayer go up that this gets us to the next step of the playoffs.

The moment the ball is released, I watch it as if it's in slow motion. I hear the swing of that bat, and all that it catches is air. Like a miracle from above, it's another out, and that one moment signifies the end of the game. The players rush the field as if this were the winning game of the season; however, it's simply a significant one to ensure they move on to the next round.

We're screaming, throwing our hands in the air, and soaking in this feeling of relief and victory. River pulls me into a huge embrace, and I can't help the screams I'm letting out. The significance of this win is exponential, and I know the players needed this to move forward with their heads held high.

All of a sudden, I hear the crowd making noise, and when I look over, I see them pointing to something in the middle of the field. It takes a second to register what's happening, but that's when I see one of my players, number thirty-three,

Garrett Nelson, on one knee, his girlfriend standing in front of him with her hands covering her mouth and nose. I can't see the details of her face, but I can only imagine her eyes are welling with tears.

I tap River to look over, and I stand there in awe. I am a sucker for proposals. I always have been. Something about that moment feels so raw and so pure between a couple. This time is no different.

The moment she says yes, I start to scream again, my heart soaring for the newly engaged couple. I catch River looking at me and then at the couple kissing and embracing in the middle of the field.

"I didn't take you for a softy with engagements, Skipper," he taunts, and I smack him on the shoulder.

"Yeah, well, I guess you have a lot more to learn about me, huh?" I toss back, and he throws his head back and lets out a big laugh. I smile at him, feeling like even if the words haven't been said to one another yet, my heart loves this man in front of me. If we weren't so stubborn about keeping from being the first to say it, I think I would belt it out now. But I keep my mouth shut, waiting for that moment when it feels right.

Later that night, we get ready for bed, Lola panting by our side, circling her dog bed until it feels right, and then plops down. Meanwhile, I pull the bedding back for River and me to get into bed. The moment I lay myself down on my side, I feel River's arm hug my middle and tug me back against him.

I instantly feel warm and comfortable. He moves his kisses from my head down to my neck, nuzzling me and breathing me in.

Since River and I reconnected, Lola has been a welcome addition to the mix. She even spends the night with me when River's pulling his shifts at the station. We've definitely moved forward without a hitch since that night, and I can't say I'm upset about it.

My mind begins to drift to earlier tonight, and I feel my heart flutter a bit in my chest. It's hard for me to think back to that proposal tonight and not let my mind wander to possibilities between River and me. I never really saw myself getting married, but now that I have this man by my side, my mind gravitates to that possibility in our future. A soft smile takes over my features as I feel my eyes get heavy, and I finally doze off, thinking of the man holding me and giving me everything.

* * *

The car feels smaller, and at first, I don't understand how that's so. But I look down, my legs longer than they were the day of the crash. It takes me a moment to realize I'm an adult in this version of the nightmare. I bring my hands up in front of me, my nails done as they usually are, and my outfit similar to the ones I use to go into the office.

I look out the window, and the scenery is the same as the neighborhood we were driving through that morning though. I'm living my dream in the same way; however, I'm grown up this time around. It takes a minute, and then I swing my gaze to the front of the car and realize there is only one body behind the wheel. I yell for my dad to look over, waiting for a glimpse of his face like I always do when I'm pulled back to that day.

The body is shifting to change the radio station, but when the person looks back, I feel like all the air in my lungs is nonexistent.

"River, what are you doing here?" I feel myself saying, panic laced in my words.

"What do you mean? I'm driving you to school," he says in a tone that makes me feel small and silly.

Why is River in this car? I'm trying to think of something to say when all of a sudden, it dawns on me that everything happening in this moment mimics that morning, except the wrong person is in the car with me.

I look around me, trying to snap myself out of this new version of hell. I feel like I live this day on repeat when I close my eyes, but today, my anxiety feels crippling. As horrible as that day was to live through, I still knew what was happening when I'd be pulled back into the nightmare.

But now I feel lost. I look out the window and recognize where we are. We're passing that part of the street where the other car goes through the stop sign at a speed that took everything from me.

I try to warn River to slow down, to look to his right, but I open my mouth, and it's too late. I feel the force of the impact, and every-thing goes black.

My eyes open in a state of pure horror, pulling me from the memory, my body shaking and the tears streaming down my face.

I feel strong arms pull me in, and all I can do is cry. I'm digging my nails into River's skin, that simple act reminding me it was all a nightmare and none of it was real.

Gasping for air, I can't calm down. River keeps shushing me, telling me I'm safe. I don't know how long he holds me, but it feels like forever before my heart rate slows, and I can take a whole breath in.

My breaths begin to even, and I peel myself away from River's chest. My tear-soaked cheeks keep my hair stuck to my skin, but River moves as much as he can out of the way, dropping kisses along my cheeks, then moving his lips down to the corners of my mouth. Eventually, he drops a small kiss to my lips, his eyes full of concern.

"Kennedy, talk to me, baby. What happened?" I feel my eyes well up again just at the thought of what happened in my subconscious.

I'm surprised it took this long for a nightmare to happen since I started seeing River. I have always been a restless sleeper and that hasn't changed since we started sleeping together, but my nightmare hadn't returned for months.

"I sometimes have nightmares about the day my parents

died. It's always on repeat, pulling me back through the steps leading up to the accident. In some morbid way, I sort of look forward to seeing them, even though the entire memory is so horrible. But it's like a window into a world I never got to see carried out past the handful of years I got with them.

"But this one was different. This one didn't have my parents in the front seats. This one had—" I choke on my words, feeling as if my breath is once again taken from me as I recall the horror that felt like reality just moments ago.

"This time, it was you sitting in the seat. And I couldn't warn you, and everything went black." I feel the tears slip free again, that fear that the one person who is finally holding my heart is going to leave me just like my parents did.

River brings me back so that I'm engulfed in one of his embraces, holding me close, and I hear the steady beat of his heart against my ear.

He's here; he's with me. He wasn't there; he's going to be okay.

I keep repeating those words, hoping they start to feel real the more I breathe him in and feel the beat of his heart in his chest.

"I'm right here, Kennedy. I'm not going anywhere." He tries to assure me, but I start to shake my head.

"You can't promise me that. You can't say those words and know for certain," I say, once again turning into a blubbering mess as I let fear overtake my emotions again.

"Kennedy, look at me." River adjusts himself so his eyes are in direct line with mine. I try to avoid his gaze, the vulnerability in my soul at an all-time high.

I keep my eyes anywhere but on him, but eventually, I give in, unable to keep from losing myself in his gaze.

"I'm not going anywhere." He moves my hand to touch his chest above his heart. "You feel that? That beat beneath my skin? It's there because it beats for you. It beats in rhythm to the love I feel for you. Because that's the thing, Kennedy. I love you, and all my steps will lead back to you. Always," he says with no hesitation.

Right now, in this moment where he confesses his love for me, I forget about how stubborn we've both been at not declaring our love for one another. This right here is about us; it's about a love that erupted from the most unlikely place.

"For so long, I pushed you away. I kept you at a distance, thinking it was a result of years of irritation and annoyance. But I think my heart knew the moment I let you in it would never be the same. And it hasn't. I have loved you far longer than I could imagine, River. You're it for me." I stroke the soft hair on his chest, trying to memorize everything about him in this moment.

"I'm scared now that I found you, I'll lose you. Like there's a dark cloud that sees my happiness, and somehow I'll lose everything once again," I say, my voice above a whisper, fearing if I confess this too loud, something in the universe will pick it up and run with it.

"Life isn't about control, as much as you've worked hard to attain it. It's about giving your heart a chance to love, even if it breaks later. It's about giving that muscle a chance to get stronger. Because without those moments, you're not living. You're simply surviving until your last breath." He drops another soft kiss against my lips.

I let that kiss deepen until I feel him get hard against me. He turns me so I'm on my back, and he pulls away, his gaze full of passion and love.

"Kennedy, you don't have to fear my love being lost with you. Your heart is safe with me. It just took me some time to figure myself out, but know that life feels fuller with you by my side. And I will not leave you behind to feel that kind of loss again." Then he brings his lips to mine, and, for the first time, I feel myself get lost, not in the physical need I have for this man, but in the love we've learned to embrace between one another.

CHAPTER 29
River

THE MOMENT I confessed my love for Kennedy, it felt like a weight had been lifted. Aside from my parents and my brother, I have kept myself from telling anyone I loved them. Now that I think about it, I don't even think Kailey and I told each other we loved one another in high school, despite how long we dated. I knew whatever I felt for Kennedy was deep, but I kept talking myself out of the fact it could be love.

That night, when we decided to make this thing between us something more than a physical need, I knew it was love that was making its way into my heart. I think I knew, even when it felt like we were enemies throughout the years, that I loved her to some degree. I look back and remember watching her movements and thinking that I would catch her if she fell.

Little did I realize that she would fall into my arms, and I would never want to let her go. I look at her, and I don't just see tomorrow; I see next month, next year, and all the other milestones with her by my side. The craziest part is this came out of nowhere for both of us. For so long, we've felt as if we were pushing away from one another, only to see us gravitating closer with each step.

I move my hand over to interlace our fingers. My mother asked, or shall I say demanded, that I bring Kennedy over for Sunday dinner.

"I can't fucking believe this is happening," my brother pipes up from the backseat.

He had the means of coming on his own, but I know he just wanted to tag along to bother us on the drive over.

"Awww, Clay, just getting a step closer to you." Kennedy winks.

"The fuck, Skipper!"

They both laugh—traitors—and I scowl. After a beat, I bring my gaze back in front of me.

"Mom is going to lose her mind. She always looked at me as the one with my shit figured out. She never imagined River would save the day and get her a step closer to having grandchildren."

I know my brother is playing around, but I see the slight change in his features when he makes that little joke. I know what he not only lost after Abby left but also what he lost when they were together. The moment she walked out, though, she took all his dreams with her.

I move my eyes to look into the rearview, catching my brother's gaze where I'm joined with Kennedy. His gaze quickly darts up to meet mine, and he gives a small smile.

As we pull up to the house, we find my mother standing in her garden, pretending to tend to her flowers. The moment we park, she acts surprised to see us. This woman is way too transparent.

My brother and I move out of the car, my brother going in for a hug when my mom pushes him aside and grabs hold of my girlfriend, pulling her into a hug.

"Ma, what the hell?" Clay exclaims as my mother hushes him and directs all her words to Kennedy.

"Come here, you saint of a woman. I know what a pest River can be, and I'm so glad you're taking a chance on him," she says, and I stop in my tracks in shock that my mom would throw me under the bus like that.

"Hey, I heard that!" I say, throwing my hands up in the air.

"It was meant for you to hear, son. Now come along, make yourselves useful, boys. The table needs to be set. Kennedy and I have some chatting to do." She gestures for my brother and me to go inside while she steals Kennedy away from me.

I look back at them, and the satisfied look moving across Kennedy's' face tells me all I need to know: she loves the fact she's the new favorite in the Nichols household.

* * *

"Oh, you should have seen him. My sister and I were exhausted, and all we wanted was to put those rascals to bed and call it a day. We came back from the beach and bathed Clay, River, and Antonia together, but the look of horror that passed across his face was priceless. He pointed at his cousin Toni and said, 'Auntie, her penis fell off!'"

Even as my mom retells this story for the hundredth time, she laughs about it like it's her first time reliving it.

"I swear I nearly peed my pants." My mother cackles, and Clay being the dick he is, laughs right there with her. Motherfucker! I'll find a way to dig up some shitty story about him and share it with the next girl he brings over.

"Yeah, yeah, River didn't realize girls had vaginas. Whoop-de-doo. Can we change subjects?" I say, a little scared of where another story may lead now that my mom brought out the big guns.

"Oh, you've got to share more. That was priceless!" Kennedy says as she wipes literal tears from the sides of her eyes.

"Oh, sweet girl, let me go get the photo album," she says, and both my brother and I moan.

"Come on, Ma, not that. Please. Kennedy does not need to see me with my ass hanging out," I beg, but my mother has already left the room.

"Yes, Kennedy does need to see this!" Kennedy responds, and I see the gleam in her eyes. She likes this too much.

My mom comes in holding not just one album but multiple, and I groan.

"Ma, we won't be here that long. Please don't tell me we're going through all of these right now." I move my hands through my hair.

"Oh hush, Riv. Let me have my moment," she responds, and the smile Clay gives me is pure evil. He's loving this too damn much.

Kennedy is moving her hands together like she's gearing up to get all the dirt on me she possibly can. My mom is kind enough to start at the very beginning, and I decide now is the time to get up and grab a drink from the fridge.

"The boys were so cute when they were little. Even the nurse said they were beautiful from the moment they took their first breath." My mom oozes pride as she talks about us.

"See, we couldn't get enough photos when they were in the nursery at the hospital. They were the only boys born that day and the only twins too." She's pointing, and I know exactly what photos they are. We're wrapped like burritos, and my brother and I were side by side in bassinets they had to keep together. We apparently needed to know where the other was at all times, even just hours out of the womb.

They're flipping through photos, and Kennedy is asking questions about Clay and me. Most of the pictures they're going through are literally just us: our first swaddle, our first bath, our first time opening our mouth. I guess that's what new parents do—they take a shit ton of photos, especially in the first hours of life.

They're about halfway through the pictures, and we finally get into more group settings, where my parents are holding us outside at the hospital, our first trip to the zoo, in the park, and around the neighborhood.

Kennedy is inspecting each photo, admiring the love my parents had for their two rambunctious boys.

"Did your dad have a mullet?" Kennedy suppresses a laugh, and I smile.

"Yeah, Dad rocked that thing, at least from what I remember," I say, although my dad didn't have that hairstyle as we got older. He grew a mustache the last few years of his life, so that's how I always envision him. He looks completely different in the first two years of my life.

But that mullet was in full force when Clay and I were merely babies, and it really wasn't in at that point. I guess the guys at the station said he lost a bet, and that was his punishment, but then he kept the style going just to mess with them.

My mom pulls out another album, and I'm immediately reminded that's the one she put together right before he died. She opens it up to the first page, and it's our birthday a few weeks before he passed.

I don't know what photo they're on, but Kennedy is silent, taking in the page. My mom is rambling about how my dad couldn't get enough of the water balloons we were tossing outside in the yard. I peer over Kennedy's shoulder and see the photo they're inspecting is one of my brother and me aiming water balloons at him, and my dad's pretending to be shocked in the center. The smiles we're all wearing are big, nearly taking over our faces.

My brother and I favor our mom in appearance, but something about the way my dad carried himself seems to be the biggest legacy we have held on to. My dad lived life largely, always chasing the next adventure. I think that says a lot about the fact he died walking toward a building that breathed instability and fear. He was ready to carry out his next assignment despite the fear that many carried as they ran away from the wreckage.

My mom keeps talking, but the more she carries on, I can't help the dread that seems to be taking over my girlfriend's face. I can tell all the color has left her face, and she looks like she saw a ghost.

"Hey, Kennedy, you okay?" I ask, putting my hand on her shoulder.

She doesn't move, and her body is rigid. I look down at the photo, wondering if there's something odd in the image in front of her. Much as I expected, the picture staring back at us is the one at that birthday with my brother and me goofing off with our dad.

Like a spark has been ignited back into her, Kennedy stands abruptly and declares, "I, um, I don't feel good. Do you mind taking me home, River?" She doesn't even turn to look at me. She's already moving along, her body language closed off and uncomfortable.

My brother keeps looking down at the picture and then in the direction where Kennedy walked off. Before I can register what's happening, Kennedy comes back in, her voice laced with unease when she speaks to me, "Please, River," and I start to move about, saying a quick goodbye.

"I'll stay here for a bit longer," Clay says, grabbing the photo album and inspecting it further.

"Thanks for everything, Mrs. Nichols," Kennedy directs to my mother flatly, and it's like she only realizes Kennedy's odd behavior right then because my mom looks over to me with concern on her features. I shrug and wave a final goodbye before heading out the door.

Kennedy is already standing next to the passenger side door, waiting for me to unlock it.

The minute the car beeps, she shoves the door open and gets inside. I make my way to the driver's side, trying to understand what just happened.

The drive back to Kennedy's place is full of tense silence,

filling my truck cab. Kennedy is pensive, her gaze glued to the outside of her passenger window.

The moment I park in the underground lot of her building, she's rushing out of the truck, trying to get as far away from me as possible. She reaches the elevator, and had I not been close behind, I'm not too sure she would have held the doors for me. The ride up is just as quiet, riddled with tension, much like the ride in my car was.

As much as I want to give her space, this has gone on long enough. I've given her time to say something, letting me into this internal freak-out she seems to be experiencing, yet she's getting more closed off by the second. The moment the doors open, she charges out, keys in hand, ready to get inside her home and away from me.

What the fuck is happening?

I stop the door from slamming, with Kennedy already moving through her home, putting her things down, trying to dispel the tension I see radiating off her.

I grab her shoulder, forcing her to turn toward me. "What the hell, Kennedy? What was that? What's going on?"

It's then I notice the tears that have started to fall down her cheeks. I'm lost and have no clue what instigated this reaction.

"What did you see at my mom's house?" I keep throwing out questions, hoping something becomes more clear.

Her eyes look around her surroundings until she brings her bright gaze to mine. She gives a small nod, and I can't help but feel it does little to soften the blow she's about to throw at me.

"Your dad, he…" She moves her hands to rub her arms even though it's a warmer day today. I wait to let her finish.

"He was the man that day," she explains, yet I'm not following.

My expression must depict a puzzled look I can't seem to hide.

When she doesn't elaborate, I push further. "He was what man?" I'm still not following.

"He was the man who pulled me out of the car that day of the accident," she says, and her voice is so small, so unlike Kennedy, I can't seem to shake the unease that courses up my spine.

She takes a deep inhale. "He was the man—the firefighter at the scene of the crash that killed my parents."

CHAPTER 30

Kennedy

HE HAS *kind eyes that are bright green with blue in the middle; I can see his smile lines, which adds to the comfort he's giving me as I am placed on the ambulance stretcher. His thick mustache is dark brown, and it looks like Mario from the Mario Bros. game I play at home.*

I feel sad, but looking at his eyes, even for a moment, and feeling him squeeze me in a hug, and just the way he looks at me, makes me feel a little better in the mess of this accident.

He hurries off to see how he can help at the scene, but he keeps looking back at me. I can see he is confused with his feelings, trying to take care of the people in the accident, even checking my parents one more time, probably to know for sure there is nothing else that can be done.

Something about the man made me think he has a kind heart just from these little movements he makes around me. As much as this feels like I'm having a nightmare, I never look at this firefighter as anyone other than kind, even in all of the pain.

Much like the warm blanket he threw on me before he left me with the paramedics, his simple looks are calming me in a way I never expected, especially from someone who's a stranger. But soon, everything comes rushing back to me, and my heart feels too heavy for my little mind to understand the pain I'm going to have to live with for the rest of my life.

The paramedics ask me a few more questions, trying to find out if I have family nearby. I tell them about my grandparents, but my mom and dad have the cell phone. "It's only for emergencies," they would say, even though they would sometimes let me play Snake when I got bored and they were working.

The lady calls over to the nice fireman and tells him to look for a phone. She doesn't say his name, so I still don't know who he is. He goes on his search, and I feel like my body is a statue, looking past him at the two lifeless bodies under the drapes. My mommy and daddy, not laughing or playing peek-a-boo, but simply there, without any kind words or ways to make me feel better.

The fireman comes back with a phone; the screen is cracked, and I can't help but think that I will never play a game on it ever again. I will never hear my mommy laugh or my daddy try to talk in an English accent when he would read me stories. In that moment, that fireman gives the last piece of my parents that I'll ever hold. Because now I'm alone, and all I want are their hugs and their laughter. All I want is to go back home and start the morning over again. I just want to go to sleep and wake up from this nightmare I've been dragged into.

The fireman stops to talk to the lady paramedic, telling her to watch over me. He says something to me about his kids being young like me and tells me about his favorite cartoon to watch with them. He tells me maybe the emergency room will have a cartoon playing when I get there, and that if it is the same one, he wants me to tell him all about it. He promises he will check on me later to see if I am doing okay with my grandparents once they meet me at the hospital.

Before I know it, I'm being rushed off in the back of the ambulance, and the lady sitting next to me with her clipboard is asking me more questions. Even though I don't know him, the more she talks, the more I wish the fireman could be with me, asking me questions instead.

My head hurts, and my heart feels like it's never going to be the *same. The rest of the day feels like a horrible dream, and I want to see the fireman again. He never comes though. The world changes from the look on everyone's face when I'm waiting for my grandma and grandpa. But I'll always remember that fireman with his kind eyes. No matter what I do, I'll always remember his eyes.*

———

Numb. That's the only word that comes to mind with how I'm feeling right now. That memory of the younger version of me in the firefighter's arms is playing on repeat. The moment River's mom flipped the page of that photo album, and I saw his face, it felt like the world around me disappeared. In previous photos, he looked so different with his hair and no facial hair. But the minute I saw that one picture, I knew who was staring back at me.

I'm hunched over, feeling violently ill and close to passing out. I look at River to find him stunned and somewhat confused. I can't imagine what I'm saying to him makes much sense.

"What do you mean he pulled you out of the car that day?" he asks, his features hard to read.

"Exactly how it sounds, Riv. Your dad, the firefighter who got me out of the car after the accident and got me to safety, is the same man in those photos."

I don't really understand why I'm so uneasy with River right now. I mean, this doesn't change my relationship with him in any way, but some part of me feels strange being the last person to see him instead of River himself. Like I got a piece of his dad right before he ran into that building and never came out alive.

River takes a few breaths and then goes to sit down, probably trying to digest what I just told him. He runs his hands through his hair a few times, a tell of his when he's uncomfortable or thinking things through. I've noticed him do it often when he's working something out, and hopefully, he doesn't pull his hair out with how much he might be repeating my words through his head right now.

"Let me get this straight. The firefighter who saved you that day, who pulled you out of the car that your parents died in, is my dad?" He chokes up at the last part like it's too much emotion for him to process.

I simply nod, trying to put the pieces together. There's so much of that morning I've tried to forget, but his father is someone who was the only light on the darkest day I've lived through.

"He had kind eyes," I can't help but say out loud.

River moves to sit down and then looks up from the couch, and I see the comfort from my words enveloping him.

He nods, and a smile finally breaks the tension on his face. "Yeah, he did. He was always happy and everyone's favorite person in the room. Even though Clay and I were young, I still remember the booming sound that would carry whenever he laughed. I remember my mom looking up at him and the pure love she had for the man, even years later. They were high school sweethearts. Did I ever tell you that?" River says, and I can see him being pulled into a distant thought, reminiscing about the father he lost years ago.

"Yeah, they met sophomore year in high school and started dating junior year after he spent twelve months badgering her to go out with him. She always tells the story like he finally wore her down, but I can tell she always liked him but just needed to play hard to get, even all these years later, and he's not even here."

He chuckles at his own words, and I feel like my heart is breaking all over again, knowing he lost his dad in a way so many others did that day.

"Can you tell me more about your interaction with him? I know it hurts, Kennedy, but it's like I have been given this little extra moment to hear a story I never got to hear about a man I lost too early in life." I can see the agony in his features. He knows how hard things are for me when it comes to recalling that horrible day in my life, but I know how much he needs this.

When I hear of people who lost loved ones on 9/11, many are saying how much they hope they know they were loved. Many will talk about their hopes that their person was happy doing what they loved. I think they just want to know that the person was at peace during such a horrible day. Add in the stories of people who missed a call from a loved one to only have a message on a machine that they play back over and over, recounting the love they shared in their message.

I take a seat next to River and pull his hand to rest in mine. "Of course I don't mind." I feel that lump in my throat try to form, but I push past it, knowing that we now share a moment we both wish would have turned out very differently.

"He was the only fireman I spoke to that day. He pulled me out of the car. He held me, and the moment I saw his eyes, I felt comforted. I felt like he could feel my pain. Now I wonder if it was sympathy knowing he had two little boys close to my age at home waiting for him. I can't imagine scenes like those are easy on you all," I say, knowing River lives a life that is very much parallel to his father's.

He nods his head, not sure if he is in disbelief or in agreement with what I said.

"He didn't say too much to me, but he made sure I was safe. He made sure I wasn't left unattended and that someone would ensure my family came to get me at the hospital. Little did anyone know how chaotic that day would turn out to be for all of us, but in that moment, I felt cared for by someone who wasn't a parent or relative, and that's all because of your dad. He made me feel seen when all I felt was shattered."

I let the tear escape my eye and fall down my cheek. The

pain from that day still lives so close to the surface, and I can't help how it takes over my body.

It's then I realize I can show River one of the things I've kept from that day. "I need to go grab something. Give me one sec," I say and scurry off to my room. I rush into my closet to find that one box I've carried with me since I moved out of my grandparent's house years ago.

I find it at the top of my closet, and I pull the top off to reveal the contents from that life I've tried to leave behind.

I pull the item out and inspect it. I get up, about to step out and back into the living room, when I bump into a hard chest.

"What's that?" River asks, and I should have known he was going to follow me here, curiosity getting the best of him.

I nudge my chin toward the bed, and he follows, both of us sitting side by side.

I put the old phone in his hand and let him inspect it. It's no longer useful, obviously, but some weird side of me felt like I had to keep it. Like it was the last thing my parents touched before getting in the car that day. Like having this was at least a way to feel connected to them in some weird way.

"That is my parents' phone your dad retrieved from the car that morning. I know it's silly," I say, feeling a little stupid that I care so much about a phone that will never work again.

Right then, River interrupts, "It's not silly at all," and I feel reassured by something in his tone that shows his appreciation more than anything else.

"Well, I find it comforting to touch things my parents touched," I shuffle through the box I brought out from the closet and onto my lap, "like the car keys they carried with them and the note my mom had packed in my lunch that morning. This phone became a piece of their puzzle I couldn't let go of. But now I think it can be a part of yours too." I hear the shakiness in my voice as I show things to River, tossing the items onto the bed one by one, still unsure how he's feeling about all this.

He stays silent for an uncomfortable amount of time. I don't know what to make of it, and I'm starting to get restless. I fumble with a piece of plastic on the side of the box, then pick up the car keys and mess with the little baseball keychain my uncle had gifted my dad that last Christmas we were all together, unease lacing all my movements.

River clears his throat and keeps his eyes on the phone I handed him. His thumb keeps grazing the plastic, almost like he's trying to feel his dad's warmth from the gesture.

"I always wondered what his morning was like that day. My mom had talked to him that morning, and he even said it had been quiet on his shift. I remember my mom giving a little chuckle on the phone, telling him to keep from saying the dreaded word: bored. I still remember my mom sitting on the couch, hours later, clutching our cordless house phone, wishing things had stayed as boring as they had been when she had spoken to him earlier."

"Was that the last time they spoke?"

"Yeah, I think so. Cell phones were nothing then as they are today. Even if he had his on him, it was sort of known to just use them for emergencies. So he didn't call again. One of the guys from another company met up with my dad, and my dad had told him to give us a message that he loved us and that he'd always be with us. Luckily that firefighter happened to survive, and he was able to pass the message a few days later. Even though my mom had a premonition my dad had perished in the collapse, that message was almost like a confirmation because my dad would never have said that had he not known what was going to happen. I think deep down he knew he wasn't coming home."

Another tear falls down my face, and River has the strength to comfort me while he's remembering his own father.

"I've always wondered where he went after that call with my mom. I wondered if he was at the firehouse that morning and saw the building on fire with the first plane and headed over. I never asked those who survived from the firehouse."

He is speaking to me, but at the same time, it feels like he's talking into the open space of the room. Like his thoughts are so jumbled that saying them out loud will make more sense.

I rub circles around his back, comforting him as he processes everything. The tables have turned from earlier when I felt paralyzed by the knowledge that River's father is the same man who cared for me hours before his own passing. Now I'm the one allowing River to lean on me.

This all feels so heavy, and it's hard to separate this emotion I'm feeling from the one he is most likely coming to terms with.

"I don't know, Kennedy. I am in shock that all this time, right in front of me, I was so close by to someone who was one of the last to see my dad before he went into that building to never come out. After you told me your parents died on the same day as the tragedy that tore through every American, I felt a deeper connection to you, but this? I never, not in a million years, would think you got to see my dad that day."

I push his hair away from his face, and we simply stare at one another. We share something unique, and even though his dad witnessed me on my worst day, there's something about the fact that I got to meet him in some capacity that makes me feel like I'm linked to River in an unshakable way.

He puts the phone down and carefully places all the mementos back in the box and move it to the ground. He places his hands on my cheeks and glides them through my hair; instinctively, I close my eyes and lean into his touch.

"You were brought to me, Kennedy. I truly believe my dad is watching us, and he knows that I finally found what he had left for me before leaving me behind." He drops small kisses along my face, catching the tears coming down.

"The way my heart has opened to you, Kennedy, is like nothing I've ever felt in my life. Thank you for sharing your day with me, even though it's one filled with so much pain. I know what you and I experienced that day is in many ways different, with similar feelings attached to it. I don't think we will ever walk a day in our future without that piece of our past latching on."

I nod, now the tears are constant streams down my face. I hold his hands over my cheeks and allow this feeling to overtake me. My love for this man may have hit me out of nowhere, but the more time we spend together, the more I'm reminded how much our past intersected in ways we never expected.

The moment he brings his lips to my own, I realize I've stepped through the worst part of life just to lead me to him.

CHAPTER 31

River

IT'S BEEN a few weeks since Kennedy and I discovered this unknown link in our lives. It's interesting how grief can hit you, feeling that loss all over again, even years after the fact.

When I first started this with Kennedy, in the back of my mind, I would wonder what my dad would think of her. I think it's only natural to wonder something like that when you lose a parent too soon. You're always looking at the life you're building and wondering how that person would take in the choices you've made.

I'm well aware that my dad had no idea who Kennedy was at that time. Nor did he understand the person she would grow to be in my life. But there is this part of me, deep down, that feels this connection to her in a different way now. It feels as though a part of her was meant for me and vice versa.

After she calmed down and we were able to talk about it without feeling an overwhelming sense of emotion, we called my mom and explained everything that had come to Kennedy's realization. Clay was still there, and the moment Kennedy explained her reaction, there wasn't a dry eye on either side.

My mom was overcome with a sense of closure, although what Kennedy experienced with my dad was so different than the last few moments of his life. But for my mom, after years of hoping to know more about how his day had gone up to the point he entered the tower at the World Trade Center, she got a little piece of him back with this story.

There's no way to look at this and feel complete though. That's something we all have to come to terms with as we realize this new link between Kennedy and my family. Three people were lost amongst us, along with thousands of others. Amidst the tragedy that day holds, we've found a way to carry on, but the pain lingers deep in our core.

I've pretty much spent every waking moment at Kennedy's if I'm not on shift at the station. I feel like I'm here more than at my own place, so much so that Lola hasn't been back to our apartment in weeks. Something feels right about it, and it seems neither of us wants to say anything to change this new normal we've fallen into.

I'm walking out of the room to find Lola snuggled next to Kennedy while my girlfriend is smiling at something on her phone. It isn't until I get closer I see it's someone on social media getting engaged.

"What is with you and proposals?" I ask, not sure if she's trying to drop hints or something.

"I honestly love proposals. I have this thing about them; they just make me smile. Even years ago, I would stop to watch a proposal if it was happening at a game or at some popular spot in the city. I've always loved them," she explains, all while watching her screen.

"Are you hinting at something?" I can't help but ask.

In all honesty, I've thought of ways I would ask someone as strong-minded as Kennedy to marry me, but I haven't thought of the best way yet. I know when the idea hits me, it will be epic.

"Oh, stop, River. That is not what's happening. I've loved

proposals since before this whole thing with us started. Come to think of it, I think it all started with my parents," she continues, smiling, this time swinging her gaze to me.

"Don't leave me hanging, Skip," I say as I make my way to the kitchen to grab some food to take to the station.

"My parents didn't fight often, but when they did, no matter what the discussion was about, in hopes of making my mom smile, my dad always asked her if she would marry him again, even after making her mad," she chuckles, "and she would always say yes." She shrugs her shoulders and keeps scrolling on her phone.

For someone who was so adamant about staying single and not committing to someone, I love seeing her melt a little at seeing people propose.

* * *

The holidays have just ended, and I am cringing at the thought of taking down all these decorations. Experiencing the magic of Christmas with Kennedy was fun for me. I remember we'd stand so far away from the mistletoe at parties, sending each other seething looks. But this year was quite different, and I know we had a lot of fun making up for lost time each chance we got.

I'm lost in thought, grabbing a snack in the kitchen, when I hear Kennedy in the other room.

"Oh my god, River!" I slam the fridge as she yells.

She comes running over, my dog at her feet, getting excited over the prospect of whatever is getting Kennedy all riled up.

"The twins are coming! Sam is in labor!" She shoves her phone in my face, and once my eyes focus, I see the text from Ashton.

"That's exciting. Are you going to head over there?" I ask, realizing the time and the fact I need to head out soon.

"I guess? I can text her and see. Last she went to the doctor, they were going to do a C-section because the babies aren't in the right position or something. I guess her water breaking means the party is happening early," she says excitedly.

"Keep me updated. I can always try to run to the hospital if it's not too busy," I say, grabbing the last of my things before I give Lola some attention and give Kennedy a kiss goodbye.

"Riv?" she calls after me before I close the door.

She comes running over and stops me by bringing her lips to mine.

"Please be safe tonight. I love you," she says, a soft smile taking over her face.

"Love you, and I promise I will," I say and then call out, "Keep me updated on the babies and Sam."

The elevator chimes, and I head in, blowing a final kiss her way. I'm officially a lovesick puppy because as I make my way out of the building, I'm already counting the hours until I'm back in her arms.

* * *

My brother and I are on shift together, and we're both digging into our dinner, nodding our heads at the same time. I doubt it goes unnoticed by the guys that some twin things are just hard to explain. We finish each other's sentences, move our bodies in the same way, and even answer things at the same time by gesturing with our bodies.

Out of nowhere, Rios comes strolling in, and I can bet money he's going to bring up the whole Kennedy and my dad connection again. He hasn't stopped talking about it.

"Dude, I'm still shocked with that story about your dad and Kennedy. I mean, what are the chances? It's wild. I can't believe it." He whistles at the end, bewildered by the news, even all this time after I told him the first time.

Now that he's made comments left and right about the fact Kennedy and I share a deeper connection, I sort of shrug because Rios is like a broken record.

It's hard to ignore what a busy night it's been so far, with a call coming in right when we came on. We barely had time to put our things down before we heard the call, sending us out.

I've gotten a few notifications from Kennedy regarding Sam and her care. It turns out the babies are still not in the right position to try a natural birth, so the last text I got was that they were prepping Samara for surgery. The babies are coming earlier than expected, but nothing uncommon for twin deliveries. Luckily, the hospital is one of the top ones for delivering multiples; they're in good hands.

Ashton texted me once, all with GiFs of characters freaking out. The last one was of that movie *Airplane* where the pilot is sweating bullets. I can't lie: that one made me laugh out loud. The last text I got from Kennedy, she was preparing to head to the hospital once Ash gave her the go-ahead.

It's getting close to midnight, but the last text was about two hours ago, so she should already be there. Sam's parents arrived before Ash and Sam did, so Kennedy was planning on hanging out with them while waiting for the surgery to end.

I can't help my mind drifting to this big moment for my best friends. The day they become parents is finally here. This pregnancy felt long for me as an onlooker because we knew about it quite early on. Now that the babies are coming, I can't wait to meet them and to watch Ashton handle this new chapter in his life.

Rios is still mumbling to himself, and it causes my brother and I to turn to one another and smile. Clay was pretty quiet when Kennedy explained the connection we had, and it took some time for all his feelings to settle. It wasn't that he was mad about it; it was just unexpected.

We finish up, and I clean our dishes while he grabs us more water. It's then we hear the breaking news on the television of a fire that broke out right outside of town. Right then, Rios grabs the remote and turns the volume up.

From the look of it, this is going to take a lot of manpower to stop. It's an old factory, one that hasn't been functional in decades, yet a fire is taking over the structure.

We get the alert we are needed, and we run toward the truck, pulling our outfits on and preparing for a long night ahead.

* * *

The moment we reach the call, we see the building engulfed in flames. Our captain is barking orders at all of us, everyone making sure their gear is set to walk into the flames.

I take in the disaster in front of my brother and me as we prepare to make our way in. The heat is immediate, and my body kicks into gear to get further into this place and check for anyone who might be injured or trapped.

We have a blueprint of the place to inspect each location. Although this building was abandoned, kids liked making their way inside, and from what some of the teens who were being cared for by paramedics in front were saying, there are two unaccounted for in their group.

I break off with my group to move through the large area, my brother going with Rios and a few other guys, and I hang back to assess some portions of the foundation below. We make good time inspecting downstairs, realizing no one is hidden in any corners, nor did anyone call out.

We make our way upstairs, going through an area my

brother and the others haven't gone. I hear a faint sound and then see movement to my right. I call out, making sure they know help has arrived. I reach the teen, who now has his shirt covering his face. I pull the face mask onto him, watching him take deep breaths of fresh air. His buddy is nearby, a gash in his leg.

One of the guys in my company, Bently Denko, is caring for the friend while I make sure the kid in front of me can get up and walk. He's limping after hurting his leg, but with the amount of smoke engulfing the room, I can't wait for him to walk slowly through the place. I have no option but to carry him out. A further inspection of his wounds will need to be done once we get outside.

We had communicated we had found the two missing teens; however, it took longer than either of us would have liked, and now we are hustling to get out. I look over to see Denko picking up the other kid, the gash in the teen's calf deeper than I imagined.

We give each other the signal to move out, the need to move fast very much at the forefront of our minds. That's when I hear the creaking take over. We begin to move faster, knowing this building is unstable and might start to come down on us.

Our radios begin to project my captain's voice, telling us to move out. I hear my brother, along with others from the station, call out that they're headed out of the building right then. We are making our way downstairs, but the stability of the wood in this portion of the building is weak. I can feel the ground beneath my feet giving out a little more with each step I take.

We're finally close to the exit, and that's when we start to see more debris falling from above us. Denko is able to get the kid out, and when I get close to the entrance we initially came through, I hand the boy off to some other firefighters from another station. Elation overwhelms me with the fact the teen got out of the burning building and should be okay. In the next second, there's a shift in the atmosphere around me, and before I can process what's going on, everything behind me gives out, and I'm engulfed in darkness.

CHAPTER 32

Kennedy

I'M in the waiting room, the anticipation of meeting these little ones causing me to pace around the small room. Sam's mother is no better, going up to the nurses' station every few minutes to ask for an update.

There aren't too many families waiting out here, so I don't feel like my movements are interrupting anyone, but I try to keep myself from walking the entirety of the labor floor waiting room as the twins are most likely delivered at this point.

The next time the large double doors open, they reveal Ashton, his smile from ear to ear. Sam's mother jumps from her seat that she occupied about fifteen seconds ago and rushes toward him.

"Sam's doing great. The babies are perfect. They look like their beautiful mama. I've fallen in love all over again. We've got twenty fingers and twenty little toes. They're fine but had to go to the NICU. They were struggling a little to breathe without the oxygen mask, but overall, are looking good. Once Sam is moving a little better, we can wheel her over to see them."

Even though the babies are being monitored in the NICU,

the smile hasn't left his face as he talks to us. All of us breathe a sigh of relief with the news, and I can't wait to see their sweet faces.

"I'm just going to swing back and check on Sam, then I can walk to the NICU and get an update on how they're doing," he says as he makes his way back toward the room where Sam is recovering.

We nod, tears falling down our cheeks with the happy news, and start to grab our belongings. Right then, I swing my gaze toward the television, not registering everything I see when I catch a flash of reflective gear that looks a lot like the kind I see at the firehouse.

I notice they're covering a fire at a local factory that has been shut down for some time. The flames are taking over the screen, and my stomach drops. My hands go numb as I feel this dread come over me in fear that River is in the middle of that chaos. I know he most likely will be, the structure is far too big for one station to cover alone.

As if I conjured him up, I see his face come through the elevator doors that just opened. I feel instant relief seeing him in front of me, but it takes an extra second to realize it's Clay, not River, coming toward me.

The look of concern on his face consumes him, and I feel all the contents in my hands fall to the ground. I start shaking my head, fear overtaking me as he gets closer.

He opens his arms to me as I rush into them, immediately talking into my ear, telling me, "He's okay, Kennedy. He got injured on the job, but he's going to be fine. I promise he is going to be okay." He pulls away, then gets at eye level with me. "Did you hear me? Did you understand what I just said?" he asks, probably feeling my body shake in fear even though I know he's going to be okay.

"Wh-what happened?" My breaths are shortening, and I can feel the anxiety taking over even as I try to calm myself down.

"He was trying to get out of the building, and it was so old, it came crashing down pretty quick. Quicker than we ever imagined. He didn't quite make it out the door completely, and his leg got caught. But in his attempt to escape getting more injured, he hit his head and was unconscious for a bit. He's downstairs in the ER waiting for orders from the doctor."

I don't know how Clay is being so calm as I'm a mess just hearing the story.

"I need to see him. Please, take me to him." I start to grab my discarded items, and I look over to Sam's parents. "Please let Ash and Sam know I'll be back later to check on all of them. Tell them congratulations for me." It's hard to muster a smile, yet I give them a small one, and then I turn and rush to the elevator.

"How did you know I was here?" I ask him, forgetting a number of people know my whereabouts.

"I knew Sam was having the babies, but then once River came to, he told me to get you. Actually, he demanded it, so here I am." He smiles, and it's hard not to see all the similarities between the two of them at a time like this. Most of the time, all I see are the two of them as entirely different people. I see little differences in their facial expressions, but that's probably due to years of inspecting their features.

I hug Clay and thank him for coming to get me. The elevator ride feels like a lifetime until it dings and opens to the hustle of the lobby of the ER. I see multiple firefighters waiting around; some I recognize, and some are new faces to me.

The nurse sees us coming and calls out, "This the wife?"

I must have a stunned expression as I look over my shoulder, waiting for someone else to be trailing behind me. To my surprise, she's directing her question to us, and Clay answers, "Yep," and the doors automatically open, and we're moving along the corridor to River's room.

"Who's wife?" I ask, still not allowing all the pieces to fall into place.

"Only family is allowed back here, Kennedy," he says as if I should have known.

I'm still digesting the idea of being River's wife when the curtain opens, and River's handsome face appears. He's got a cut over his eyebrow that is being stitched by the nurse. A pretty nurse, might I add. If she could focus on her job and not on my boyfriend's gorgeous features, maybe she'd be done already.

She snaps out of it to look over at us making our way into the room. "Oh, are you the wife?"

I don't hesitate this time and make my way toward River's side, grabbing his hand and squeezing it.

"That I am," I say, making sure I lay claim on him before she decides to try anything further with him. She's already a bit closer to him than I would like, but she's fixing him up, so I'll keep the green-eyed monster at bay for now.

The nurse must sense the tension I'm giving off and blushes slightly, returning to the cut on River's face.

I move my gaze to him, and he's smiling like he's enjoying the fact I'm jealous a little too much.

"Hey, baby, or should I say wife." He waggles his eyebrows and quickly winces.

"Stay still, please," the nurse says, clearly disappointed her hot patient isn't available.

"Are you okay? You're scared me!" I complain, yet all of the cells in my body are relieved seeing him mostly intact.

I look down and notice his right leg in a splint.

"Did you break it?" I move my hand down his leg, careful not to put pressure on it.

"Nothing a few kisses won't fix." He winks with his good eye.

"I see." I smirk yet squint my gaze in his direction.

Working a little faster, the nurse finishes patching him up

and stands, grabbing all the supplies she was using on her tray.

"Okay, Mr. Nichols, you're all stitched up. We'll be right back to do an X-ray of that leg to make sure nothing is indeed broken. No falling asleep. Remember, you're on concussion protocol," she explains, not once making eye contact with me.

I stand a little closer to River and drop a kiss on his head. I still see the dust from the debris that fell on him, and I close my eyes and throw a quick thank you to my angels above for watching over him.

"So, what do you think, wife? You ready to take care of me for a few days?" River says while Clay snorts in the corner.

"Yeah, right. That'll be the day," his brother says, and I look over and cut him a look that shuts him right up.

My gaze returns to River. "Sweetie, you can call me Skipper, girlfriend, or baby, but there's no wife here today. You're going to have to put a ring on it for that dream to become a reality."

"I'm injured, baby. You've gotta cut me some slack." He gives me his big, hazel eyes, pleading with me.

"Not today." I shake my head. "You may be hurt, but it's going to take a proper proposal to get me to marry you," I say.

River mocks hurt by placing his hand on his chest. "Wow, for someone who loves proposals, you're sort of cold."

"You never proposed, Riv!" I whisper-yell his way.

"Fine, then I will cross out 'near-death experience' as a means to ask you to marry me," he says, and I start to laugh until I realize he's seriously talking about marrying me like it's really in his plans.

He must read the confusion on my features and adds, "Oh, don't worry, I've got something planned. You'll just have to wait now, Skip." He's taunting me, asking for me to bite, but I let this conversation die down and pull a seat next to his gurney.

"Okay, buddy." I chuckle and lift my head to look at Clay. "How hard did you say he hit his head?"

"You think I'm kidding, Kennedy? I'm serious. I'm going to propose to you so hard, you're not even going to see it coming," River teases.

Before I can answer, a tech comes to get him x-rayed. River is wheeled out to radiology while we stay behind and wait for his return. We had moved to the hall to see River out but stayed for a few extra moments, no rush to sit back in the room.

While staring toward the door River just left through, I hear whispers in the nurses' station. "See, that's her. He's taken ladies. They're always taken."

I just smile to myself, and I look over to see Clay suppressing a laugh. The chatter continues, and it's proving to be quite entertaining.

"He's got a photocopy right there. Just ask him out," another voice chimes in, and now it's getting hard to hold in the laughter.

Clay moves closer to me to whisper, "It's always so reassuring to hear you're second-best."

I smack him on the chest and let out a laugh. To add to the entertainment, someone taps Clay on the shoulder. The moment we both turn around, I'm instantly greeted by the nurse who was stitching River's gash.

"Hey. I'm Jamie. I, uh, am your brother's nurse. I wanted to see if you wanted to grab a coffee sometime." I can hear the nervousness in her voice, and I let my eyes dart from her to Clay, waiting to see how he tackles this one.

"Sure, why not?" He extends his hand. "I'm Clay, by the way," he says to her, and her smile beams his way. She puts a paper in his hand with what I assume is her number.

"Great. Give me a call." She saunters off, giggling as she joins the rest of her nursing friends.

"Wow, I guess second-best isn't too bad after all," I tell him, and he pockets the number.

"I guess not," he says, turning to face River's room again.

"She's cute. I bet it would be fun," I say, taking a quick look back at the nursing station again.

"Yeah, only one way to find out," he says, sounding a bit defeated in his tone.

"So you think you're ready to get back out there for real now?" I ask, sort of surprised he's ready to start dating now. From what I've seen, he's seemed more caught up on Abby than wanting to move forward.

He looks down at his hands, wiping at some soot still left near his wrist. "My marriage crumbled, but I think it's time I start dating again. It's weird. When Abby first left, I was adamant I hated her. I was so mad, but then it took a few months and many drinks later to see that I wasn't mad at her. I was still in love with her.

"And no matter how much I tried to deny it, it wouldn't change that fact. So now I own up to it, and hopefully, one day, it won't feel so heavy to get someone's number and actually pull the trigger and call them. And maybe that day will be today with Nurse Jamie. Maybe it's with someone else. But I can't keep waiting around and sulking. What I had with Abby is in the past. I can't go backwards anymore. I have to look ahead."

As much as he's saying these words, I a see the look of defeat in his features. It's in moments like these I see the differences between the brothers come to the surface. River has always been sarcastic and ready to goof off. Clay has always had a softer side. That's probably why I never felt an attraction to Clay. I preferred the side of River that was always wanting to spar with me. Clay was the one I went to for a comforting hug and something kind to say.

"I'm sorry it still hurts," is all I can think of to say. He nods and puts his hands in his pockets.

Once the X-rays are done, we return to the room and sit to wait for the doctor on call to come in and give us results.

"You're lucky, Mr. Nichols. Looks like it's just a bad sprain. The swelling should subside after a few days, but no fracture is evident. If, for any reason, the pain worsens or you notice more swelling in that portion of the leg, please don't hesitate to return. You'll be off duty for the next two weeks. Don't try to be a bigger hero either and disregard my orders." Dr. Jonis looks at River, hoping to get through to him.

"Don't worry. We'll keep an eye on him," I reassure the doctor. "Thank you for everything."

"You're still on concussion protocol even though there's no indication you have one. I'd feel better if you have someone with you tonight. The nurse will give you discharge papers with a list of symptoms to watch out for," he explains.

"Oh, my *wife*," River emphasizes the word, "will be with me all night. She's a great nurse." River has the nerve to wink at me, and I roll my eyes. Seems that head injury isn't messing with him right now.

The doctor nods and turns to leave when River chimes in again, "Uh, Doc, what about other things? You know, other extracurriculars," he asks with no shame while Clay lets out a loud laugh by my side. I simply shake my head. I cannot believe his mind is on *that* right now. Of course, my face goes crimson.

"As long as you continue to do well and don't feel any headaches, dizziness, nausea, vomiting, or double vision, you should be good to go in twenty-four hours. Just be careful with the leg. Make sure you're staying off it while you recover." With that, the doctor leaves, and we wait for the nurse to come back with discharge paperwork.

Clay leaves to update the firehouse with the news, and then it's just us in the room. I sit there and continue to look at River with a baffled expression.

"Oh, come on, Skipper, you had to know I would ask. I'm

injured, not dead. I have needs, and so do you." He smirks, and, once again, I can't help the eye roll.

"Your safety and health come first, Riv," I say as I stand and get closer to him.

"Believe me, all that is part of my health." He moves his hand onto my cheek.

The feel of his warmth against my skin calms me, and I close my eyes and lean into his touch. The fact he could have been severely injured or taken from me is not lost in that moment, and I can feel a tear fall down my cheek.

"Hey, why are you crying? Look at me. I'm fine," he says as he moves his thumb to catch the tear.

I move closer to him, kissing his face, careful not to hurt the patched-up spot above his eyebrow. I move my lips over his and just savor that moment between us.

"I love you so much, and I just can't fathom a moment where you're not here with me, that's all," I say, vulnerability etching my words.

"I love you too, and I told you nothing is going to happen to me." He moves his hand into my hair and brings my lips to his again, deepening the kiss.

"You can't promise me that though," I whisper.

"Let's move in together, Kennedy," he says, and I can't help the gasp that escapes my lips.

"River, listen, I am not expecting you to make big decisions right now. Let's get you better, and if you still want that, then we can revisit this at another time." I think he does have a concussion. There's no way.

"Kennedy, you want to know what gets me through my day when I'm not with you?" I give a slight nod, and he continues, "Knowing I'll get to spend my nights with you. The fact Lola is there waiting for me and so are you. Getting home after a long-ass shift knowing I can hold you and breathe you in. Those are the things I put high on my list. But tonight, all I wanted was to come home to you. Our home.

Not my apartment or yours. I want us to be under the same roof, sharing things, annoying each other. Everything. I'm not kidding when I say I want everything with you."

I look at him as he speaks to me, my eyes taking in his big hazel irises, sincerity and truth behind his gaze.

Without thinking through it too much, I start to nod, the smile on my face growing.

"Yeah? Yes? Fuck, Kennedy, baby," he says, bringing my face closer to his and kissing me. "I'm so happy right now." He kisses me, and I swear I see stars.

In that moment, I fall a little deeper for the one man I pushed away for so long.

CHAPTER 33
River

IT'S BEEN a month since my injury, and I'm finally starting to feel like myself again.

Kennedy and I are unpacking my last box. She held off on accepting my offer that we live together because she said I was just feeling the effects of the adrenaline pumping through my system after my injury. It took literal begging for her to finally cave, and now we share space together.

The fact I'm living with her after years of needing to keep my distance just shows how life can change in an instant. I was already thinking about taking this next step before hurting myself, but when I was in that hospital bed, the first thing I thought of when I woke up was how short life truly is. If there are two people who understand that, it's both Kennedy and myself.

"Hey, you never wear this for me." Kennedy huffs as she pulls one more item from the box of my clothes.

I look at her, holding up my gray sweats.

"I think I could manage to put these back into the rotation. Why? You like sweats or something?" I look over, a little confused.

"Well, yeah, it's like in all my romance books. If I have a

boyfriend living with me who I can ogle at, it just makes it more fun," she says, looking at the sweats one more time before putting them in the drawer.

"Hold up, you don't ogle me all the time now?" I gasp.

"Not really. You're not really that fun to look at that much." She laughs then squeals as I start chasing her around the room—our room.

The moment I grab hold of her, I throw her onto the bed, where I follow suit and cage her between my forearms. I look down at her, both of us catching our breath, and I can't hide how mesmerized I am by her.

This woman who started our first interaction with judgment and anger is now the one person I run to on my worst days. She's the person I close my eyes and envision standing at the altar waiting for me. She's the one I hope to one day put my hand over her belly and feel our baby kick.

"Where did you go?" She moves her hand to touch my cheek, her soft touch such a contrast to the hard edges she showed just months ago.

"In the future," I say, smiling and letting my dimples I love pop and make her melt a little more with.

She moves her hand through my brown hair, the feel pushing me to close my eyes and relish how her touch sets fire to my soul.

"Mmhmm." I can't really form words, and I already feel myself getting turned on at the prospect of what we could do instead of continuing this unpacking mission we started with.

"And what did that future look like?" she asks, and I see her looking at me when I open my eyes, and I have no shame in telling her exactly where my mind is.

I reach down and kiss her nose. "I see you in a white dress walking toward me to become my wife." I move my lips to her temple and drop a kiss there. "I see you holding a pregnancy test and telling me we're going to be parents." I move my lips to the other side to kiss the skin right below her earlobe, knowing it sets her off in the sexiest way.

"I see you standing in our kitchen, your belly swollen with the life we created together," I finish off, causing her breath to hitch.

For someone who always kept such a shield up, Kennedy is more sensitive than I would have pegged her to be. Tears well in her eyes, and I take the opportunity to drop my lips to hers.

The moment we connect, it feels so much like the first time, full of passion and a bit of desperation to feel one another bare. My skin tingles as I move my body over hers, letting her feel what she does to me.

She moves her hips up to meet mine, and before we know it, we're pulling our clothes off one another.

She moves me to lie on my back, pushing my pants off. Next she pulls at my shirt and lets her hands roam my upper body, and I'm relishing the feel of her fingertips moving along my skin. She sets every part of me on fire, and I reach over and cup her sex through her leggings. I need her naked, and I need to be inside her.

I move her sweater over her head, and I see she's wearing a nearly sheer lacy bra, her nipples peaked under the soft fabric. I cup her breasts in my hands and move my thumbs over her nipples, eliciting a moan to drop from her lips.

"You need to catch up to me," I say before I move her to lie down on the bed and pull her leggings and underwear off. She makes quick work of her bra, and I just watch as she lies there, naked and ready for me.

"I think you need a little warm-up, Skip," I say as I lick my lips and move to my knees, throwing one of her legs over my shoulder, ready to devour what's mine.

The moment I connect to her center, her hips push off the bed, as if she hasn't felt my touch in years instead of the few hours it has been since I've been inside of her.

She moves her hands through my hair again, assisting in the movements of my head to catch her release. And it doesn't take her long to get there. She starts to scream out my name, and I lap up her wetness as she lets out a few giggles while coming off her high.

I drop kisses along the inside of her thigh and make my way up her torso, nipping at her abdomen and then giving attention to both her breasts, tugging on her nipples to push her a little further.

I move my body to grab a condom, and she stops me. I look over at her, trying to figure out what's going on.

She shakes her head. "I don't want anything between us anymore. I'm on the pill, and I want us to have this together."

We haven't gone unprotected since that night in my truck, and I won't lie and say I haven't been fantasizing about it since. The idea of going in bare right now has my dick pulsing with need.

I bite down on my lower lip and grab my cock to give myself a few strokes, looking down at this goddess I can call mine.

"Fuck, River, you're so hot. I swear I could get off just looking at your muscles flexing in front of me," she says, and I continue my strokes to emphasize the muscles moving as I do.

"Maybe you should show me what you'd do if I weren't here," I tease.

The moment she takes me up on my offer, moving her hand down toward her pussy, I'm instantly regretting it. I don't want to blow my load before I even get inside her. If she starts moaning as a result of those strokes her fingers are making along her clit, I may combust.

I bend down and pull her into another blinding kiss and start moving my dick through her wet folds and plunge right into her without any warning.

She pulls her lips away and moves her head back, pushing

her chest into my face. I pinch her nipples and kiss down her sternum and then back up again.

I pound into her at a punishing pace, hoping to make this last long enough to get her to climax yet again. To feel her walls pulsing around me, feel her tighten as I push her further into the abyss of ecstasy, only makes me want to move faster.

Soon, her legs begin to shake, and I know she's there. I move my thumb to touch that sensitive bud, and she detonates beneath me. That spurs me on to chase my own high, and I feel that tightness from the base of my spine move up. My climax takes over, and I'm shooting into her, feeling like I've laid claim to this woman.

A smile crosses over her face, and she drops soft kisses along my neck and jaw. I pull out of her and rush to the restroom to clean up and bring a washcloth for her.

She's still smiling when I reach her again, and I decide to clean her up myself.

"That was incredible, River. I like it better without anything between us," she says, and I couldn't agree more.

"Only a lifetime to go of that, baby," I tell her and drop a kiss on her left breast.

"Getting a bit cocky, aren't we, Mr. Nichols? I mean, you haven't even asked for forever," she says, following me with her blue eyes as I return to the restroom to leave everything there.

"Oh, you think I won't?" She's made this comment before, and I don't know if it comes from a place of concern that I won't commit or if she has to keep reminding herself that she wants that.

"Well, you keep making all these grand plans. I just think now that we've taken this step to live together, it's best I let you know I don't take this lightly. Marriage is something I'm thinking about often, even though before you, I didn't really put much thought into it." She shrugs her shoulders as she makes her way through to the bathroom to clean herself up a bit more.

I follow her, then turn her so her back is to the counter and cage her in with my hands beside her. "Well, Kennedy, don't you worry. Message received."

I move myself to get down on one knee, and that causes Kennedy's breath to hitch.

"What are you doing?" she nearly screams.

"Oh, me? I'm just grabbing that earring you dropped and couldn't find earlier." I hand her the little stud she had lost last night.

"You fucking dick!" She smacks my shoulder, and I can't help the laugh that comes out as a result. This is going to be fun, but one day, I will get down on my knee, formally ask her to be mine, and will marry the fuck out of this girl. This attraction between us may have come out of nowhere, but now all I see is everything when I look into her eyes.

CHAPTER 34

Kennedy

"SO, IS HE A GOOD SLEEPER?" I can't stop staring at little Jacob Caldon while River holds Annabelle.

"Let's just say he calls the shots. If he wants to be pissed, his sister falls in line with him," Ashton says from the kitchen while prepping their bottles.

"He's getting better, and in no time, they'll be sleeping through the night. Until then, I just need one of these," Sam holds up her coffee mug like it's a trophy, "and I should be set."

It's been two months since the twins were born, and they are growing by the day. They got out of the NICU a month ago and have been adjusting well to their life at home. I swear they've grown by at least a pound since two days ago when I came to visit.

"Well, I can see that Anna loves her Uncle River, don't you, sweet girl?" he coos, and she squirms in his arms, still completely asleep with her arm sticking out of her blanket.

"Yeah, well, your brother said the same thing, so you've got competition." Sam laughs, and River looks up at her like she's gone mad.

"No, no, sweet Annabelle. Uncle River is the better one, I

promise you. Uncle Clay is no fun," he continues in that little voice he only uses for the babies.

"How are you doing, Sam?" I look up at my best friend, knowing it's been tough adjusting to motherhood.

She attempted to breastfeed when the babies were in the NICU, but her supply just never exceeded the amount the twins needed. For two babies, she needed to have a bigger supply, and the stress of it all really took a toll on her.

After weeks of crying over the fact that she was failing as a mother, she finally threw in the towel and bought formula. She said she was sick of people telling her what was best for the babies when she knew she needed to take action, and so she did. They've been thriving, so she hasn't looked back. But there are moments, per Ash, where she breaks down and feels like she failed them already, this early on in life.

"I'm okay. Still exhausted, but I think Ash and I have a system now. He takes certain feedings, and I do others, giving each of us a space to rest when needed. Sometimes, we're both dragging as the babies are awake past their routine sleep times, but we're getting there." She gives me a soft smile, and I see some relief etching her features.

I reach over and grab her hand and squeeze. She's been a trooper with all of this. I'm not too sure I'd handle it as well as she has.

"So, what's the plan for you two? Wanna babysit soon so I can have some time with my wife?" Ashton walks over and leaves a bottle each for River and me to feed.

I look over at River and respond, "Yeah, I think we can do that."

Both Ashton and Sam throw their hands in the air and high-five each other. "YES! Thank you!"

They start to get up and make their way to the stairs.

"Hold up, you mean now?" River says, a bit of panic in his voice.

"Yes, now! I need some time to hang out with Sam

without spit-up on our clothes. You said earlier you both have nothing going on today. Are you saying you lied to your best friends?" Ashton gives us a pointed glare.

River and I both shake our heads, a bit scared of this man in front of us right now.

As scary as Sam was when she was pregnant, it seems she's transferred her attitude over to her easy-going husband. Hopefully, it's an exhaustion thing because he's a bit much to handle.

They hustle upstairs, and I hope it's to change and not do other things because I do not need to relive my college years right now with sounds of them.

"You think they're going to fuck or go out?" River and his dirty mouth ask.

"Probably both." I roll my eyes and grab the bottle to start feeding Jacob before he gets angry. The boy's got a set of lungs on him.

River does the same with Anna, and we both sit and soak in the newborn cuddles while we can. There is something really nice about watching someone's baby but then handing them back at the end of the day. I'll take auntie cuddles anytime over full responsibility of little humans.

"Does this make you want to have kids?" River asks.

I look over at him, wondering why he's asking me this. "I guess? I mean, I never saw myself doing the parenting thing. But then we got together, and now I feel like I'm constantly changing my mind. Do I dream of endless diapers, lack of sleep, and likely leaking out of my boobs? No. But do I see these babies and wonder what our kids will look like or if we'll be fun parents together? Absolutely. It doesn't mean I don't get scared though."

He nods in agreement. "Well, that's good." He drops the conversation there, and we feed the babies in silence, giggling when they make funny faces as they down their bottles.

After they both get burped and a clean diaper, we put them in their bassinets to take another nap.

We're sitting on the couch when Sam and Ashton make their way back downstairs. The flushed look on their faces and her "freshly fucked" hair leaves little to the imagination.

"Okay, we're off." Ashton tries to play like they didn't just do the deed.

I look over to River who's giving his best friend a thumbs up, and I realize men never really grow up.

We say our goodbyes, and I hope they're back soon and not gone until god knows when. The more I see River holding a baby, the more I just want to jump him myself.

River goes to the kitchen to get us drinks and snacks, returning with an armful of treats. He puts everything down on the table in front of us, and the moment I stand up to grab some napkins, he halts me in my tracks. He brings himself to the floor on one knee, and my eyes must mimic the size of saucers as I see what's about to happen.

"Kennedy," he begins, and I swear I feel my heart start to race. I bring my hand to my face, trying to temper my emotions.

"You are everything to me, and I can't see beyond today without you by my side," he continues, and I swear, of all places and times for him to propose, he's choosing now.

He adds, "If I don't tie your shoes right now, I'm scared we won't make it to tomorrow. I don't want you to fall, sweetheart." The fucker looks up and winks. He's such a dick.

"You motherfucker!" I seethe. "What is wrong with you?"

I smack his shoulder once he's done tying my laces and stomp into the kitchen.

"You didn't really think I was going to propose when you have baby formula on your shoulder, did you?" He chuckles in the living room as I try to compose myself in the kitchen.

I look into the small mirror positioned on the wall, and

sure enough, there's a massive blob of white gunk on my shoulder. Damnit!

"Ha ha, very fucking funny, Riv. You know, I can still say no when that day comes, right? I hold that power," I say as I make my way back to him in the other room.

He's shuffling through shows for us to potentially watch, and he looks my way, "Yeah, right. You like my dick too much."

I smack him upside the head. "Keep telling yourself that."

I squeal as he pulls me in and puts me on his lap, kissing me hard.

"Baby, you know I will not stop bothering you about this because you make it too easy. Plus, you and I are it for one another. You know you love me." He brings his lips to drop a kiss on my nose.

"Yeah, I'm starting to question why that is right now." I shrug but still smile at the same time.

"You know you can't get enough of me. I'm irresistible."

We pick a movie, and I feel my eyes get heavy. Despite years of nightmares, I finally feel at peace within myself, and my thoughts wander into a dream of forever with this man by my side.

Epilogue

RIVER

I CAN'T BELIEVE it's been a year since Kennedy and I started this whole thing between us. What began as a way to satisfy our needs has morphed into something so much bigger than either of us ever imagined.

That being said, I still look at her every day and realize how fucking lucky I am that we're here, together, and in many ways happier than I ever gave us credit for. We walk into the restaurant with a view of the water. As the sun sets, the colors in the sky reflect, and it's hard to look away.

We're celebrating Ashton and Samara's one-year anniversary; at least, that's what Kennedy thinks. But I've got a few surprises up my sleeve, which I've been sweating bullets making sure everything is in order.

I won't lie; since I started fake proposing to Kennedy months ago, it's been fun to watch her face morph into excitement only to realize I'm fucking with her. If there's anything we love to do, it's taunt one another. So I've continued, making sure we're in public to ensure she really gets thrown off the scent of the actual proposal.

The last time I got down on one knee, it was only to give Lola kisses while we were on a walk. She nearly kneed me in the nose after that one. The way she stormed off only made me want her more, and I fucked the anger out of her that afternoon. She wasn't complaining after that.

We walk into the restaurant, and I immediately feel my palms sweat. I have to find a way to make sure everything goes well. Everyone knows their part, so let's just hope things go off without a hitch because I cannot fake this one. I have put way too much effort into this evening.

The moment we walk in, Ash and Sam are at the table we reserved. It's only got seating for the four of us, but that will soon change. I guide Kennedy with our hands interlaced, praying she doesn't feel the moisture building as my heart races in my chest.

Ash gives me a hug that nearly pulls all the air from my lungs, whispering, "You look like you're going to be sick, Riv." When he pulls away, he has a huge smile on his face, and I respond with, "Thanks for the confidence boost."

I move to pull Kennedy's chair out and take a few calming breaths as she scoots in. The moment I'm seated, she pulls herself close to me. "You look a little pale, babe. Need me to get you some juice or something?" She moves her hands to my forehead to check for a fever.

I shake my head, hoping I can pull myself out of this nervous state and enjoy the moment. We start drinking our water while we wait for the server to come take our orders.

The conversation flows as it usually does, this time focusing on the twins and how much they've grown. Sam is beaming, talking about the latest milestones they've reached, and Ash is scrolling through pictures to show off his kids. The more they talk, the calmer I get.

I'm starting to doubt myself for fucking around with Kennedy for so long and fake proposing. What if she thinks I'm faking it?

No, no, she can't. There's a ring involved this time. There's not faking it this time around. I have to be romantic. That's what Clay keeps telling me. He gave me some pointers so I don't spoil it when I ask. Highlights from his pep talk: don't say you want to fuck her. My brother, ladies and gentlemen.

The server comes by and takes everyone's order. I look over the menu and put it down, looking right at Kennedy when I do.

"They don't have what I want," I protest, looking angry.

"What do you mean? What did you want?" Kennedy picks up the menu and looks it over again. Her brows come together with a concerned look, and then she looks at me.

"You love steak. Get that," she says, then looks around to make sure we haven't gained an audience at my outburst.

"Steak won't do for me tonight. I think I need something bigger."

"Bigger than a steak?" I can see she wants to protest further at my childish ways right now.

I get out of my seat, not looking behind me, and bump into the server who was coming by to assist another table.

Everything in his hands comes tumbling down, but luckily, just menus flying through the air and hitting the floor.

Right then, I get on my hands and knees, hoping to veer this embarrassing moment away from me.

All I hear above me is how sorry Kennedy is for my outburst, and from her tone, I can tell she's incredibly embarrassed. She's apologizing while I'm gathering things in my hands. I hand the menus to her, and she places them on the table in front of her.

Once she grabs all the menus that fell, she moves her body to face the table once again, and that's when she stops and looks down at her place setting. She's focused on the contraption in front of her, confusion on her features. I take this opportunity to move into position and get down on one knee.

"Um, where the hell did this come from?" She keeps looking down at the item she never thought she'd see again.

She keeps her eyes on the crocheted dick that Aunt Kay

made for Samara when things start to fall into place. She swings her gaze back toward me and realizes my position. She gasps, bringing her hands up and burying her face in them.

Her eyes are filling with tears, and it's a good sign because at least she has clued in that this isn't a joke.

"Kennedy, I think we both remember how things went down when we first met. You and I weren't on the same page, and we continued to live our lives parallel to one another but never seeing the world together. A year ago, something shifted, and we finally took the leap to explore what it could be like to build a life in the same orbit together.

"It took some of us longer than others to truly appreciate what we had." She chuckles at that part. "But, no matter what direction I turn my head, all paths lead to you. I love you beyond myself. I'll always look to you for guidance, for comfort, and for leading me in the right direction. Please be my wife. Will you marry me?"

She's been nodding her head from the moment I started my speech, but the minute I stop what I'm saying, she's leaping toward me and screaming a resounding "Yes!"

The entire restaurant starts to clap and yell their congratulations. She pulls my face toward her and kisses me, letting us relish in this moment together.

We disconnect, and it's only then she realizes Sam and Ashton are recording everything. She starts to laugh, and then the tears start streaming down once again when she looks beyond our best friends to find my brother, mother, her uncle and aunt, our friends, and some of the guys from the firehouse hooting and hollering their congratulations.

She brings her eyes back to meet mine, and she smiles and takes me into another hug.

She brings her lips to my ear and tells me, "You are the dream to pull me out of my nightmares, River. And as much as I love you, we're burning that purse."

I laugh and squeeze her tighter, telling her I love her too.

"Before you burn it, maybe look inside at least." I bring my lips to plant a soft kiss on her lips while confusion consumes her features again.

Before greeting our family and friends who have made their way into the restaurant, she opens the little clasp and pulls out the note along with the ring I left inside:

Unlike the destiny of this purse, I want forever with you...

The End

$$Clay$$

"SO YOU TEST DOG FOODS?" To be completely honest, I had no idea that was a thing.

"Um, yeah," she says in between bites of her dinner. "I'm a dog food tester. Cool, huh?" She beams a smile my way.

Odette is pretty and definitely someone I feel attracted to, but that might be it. We lack similar interests, to say the least. Her profile on the app said she worked with animals, but apparently, she's not a dog-walker or a veterinarian. Never in my wildest dreams did I guess dog food tester.

"How does one get into that line of work?" I can't help being fascinated with this profession of hers.

"Well, it was sort of random. I was working at a local pet shop back home, and one of the reps came in, and we got to talking. Before you know it, I'm signing up to try it out and haven't looked back since." She holds so much pride in her voice as she speaks. I have to hold back a laugh.

Listen, I'm all for different lines of work. I'm open to whatever makes someone happy, but the randomness in this job is really throwing me off. It's all I can think about. Now my mind is moving in so many directions, I don't know what to focus on.

Hold on. Does that mean her breath smells like dog food? I can't help the chill that runs through me. No thanks.

The rest of the evening is uneventful, probably because nothing compares to being a dog food tester, so I feel anything beyond that fact isn't at all fun.

I hug Odette goodbye and make my way back home. The weather has turned, and I tighten my jacket around my chest to keep the cold from coming through. I'm shaking my head at the thought of the date I just went through and the way my mind wanders to the one question that keeps coming back to me: is this how it's going to be now?

How did I go from being married roughly a year ago to going on dates with a dog food tester? I mean, where the fuck do I make a U-turn and go back to what my life was?

The thing is, now that I've had some perspective, I realize what Abby and I had wasn't at all in a good place at the end of our marriage. We had become shells of ourselves because life has an ugly way of showing how difficult it can get. And it was hard for us those last few years. The sad part is that I never told anyone around me the whole truth of what went down.

It's been a few months since I saw her come into the bar with Malloy, and the thought of that still gets my blood boiling.

I cannot believe she went out with that schmuck. And of all the dipsticks she decides to date, she chooses a fellow fire-fighter—Malloy from Station 7—to be the one to rub this in my face.

I feel my hands ball into fists by my side, remembering her walking out with him latched onto her arm. I remember my gaze staying on them for the entirety of their exit until they were out of my line of sight.

The aftermath of that night is cemented in my mind, and it's something I'm constantly pulling myself out of each time I find myself hovering over her number on my phone.

I've reached a stage of pathetic if I'm being completely transparent. I love her. My love for Abby has not diminished, nor has my anger at that night or even the year prior, with her blindsiding me with a divorce, deterred me from giving her my heart. I never got it back, actually. She left me behind, and she never sent back the most valuable pieces of my heart and soul.

I've been in love with Abby Morris since the moment our eyes locked years ago. That cold Boston day where a twenty-year-old version of myself was still in college and needing the caffeine to get through my midterms.

I walked into *Amazonia's Bean Co.* naïve and looking for the strongest shot of coffee, only to come out knowing I was going to marry that girl. She sat in a corner with her beanie pulled over her ears, yet her eyes locked with mine the minute I walked in, and I haven't looked at another girl the same ever since.

We instantly connected, and from there, my heart started to beat outside my chest. She became my everything, and I became hers, until one day, all that shifted, and I was no longer what she needed in this life. Or, from what she told me that morning when I got home, was that looking at me only reminded her of the pain and the loss of the life we should have been leading.

I think that right there gutted me more than anything else she did or said regarding the divorce. Knowing that when I looked at her, I saw beauty and love, but when she looked at me, all she saw was sadness and an emptiness I couldn't fill—it felt like the ultimate slap in the face.

She left me, walking away from all we made together, because life decided to deal us a shit hand. I thought we would get through everything together, no matter the heartache, yet I was on that island alone. While I was finding ways to connect to her, she was finding ways to separate herself from me. The distance just kept growing until she chose to leave.

She walked away from not only me but our future. She told me she didn't feel like herself anymore; therefore, she couldn't be with someone who was in love with a different version of her. Little did she know I loved all the different parts of her, even if she didn't understand them.

Hell, I would have walked the surface of the sun if it meant she was waiting for me on the other side. For so long, I looked at all my buddies and felt lucky to have so much stability with the woman I chose to call my wife. We did everything together until the day came when she felt like she would rather walk alone instead of by my side.

That's the thing though; she left me behind, and I'm here like a love-sick fool, and I don't know how to pull myself out of it. I've looked into the future, and all I see is Abby by my side. I've tried to look at someone new, hoping I would find something, anything, to pull me into a new love. But I'm starting to think my heart is permanently broken. It feels like it beats differently now that I lack her presence daily.

River is now in a place where he's happy and looking at his girlfriend like she is everything to him, and I'm now looking for a life I recognize. I have no jealousy toward my brother and Kennedy. In all honesty, it's been fun to see him fall head over heels for the one girl who drove him mad for so long.

I walk up the steps to my apartment, and the loneliness feels like it engulfs me even more when I make my way up the elevator. My brother used to live in the building, but now he's all cozy with Kennedy at her place.

Each time I step foot in this building, I'm reminded I live here, in my sad little apartment, because my life went to shit. I'm completely stuck in the past, even as I go on dates trying to forget about the woman who stole a part of me only to never give it back. I go out in hopes of finding something new to latch onto, but I always feel disappointed when they don't live up to my expectation.

I feel no rush to get home, so I nearly miss the elevator doors opening on my floor. The moment I walk into the hall-way, I feel her before I see her. I squint my eyes, rubbing them to ensure I'm not hallucinating.

But there she is, as clear as the day I met her. Abby Nichols—now back to Morris—sitting in front of my door. I keep forgetting she's back in Boston after she had left me to go be with her parents in California.

I straighten my spine and try to stay strong, hoping my heart can handle this close proximity. But nothing prepares me for the words she's about to utter. She opens her mouth and I feel the pull this woman has on me when she simply looks up at me with tears pooled in those big blue eyes, and says,

"I'm pregnant."

Learn how **_Clay and Abby_** forge a new path after they've burned down everything they built in *Embers in Our Past*, coming *February 2025*. Preorder using the QR Code Below

Acknowledgments

To say this book was one of the toughest for me to write is an understatement. River and Kennedy spoke to me early on, then changed their story so many times, it drove me crazy. To write two characters that had banter and sass turned out to be more challenging for me than I originally expected.

Life got hard in my household in the beginning of 2024. Some unexpected challenges arose and my writing was put on hold. The *If Only* series had been completed by the end of 2023, so this was the first book I had tackled for 2024 and it proved to be a hard task for me mentally. My mind needed some healing and this was a journey for me in ways I simply struggled with.

I don't think I would have really gotten through the task of writing this book if it hadn't been for my PA, Meghan. I have to shout her out first in this section because she truly let me lean on her for all my bookish moments pertaining to this project. She was my alpha reader, my sounding board and the first person to simply tell me she loved these characters and that I was onto something with this storyline.

Writing is incredibly humbling and sometimes we just need someone to point us in the right direction. Meghan helped guide me in so many ways. She cheered me on, got this playlist underway, helped me with my hype team and simply got me through so many projects as I got through each task to complete this book. This was a huge undertaking for me mentally and Meghan was pushing me forward every step of the way. Thank you Meghan for your kindness and patience.

To my beta readers: Noelle, Allie and Joanna—I appreciate you so much and thank you for always being available to take on a new read. Thank you for your feedback and kindness always. I don't know what I'd do without you reading my books and falling in love with my characters.

To my husband and kids—thank you for enduring me sitting on my computer for endless nights and weekends working after I've already worked my regular job. Thank you for your patience and giving me the space to be creative in this way. I know I have dedicated so many hours and days to this craft and I appreciate the help you give to let me thrive in this field I'm still learning how to grow in. I hope you know it's due to you I can get this work done. I love you three so much.

To Joanna for always listening to my endless characters that are in my head and knowing that I can't stop the loop that plays on repeat like a movie. You have to hear about the storylines that I want to get out on paper and you're always the first to hear about them before I get to write about them. Thanks for patiently being the person to listen to my ideas and helping me plot things out before I move forward to writing them out. I love you sissy.

I have so much appreciation for my editing team at KLS. To my editor extraordinaire, Steph White. You are brilliant! Your feedback on River and Kennedy was so fun to read because these characters seemed to bring out a good laugh from you and that made my day. Now I will get to share Clay and Abby with you and I know that will be another fun adventure together. So here's to another great ride coming soon!

To Christiana at Concepts by Canea, you were my savior redesigning these covers. I saw a new vision midway during this series and you took it on and made it a reality. River and Kennedy came to life with your illustration and I'm in love.

You made this so much fun for me and I can't wait to see the rest of this series come to life. You are truly gifted at your craft. Thank you so much and for all your hard work! I had so much fun working with you on this project 🤍

The Author Agency has been an absolute treasure of a team. Thank you for being so fast with communication since we started working together earlier this year. Things had been tough for me when we first teamed up and you took a lot of the stress off my shoulders at a time I needed it. Since then, you've helped continue foster that same care with each book release and it's been a fun process for me moving forward. Thank you for assisting me when needed and seeing me through each release with grace and professionalism. Looking forward to the rest of this year and what 2025 has to offer.

To my hype team: even though we don't know one another in person, I love messaging with all of you. You're always so supportive and kind to take the time to share my work on socials. I know how much effort goes into reading someone's book and sharing what you've read on social media. It's not easy and you take the time to put my stuff out there for others to find. It means so much to me and I truly don't take it for granted. Thank you from the bottom of my heart.

To my ARC readers, I appreciate every single one of you for taking the time to not only read this indie author's work early, but for reviewing it as well. I was once in your shoes so I know what it's like to take a chance on an author. When you review my work, I see it and I appreciate it. It goes a long way to getting my book seen by others. It makes a difference to me and my family. Thank you so very much.

I hold so much gratitude to all my readers! Anyone that picks up my books—if you are new to my books or someone that has been reading from the very beginning, thank you so much. It means so much to me that you are here and supporting me in this way. I started doing this for the simple love of writing. It is a form of expression and love of the work. And it has taken off from there.

To all those I have gotten to meet from recent book events: meeting you in person is a gift that has uplifted me and given me a new purpose that I am using as I write moving forward. I have many things to look forward to as I go into my projects ahead and I want you to know you have filled my cup in a way I didn't expect. Thank you so much to all of you for making me smile a little bigger. You have truly brightened my day.

Again, I appreciate all of you for taking a chance on this little author who simply had a story pop in her head last year and took a chance on herself.

Stefanie xoxo

About the Author

Stefanie Castro is a Registered Nurse, certified doula and yoga instructor. She specialized in the field of obstetrics and loves everything about her career. She is a first-generation Brazilian American and is fluent in English, Portuguese and Spanish. Stefanie is a wife of 18 years and mother to her son and daughter, along with her very rambunctious Cavalier King Charles dog.

She has grown in her love of reading throughout the years and now it's hard to find her without her kindle by her side. Her favorite foods are popcorn and sushi. She is also very excited about Christmas and begins plotting her next year's decor on December 26th. Stefanie has started two bookclubs and is avidly reading whenever she has a free moment in her day. She loves to cuddle on the couch with her dog, along with a great book and a cup of tea.

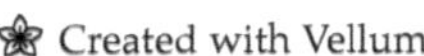 Created with Vellum